BEHIND THE NIGHT BAZAAR

In 1992 Angela Savage travelled to Laos on a six-month scholarship, then spent the next six years living in Asia. Based in Vientiane, Hanoi and finally Bangkok, she set up and headed the Australian Red Cross HIV/AIDS subregional program. *Behind the Night Bazaar* won the 2004 Victorian Premier's Literary Award for unpublished manuscript. This debut novel launches a series featuring Jayne Keeney PI. Angela lives in Melbourne.

D0925750

Behind the night bazaar

ANGELA SAVAGE

Text Publishing Melbourne Australia

The Text Publishing Company
Swann House
22 William St
Melbourne Victoria 3000
Australia
www.textpublishing.com.au

Reprinted 2012

Design by Chong Weng-ho
Typeset by J & M Typesetting
Printed by Griffin Press

National Library of Australia
Cataloguing-in-Publication data:

Savage, Angela, 1966- .
Behind the night bazaar.

ISBN 1 921145 22 6.

I. Title.
A823.4

This project was assisted by the Commonwealth Government through the Australia Council, its art funding and advisory body.

To Andrew Nette

All roads I travel lead home to you

The sluggish Bangkok traffic forced Jayne Keeney to slow to a crawl at Siam Square. To her right, a motorbike the same as hers carried a family of five: father driving, mother and two children in school uniform riding pillion, infant perched on the petrol tank up front. In front was a blue pickup truck, its tray full of plastic water bottles, a young man sprawled across the top of them, sound asleep despite the car horns.

Coming to a halt, Jayne placed her feet on the road either side of her bike, taking care to avoid a squashed rat in the gutter. It was late afternoon, the hot bitumen sticky beneath her sandals. She removed her helmet and shook the sweat from her long, dark curls. Reflected in the rear-view mirror, her pale skin had the rosy flush of someone emerging from a sauna, and she wiped smudges of mascara from beneath her amber eyes.

She smelled the garlands of jasmine an elderly woman was selling as temple offerings from a cart on the footpath. A tattered Happy New Year banner hung over the cart. It had been there long enough to cover several new years, from 1 January, the Chinese new year in February, and the mid-April festival of Thai new year the previous week. Beside the banner was a gaudy red and gold picture of a rat, the symbol for 1996.

On the facade of the department store behind the flower seller, a wall of televisions advertised skin-whitening cream. Opposite, a hand-painted billboard announced the release of another American action movie, while next door the evening's special at the Dok Bua Restaurant was spicy fish-head soup.

Despite the atmospheric cocktail of high octane petrol, humidity and dust, Jayne felt invigorated. Not even the sight of a couple of Western backpackers kissing on a nearby corner could dampen her mood. The jaded charm and polite anonymity of the Asian metropolis suited her. Even the congestion on the roads worked in her favour: tailing someone was easy in a traffic jam.

Her target was a Thai woman whose American spouse suspected was having an affair with a colleague. The wife had told her husband she was flying to Udon on a business trip. But the taxi Jayne was following had bypassed the airport turn-off and headed into Bangkok's city centre. Or one of them. The Thai capital was too much of an amorphous sprawl to be restricted to a single hub.

The traffic jerked forward and the sleeping man rolled over the water bottles undisturbed. Jayne replaced her helmet and joined her fellow commuters in honking at the backpackers. The Thais considered public displays of affection rude, though if Didier could see her, he'd say she was jealous. The lovers remained oblivious to the attention they attracted, love being not only blind but also deaf in this case.

She accelerated to gain on the taxi as it turned up Phayathai Road towards the Asia Hotel. The hotel's lobby bar looked like a 1960s film set—dim booths and low-hanging lights—and Jayne had fond memories of seeing a Thai Elvis impersonators show there a few months back. As she inched her motorbike past the hotel onto a bridge, she caught a whiff of fetid *klong*, its contents the colour and consistency of sump oil. The canals were once the lifeblood of the city, where people drank, bathed, commuted and traded. These days the remaining klongs stank in the summer and flooded in the wet season, a reminder that Bangkok was built on a swamp and might easily become one again.

The taxi pulled over at the entrance to a *soi*, one of the numbered streets that branched off Bangkok's main roads like tributaries from a river. Jayne parked and slung her helmet over the handlebars—headgear was so unpopular there was little risk of it being stolen. While the Thai woman paid her fare, Jayne waited by a fruit stall, rolling a rambutan around in the palm of her hand. The fruit's egg-shape and hairy texture made her think of testicles—though it was a long time since she'd handled any of those. She put it aside as the woman emerged from the cab and paused to fold a piece of paper, probably a falsified receipt showing an airport drop-off. Jayne had seen it all before. In a city awash with sexual intrigue, spying on unfaithful lovers had been her bread and butter for over two years.

The woman adjusted a large tote bag over one shoulder and dragged a small case on wheels into the soi. The area was affluent but modest, low-rise apartments dotted among Thai homes with established gardens—the sort of place where Buddhist monks still begged for alms in the mornings and tailors made house calls. The woman headed towards a newer block of flats, a mishmash of architectural features including iron balconies, faux-marble pillars and a portico suitable for a Greek temple, complete with ornate caryatids.

Jayne ducked behind a large rubbish skip on an adjacent building site and opened her backpack. Her camera would record the time and date of the woman's arrival and departure, which Jayne knew was the residence of the colleague under suspicion. This should give her client sufficient grounds to confront his wife, though whether she would fess up was another matter. In Jayne's experience, circumstantial evidence was grounds for separation only if either party wanted out of the relationship. The need for proof was greater when there was more to lose.

It was a safe bet her subject would be spending the night. Jayne anticipated a stake-out and came equipped with water, a notebook and a novel. She didn't bother carrying food, given the round-the-clock supply available from the street vendors. A local joke was if more than three people gather in the same place for upwards of two days, a food stall will appear. Indeed a group of women had set up a narrow strip of kitchen-cum-cafes on the footpath nearby. One of them, wearing a white chef's hat and an apron advertising MSG, tossed noodles in a wok large enough to bathe a baby in. Another offered flattened half-chickens on bamboo skewers and catfish speared from mouth to tail, both grilled over hot coals and accompanied with plastic bags of pickled vegetables and whole chillies. The aroma of frying garlic and barbecued meat was enticing, but Jayne was too hot to eat.

She eyed the entrance to the apartment building where a security guard was dozing. It would make for a much more pleasant evening if she could conduct her surveillance inside. Although the sun was setting, the temperature rarely dropped below thirty at this time of the year. Jayne wiped her forehead, dirt and sweat coming away in greasy balls on her fingertips. The least she could do was suss out the possibilities.

Taking one of the caryatids by the waist like a dance partner, Jayne sidled around the statue-cum-column, slipped past the guard and entered the building through tinted glass doors. To the left was an unmanned reception desk, concealed from the entrance by a row of potted bamboo. On the opposite side of the foyer was a lift. A glance at the residents' directory confirmed a match with the name supplied by her client.

Jayne checked out the view from behind the reception desk, the ideal height for her camera. The terracotta pots containing the bamboo were heavy, but the airconditioning gave her new energy. She dragged a pot around to the front of the desk, concealing her camera and ensuring the lens poked through the bamboo stalks. She checked the focus, activated the remote control and had just taken a test photo of herself, when she heard the lift rumble behind her.

The doors opened to reveal her client's wife locked in a passionate embrace. Her lover's face was obscured against the woman's neck, his hand on her breast. They didn't seem to notice that the lift had stopped. The woman's eyes were closed. It was an opportunity too good to miss. Jayne pressed the remote control button and released the camera shutter.

The Thai woman's eyes snapped open and the couple sprang apart. The woman pressed herself against the back of the lift, holding her tote bag against her chest like a shield. The man started shouting, an Australian accent. Jayne turned to the reception desk, relieved to see she hadn't blocked the shot with her body. Through the glass doors, she saw the security guard had woken up, roused by the noise. She stepped quickly over to the reception desk to retrieve her camera.

She turned back to the Australian, ready with her usual spiel about acting within the laws of Thailand, when she felt something wet and warm running down her left arm.

Jayne saw the blood but couldn't feel the bleeding, light travelling faster than pain. She looked up from the gash in her arm to the knife in the Thai woman's hand. Her face was a mask of fury, her arm raised to strike a second time.

The Australian man moved towards Jayne from the left, the security guard from behind. Shouting in Thai and English, they lunged forward.

But it wasn't Jayne they were after. The two men grabbed the Thai woman's arms and the knife clattered to the floor. The guard kicked it out of reach, and the woman slid to the ground. 'Are you all right?' the Australian man said, but Jayne couldn't tell who he was talking to. The guard looked at her wound and blanched. At that moment, the pain set in.

Her legs shook and she crumpled to the floor. Still clutching her camera, she took the weight of the fall on her right shoulder, bringing her eye-to-eye with the Thai woman. They met each other's gaze and in that moment,

Jayne understood her mistake. It was, she realised, her first case in which the unfaithful party was a Thai female. And she'd seriously underestimated her quarry.

Her girlfriends would give her hell about it. But she could rely on Didier to make her feel better. An overwhelming urge to be with him was the last thing she remembered before passing out.

Jayne sank into a rickshaw outside Chiang Mai station. Two weeks had passed and the stitches were gone, but the wound was still tender enough for her to accept the *tuk-tuk* driver's help with her backpack. Her luggage was mostly books. When she'd phoned Didier from Bangkok, she called a book club meeting as an excuse to see him. She planned to tell him about the attack in person—once she figured out how to bring it up.

She directed the driver to head for the Rama IX Bridge, then turned around to take in the view. Chiang Mai was no longer the sleepy town it was when Didier moved here fifteen years earlier—'so quiet, you could hear the chanting of the monks in the middle of the day'. Thailand's second-largest city now had its share of traffic, high-rise buildings and fast-food restaurants, though trees still lined the roads and there were almost as many push-cart vendors as cars. At the town's centre, ancient ruins were surrounded by immaculate gardens and a square moat, which was lined with flaming torches during festivals.

But the biggest difference between Bangkok and Chiang Mai was the sky. In Bangkok towering office blocks and condominiums obscured the horizon, freeways stacked like shelves. Pollution turned visible patches of sky a noxious shade of grey that at dusk blazed red like a chemical fire. In Chiang Mai, Jayne could breathe again.

The tuk-tuk turned onto the road that curved along the Ping River, and she drank in the sunset, the sun dipping behind the jagged mountains that ringed the town, turning the sky and water a matching shade of pale gold. Jayne felt like a creature coming out of hibernation, revitalised by the light after months in a cave.

Not that she would admit this to Didier. Almost as much debate took place on the merits of 'The Big Mango' versus 'The Rose of the North' as on their other favourite topic, crime fiction. Didier read what Jayne scathingly referred to as 'cosy' authors, while she preferred darker fiction, which he found 'unnecessarily grim'. Perhaps that was how she could raise the issue of her injury: proof that the violence in modern detective novels wasn't exaggerated.

The tuk-tuk driver veered left after the bridge, passed the market, and stopped in a narrow soi. Didier's place was built in the traditional Thai style. At the front of a lush, tropical garden was a *sarn phraphum*, a small house-shrine for the land spirits, piled high with offerings of fresh marigolds, rice balls and smoking incense. Set back from the street, the house was made of teak and built on stilts. A steep staircase led to a large verandah furnished with triangular pillows and rattan tray tables. Didier and Jayne had spent many nights lounging there in the mottled light cast from lampshades made of eel-traps and sticky-rice baskets, drinking gin and tonics and arguing about books. While the interior of the house reflected his Thai partner's love of all things modern, preferably plastic, the charm of the balcony and garden was all Didier.

Jayne was paying the driver when Nou came to the gate. He was wearing a grey Calvin Klein T-shirt, which Jayne suspected was an original. Didier's boyfriend's real name was Sanga. His nickname, Nou, meant 'rat' in Thai, an apt moniker in Jayne's opinion. Though Nou was always polite to her, she sensed the dislike was mutual. They greeted each other with a *wai*—the prayer-like bow—and he insisted on carrying her backpack into the house. It was a gesture of hospitality and she let him do it, but after more than three years in Thailand she still felt uncomfortable being waited on by Thai people, and especially by Nou.

None of that mattered when Didier appeared at the top of the stairs. His face was perfect—strong chin, straight nose, high forehead, thick, honey-coloured hair. And at this point in the hot season, his skin was at its deepest shade of olive. He hid hazel eyes behind black-rimmed glasses in an effort, she suspected, to make himself look less attractive. But the ugliness of the glasses only enhanced his beauty. Jayne felt better just for laying eyes on him.

He stood aside to let Nou pass and held out his arms.

'It's good to see you, *chérie*,' he said, pulling Jayne close and kissing her on each cheek.

She winced as his hand gave her injured arm an affectionate squeeze.

'What is it?' Didier said, holding her at arm's length. 'What's the matter, Jayne? You look pale.'

'I always look pale,' she said, shrugging off his hold. 'Besides, I've been on a train for fourteen hours and desperately need a gin.'

'Of course,' Didier smiled, though the concerned look

10

remained. 'You settle in, I'll make the drinks and then we can talk. We'll sit outside, yes?'

'That's a rhetorical question, right.' Jayne returned his smile.

Didier held the door open. 'I'm so glad you've come,' he said. 'We have so much to talk about.'

Nou watched Didier hand Jayne a drink then take a seat on the balcony beside her. They were talking about books. Nou had a reasonable grasp of English, but he wasn't interested enough to keep up with what they were saying. He wondered why Didi wanted him there, since he never paid him any attention when his *farang* friends were around. The farang friends didn't pay him much attention either. Jayne only talked to him when Didi was out of the room. Otherwise her focus was on Didier, one hundred per cent.

There were often nights like this when Jayne came to stay. Their friendship did not surprise Nou: he knew plenty of Thai women who preferred the company of men who were *gae* because it was safer than going out with normal men. But Nou did resent the effect Jayne's presence had on his boyfriend. She seemed to bring Didier to life. He talked faster, used his hands when he spoke and smiled more than usual. Didi never paid attention to Nou the way he did to Jayne. With her there, Nou might as well have been a dog asleep at the foot of the stairs. As he slipped inside to change his clothes, he was glad he'd made his own plans for the evening.

He and his friend Jet were dropping by Loh Kroh to turn a couple of tricks before heading off to the card game

Jet had set up. They were going to take on a couple of southern Chinese tourists with more money than brains. It would be easy to outwit them once they started to play by Thai rules.

Nou chose his clothes with care. He selected a new, black Boss shirt and clean beige slacks, fixing his hair in place with a trace of oil. He checked his appearance in the mirror. Though he wished his skin wasn't so dark or his nose so flat, he was otherwise pleased with what he saw. His cheeks were smooth, his eyes round, and his lips looked ready to be kissed—or so more than one customer had told him. Nou pulled a lot of business with those lips.

He looked smart but not slick. He wanted to put his opponents at ease, lose a few hands to begin with, before going in for the kill. Nou needed a big win. His creditors were not men who liked waiting.

He didn't mention any of this to Didi. Sometimes he needed to prove to himself—and to friends like Jet—that just because his boyfriend was a farang with plenty of money and a good education, that didn't mean Didi controlled Nou's whole life.

Nou returned to the balcony. Didi and Jayne were arguing now, their voices growing louder as they fought to interrupt each other. It baffled Nou the way farangs appeared to enjoy conflict when Thai people worked so hard to avoid it.

He busied himself with clearing away the empty plates and glasses, keeping an ear out for Jet's motorbike.

'Oh, Nou, you don't need to do that.' Jayne followed him into the kitchen and opened the fridge door. 'What will you have to drink?'

'Never mind,' he said. 'I'm going out.'

He saw her smile as she leaned down to get the tonic water.

'Why don't you and Didi get married?'

'What?' Jayne blushed.

'You're both getting older,' Nou said. 'You should think about having children.'

To his satisfaction, he seemed to have left her speechless. But he didn't have time to savour it. Hearing a motorbike, he hurried out to the balcony. Didier was sitting on a cushion, leafing through a book.

'*Nong pai tieow*,' Nou said casually, smoothing back his hair.

Didier looked up. 'Going out where?'

'With friends, to talk, you know, like you and Jayne.' He nodded towards the kitchen.

'Do you want to take the motorbike? It's OK if you do, I mean, if you're not planning to drink and—'

'No.' He waved towards the front entrance. 'Jet's here to pick me up. I won't be late. But don't wait up.' Nou slipped on a pair of loafers and, calling out '*chowk dee*' over his shoulder, jumped down the stairs two at a time. He skipped to the gate and climbed up behind Jet.

'All set?'

'For sure,' Jet said.

'This is gonna be our lucky night.' Nou grinned. '*Ja pai rew rew*!'

But Jet had revved the accelerator and Nou's words were lost.

Watching Nou sprint down the front steps made Didier feel older than his thirty-seven years. Old and foolish. Nou often withdrew when his farang friends were around, but he thought things were different with Jayne. Didier had hoped the three of them might spend a relaxing evening together.

He knew his life would be a lot easier if he found a partner within Chiang Mai's community of expatriate gay men, but he hadn't met any who appealed. It wasn't merely a question of aesthetics. It was as if the very factors that complicated his relationships with Thai men—the differences in culture and class—were part of the attraction.

Didier had met Nou in one of the bars where he did his outreach work. Nou had sauntered over to his table with an offer to suck his cock for 1000 baht, 'fixed price'.

'It's good to hear you charge such high rates for your services, younger brother,' Didier had replied in his most polite Thai. 'That's the mark of a healthy self-esteem. But I'm not in the market for a blow-job. Ask the other boys about me.'

When Didier returned to the bar three nights later, Nou approached him again, this time with less attitude but with no sign of embarrassment from their previous encounter.

'*Sawadee krup, Khun Di*,' he said, taking an adjacent seat. 'So you think I have a healthy self-esteem?'

'Well, the boys here usually ask only 500 baht to *samoke*,' he used the Thai slang, 'and most of them will let themselves be bartered down.'

'That's because they have no ambition,' Nou grinned.

'And what's your ambition?'

'I want to settle down with a nice farang who'll take care of me.'

Didier had smiled with genuine delight.

Because Nou was up front with him, Didier believed he'd be spared the tortuous second-guessing that characterised his other relationships with Thai men. But despite three years together, Nou's behaviour this very evening suggested Didier still needed to expect less.

Jayne reappeared on the balcony with fresh gin and tonics and a bowl of peanuts, looking slightly flustered. Didier smiled. Here was one relationship that never disappointed him. Even if the rest of his life was going to the dogs, he could rely on Jayne to make him feel better. When she phoned to invite herself to Chiang Mai, Didier took it as a sign: he'd been meaning to bring her in on a situation he'd uncovered through his work and it seemed like perfect timing. But now that she was here, with Nou gone, all he wanted to do was to forget about his problems, have a few drinks and get on with arguing about books.

They raised their glasses in a toast and both drank deeply.

'So,' Didier said, '*The Big Sleep*.'

'I really liked it.' She leaned against a triangular pillow and picked up the novel.

'You sound surprised.'

'I am,' she said. 'This is the third Raymond Chandler you've recommended and I've enjoyed them all. I'd have thought he was a bit hard-boiled for you, more like the authors I usually read.'

15

'He's not as mindless as that,' he grinned. 'Philip Marlowe isn't just clever at solving crimes, he wants to right social wrongs. I like that he cares about justice.'

'That makes sense,' Jayne muttered, adding, 'The language was great—quite poetic.'

'And the character descriptions are wonderful.'

'True,' she said, 'though there was one part I thought would put you off.' She turned to a page marked with a postcard. 'The bit where Marlowe meets Geiger's boyfriend. First he calls him a queen and a fag and then—here it is. "I still held his automatic more or less pointed at him, but he swung on me just the same...I backstepped fast enough to keep from falling, but I took plenty of the punch. It was meant to be a hard one, but a pansy has no iron in his bones, whatever he looks like."' She looked up. 'Pretty disparaging, *n'est-ce pas*?'

'OK, so Marlowe's not exactly enlightened,' Didier said. 'But remember, *The Big Sleep* was written in 1939. It's remarkable there are even gay characters in it. In that sense, Chandler was ahead of his time.'

'Well, I think you're being overly generous,' she said.

Touched by her loyalty, he leaned over and squeezed her hand. Jayne met his eyes and looked as if she wanted to ask him a question. Instead, she freed her hand to sip from her glass.

'I've got to warn you, Didi, just because I like Chandler, that doesn't mean you've converted me. Some of the other stuff on your reading list was a bit much.'

'Meaning what?'

'The plot device involving invisible ink in *Hidden*

Meanings wasn't very convincing.'

'At least it *had* a memorable plot,' he said. 'I forgot the storyline in your latest Ms Paretsky as soon as I finished reading it.'

'That's a bit harsh.' Jayne extracted a packet of cigarettes from her pocket. 'Do you mind?'

'They're your lungs,' Didier said, 'but you'll have to get your ashtray from the kitchen. Nou actually washed the filthy thing.'

Jayne gave him a withering look and, leaving her cigarettes on the floor, headed back inside the house.

'While you're there, can you bring the spring rolls from the fridge?' he called after her.

Taking another sip of his gin and tonic, Didier caught sight of Jayne's bookmark, jutting out from the pages of *The Big Sleep*.

It was a postcard of the century-old trees that lined the road from Chiang Mai to Lamphun. Several years earlier, a prominent city official announced they were to be cut down to make way for a new thoroughfare. But the citizens of Chiang Mai, smelling a rat, had risen in protest, enlisting the help of the Buddhist *sangha* to preserve what they saw as their heritage. With due ceremony, the monks ordained the trees, transforming each one into a shrine. Not even a corrupt city official would risk the terrible karma from destroying such sacred sites, and the logging order was revoked. To this day, the trees still wear the bright orange and ochre robes of the Buddhist clergy around their majestic trunks.

Didier smiled and had just replaced the bookmark when the phone rang.

Jai yen-yen, Jayne chanted to herself, the Thai equivalent of 'be cool'. She looked at her watch. Surely Didier wasn't going to work at 9pm? She'd thought once Nou left they'd finally get some time alone. But as Didier hung up the phone, he tugged at his hair, a gesture she recognised as a precursor to bad news.

'Jayne, I'm sorry,' he said. 'I'd hoped to get this out of the way before you arrived. You know my outreach work with some of the young guys in town? I've just got some new material—clear, explicit stuff—and I've finally found someone prepared to do the distribution.'

'Does it have to be tonight?'

She regretted her whining at once. Reducing the spread of HIV among young men in Chiang Mai was a personal crusade for Didier. 'Sorry, Didi, of course you have to go.'

'Why don't you come? It shouldn't take long. The friend I'm meeting runs one of the bars behind the Night Bazaar.'

'I didn't even know there were bars behind the Night Bazaar.'

He heard the curiosity in her voice and played to it. 'Come on, you've got to see this place to believe it.' He rattled his keys and grinned.

It was pathetic how easily he could win her over. Jayne grabbed her wallet and cigarettes and followed him out—he always left the door unlocked—climbing on the back of his motorbike.

'The guy we're going to meet, Deng, used to be a sex worker,' Didier said over his shoulder. 'But his German boyfriend gave him the money to start up a bar that he now runs full-time.'

He swerved to avoid a push-cart vendor selling dried squid pegged like dun-coloured socks in lines across the top of the cart.

'Is Deng's bar a pick-up joint?' Jayne shouted to be heard.

'Not in the commercial sense. There's a whole strip of bars, meeting places for gay men and *kratoeys*. Deng still has friends working in the sex industry and I want him to circulate these new materials through his networks.'

Steering the bike with one hand, he took a pamphlet from his bag and passed it over his shoulder. On the cover was an inverted pink triangle above a heading in Thai script: 'AIDS Prevention for Men Who Have Sex with Men'. Inside were graphic illustrations of anal and oral sex and step-by-step instructions on correct condom use. Jayne wasn't shocked so much as surprised that he could get away with it.

She slipped the pamphlet into her pocket as Didier parked near Chang Klan Road, the town's main tourist precinct—or, more accurately, the area where tourists were most tolerated. Foreigners could find the burger joints, banks and supermarket chains they recognised, while Thai village life went on around them. By the entrance to McDonald's, a plump woman pounded shredded green papaya, chilli and limes in a mortar and pestle to make spicy *som tam* salad, the fast food of the northeast. A man pushed a cartload of durian through a beer garden, offering a gap-toothed grin to the backpackers who wrinkled their noses at the sour smell. Money-changers clutching wads of baht notes circled the currency exchange booths like sharks, while the soothsayers and amulet traders thought nothing of blocking the entrance to the 7-Eleven by laying out their wares on plastic sheets. Jayne would have stopped for a closer look at the traditional medicine booth—she had a macabre fascination for shrivelled animal parts and desiccated reptiles—but didn't want to lose Didier in the crowd.

She followed him into the Night Bazaar, a concrete building that could pass for an underground carpark. As they zigzagged along aisles laden with clothing and souvenirs, she wondered who created the demand for stuffed cobras wrestling with mongooses, scorpions in glass boxes and metre-long wooden penises. She paused briefly to feel the fabric of a crimson and black sarong: one hundred per cent polyester.

They took a side exit, ascended a short set of steps and reached a narrow alley running between the bazaar and the next building, the glow of coloured lights ahead. The sound of dance music grew louder as they approached the strip of bars, each separated from the next by bamboo partitions. Between Tarzan's Vine and Climax was Man Date, where Didier was greeted warmly by the barman. Deng, the man they'd come to meet, was elsewhere and Jayne agreed to wait while Didier looked for him. She took a seat at the bar and ordered a beer.

The walls of Man Date were a patchwork of beer coasters from around the world, interspersed with posters of male centrefolds. There were more photos of naked men on shelves adjacent to the bar, together with a stereo system, a stack of CDs and a display of ornamental fruit—a large banana flanked by two brown lychees. On the top shelf was a small bronze Buddha, respectfully placed above head height. In front of the bar, an ornate water feature contained fresh lotus flowers and a ceramic figurine of a Chinese fisherman. Two young men and a kratoey sipped drinks at one of the club's three tables, the kratoey's red lipstick a perfect match for his mules and handbag. A neon tube lit the place, and Barbra Streisand struggled to be heard above the *Priscilla, Queen of the Desert* soundtrack blasting out from Climax.

Jayne tried to chat with the barman, but he laughed nervously and focused on rearranging the flowers. The three patrons eyed her with amusement, one muttering something behind his hand. When the kratoey responded with a high-pitched laugh, Jayne cursed Didier then herself for joining him on this errand.

She was halfway through her second beer when he reappeared with a young Thai. Smiling through gritted teeth, she returned Deng's wai and followed them to an unoccupied table. Seeing she had company, the patrons breathed a collective sigh of relief and one even leaned over and introduced himself.

'Hello. Ex-ca-use me, where are you from?'

'Australia,' Jayne said, 'but I live in Bangkok,' she added in Thai.

'You sa-peak Thai very well,' the young man pressed on in English.

'No, not really. You speak English very well.' It was an exchange she'd played out a thousand times.

The young man flushed. 'Only a little. What is your name?'

'Jayne. And you?'

'Mana. Pleased to meet you.'

'*Mai cheua*!' Didier's voice cut across their small talk. 'I don't believe it! I can't believe he'd be so stupid!'

'I'm sorry, Mister Di,' an ashen-faced Deng said. 'But you know Nou, he's got a problem with gambling. He owes a lot of money.'

Jayne frowned, wondering how Nou had come into the conversation.

'But I would've given him the money!' Didier said, tugging at his hair. 'He didn't need to go back to Loh Kroh. Why didn't he just ask me for it?'

'I don't know.' Deng bit his lower lip. 'Maybe he feels too ashamed…Ah, look, he's here now!'

Didier leapt to his feet as Nou and Jet sauntered in with two Chinese-looking men. If Nou was surprised to see Didier, he hid it well. Gesturing for his companions to wait, he approached their table.

'*Sawadee krup*—' he began. But Didier cut him off.

'Nou, what the hell's going on?'

The young man shrugged. 'I needed money.'

'Well, why didn't you ask me for it?' Didier's face was flushed, his hands curled into fists.

'Didi, please sit down,' Nou muttered. '*Jai yen-yen*—'

'I will *not* be cool!' His voice rose dangerously. 'I can't believe after all we've been through, you'd go off selling sex again.'

'You know I love you,' Nou said feebly. 'I was only doing it for the money…'

'God, you don't get it, do you? I don't give a shit about you having sex with other men.'

In the two years she'd known him, Jayne had never seen Didier this angry. Customers were turning to stare and she reached out and put a tentative hand on his arm. Didier glanced down and she felt a slackening of tension beneath her touch.

'I'm sorry,' he said, lowering his voice and releasing his fists. 'Look, I care about you, Nou, about your health, your self-respect. Don't you understand that?'

'Yes Didi, I understand,' he said, eyes downcast. 'But I thought you'd be angry with me…You always say I should stop gambling and…' He left the sentence incomplete.

Didier looked away, shaking his head.

When Nou raised his eyes, Jayne saw a flash of steel in them. Deng grabbed the pamphlets and excused himself, and Mana returned to his companions. Donna Summer had joined Barbra Streisand in 'Enough Is Enough' and Jayne took it as her cue.

'Didier, I'd better go.' She rose to her feet and slipped two hundred baht under her glass. 'You and Nou have a few things to sort out and you'll need the house to yourselves. I'll stay in a hotel tonight and call you in the morning, OK?'

'But Jayne—'

'Don't worry about it.'

She allowed him to kiss her on both cheeks and, with a perfunctory wai to Nou, turned and made her way back out through the Night Bazaar.

She kept it together until she'd waved down a tuk-tuk and given directions to the driver. But once they took off, she fired off a string of expletives under her breath, cursing Nou for having spoiled her evening and Didier for letting it happen.

Jayne was at a loss to understand Nou's attraction for Didier. Either Nou's talent in the sack was enough to sustain Didier's interest, or her friend was like any other 'rice queen' who got off on being the wealthy white partner of a younger Asian man. But this didn't fit with Jayne's image of Didier.

He should be with someone who understood him, who loved him for his idiosyncrasies—not some little bastard who was more likely to squander large sums of money over a card game than ever to read a book.

And what of Nou's bizarre suggestion that she and Didier get married? While it might be the done thing in Thailand for gay men to marry to have children, what made Nou think she'd enter into such an arrangement? His presumption unnerved her, as if he'd trespassed into her most private thoughts.

A sudden downpour hit as the tuk-tuk reached the market near Didier's place. Despite the driver's attempt to lower the plastic flaps over the passenger tray, Jayne was drenched by the time she reached the house.

She headed for the guest room, leaving a trail of wet

footprints on the wooden floor. Flicking on the bedside lamp, she peeled off her wet clothes, wrapped herself in a sarong and set about re-packing. Too miserable to care as water dripped from her curls onto her gear, she vented her anger with more muttered curses.

'I knew you were cross with me!'

Didier stood in the doorway, towel in hand, smiling sheepishly. He'd removed his glasses and his wet shirt was unbuttoned.

'I didn't think you'd be back so soon,' Jayne blushed. With the drumming rain on the tin roof, she hadn't heard him come in. 'I thought I'd dry off before I leave.'

'I came back to apologise, and because I do need to see you. There's still so much we need to talk about and—'

'What about Nou?' she interrupted him.

Didier shrugged and gave the half-sigh, half-scoff unique to francophones. 'It's the same problem we've always had. One more night's not going to make any difference.'

He handed her the towel and sat down on the edge of the bed. 'I really am sorry,' he said, staring at her half-packed backpack.

'For what?' Jayne said, wringing out her hair.

'For dragging you out tonight, for losing my temper, for not being a better friend.'

'Don't worry about it,' she said, nervous that he'd overheard her mouthing off about being taken for granted. She put the towel around her neck and wondered if she should keep packing.

'I mean it, Jayne,' Didier said. 'I don't know what I'd

do without you.' He held out his arms. 'Forgive me?'

'You know I do.' She sat down next to him.

He put his arm around her and she rested her head against his damp chest. They held each other without speaking, Didier rubbing the top of her arm. Soothed by his touch, Jayne closed her eyes.

'What the hell is that?'

Jayne recoiled, covering the still-fresh scar with her hand. 'It's nothing, an accident.'

'What happened, Jayne?' Didier removed the towel from around her neck and gently lifted her hand away. 'Tell me.'

'I–I got stabbed—'

Stabbed. It was the first time she'd said it out loud. And for the first time she realised the danger she'd been in. She burst into tears.

'My dear Jayne, *ma chérie*.' Didier took her in his arms again, holding her tighter than before. 'My precious friend, are you OK?' He rubbed her back. '*Je suis desolé, mon trésor*. I'm so sorry.'

Pressed uncomfortably against the glasses in his clammy shirt pocket, Jayne moved her head against his skin. She closed her eyes and sniffed, shock subsiding as she became more aware of Didier's hands on her bare back. Without thinking, she wiped her eyes and slipped her hands beneath his shirt, putting her arms around his torso. He shivered and moved one hand to the back of her neck.

Jayne raised her face and he kissed her lips, lightly at first, then with hunger. They opened their mouths wide, kisses growing deeper. She tilted her head back as Didier moved his mouth to her throat. He bit the skin between her neck and shoulder, making her body quiver. This loosened her sarong which fell open to her waist. She slid her hands under his wet shirt and helped him shrug it off so they were skin on skin. They lay down on the bed between the pillows and her backpack.

It was not her desire that surprised her but his. Didier kissed her mouth again, drawing her closer to him. His hand was on her breast, playing with her nipple. He hooked one of her legs over his hip so their crotches were pressed together and she felt his erection through his damp jeans. He traced the length of her spine, his fingers gently stroking the crack in her arse.

Ever since they'd first met, Jayne had fantasised about having sex with Didier. Now that it was actually happening, she should've felt ecstatic. Instead, doubt snapped at her heels like a puppy that refused to be sent outside. Didier was gay — she was under no illusions about that — and no matter how good it felt to kiss him, to touch him, to feel his skin on hers, Jayne couldn't shake the feeling that something was wrong. It wasn't in his nature to want her like this. Was he simply curious, or did he think he was doing her a favour? Was she too drunk to figure it out, or too sober not to care less?

'Didier?'

'Mmm?' he murmured from between her breasts.

She took his face in her hands to stop him kissing her. 'Sweetheart?'

'What?' He raised his head so they were eye to eye.

'I don't think I can do this,' she said.

'Why not?' He sounded offended.

'It's not that I don't want to,' she said quickly. 'It's just…to be honest, this is fucking with my head.'

'Well, it's not your head I want to fuck with.' He squeezed a nipple between his fingers, a spasm of pleasure ricocheting to her groin.

'That's not fair,' she said, flustered. 'I mean it, Didi. I'm not comfortable with this.'

'Shit, I'm sorry.' Didier rolled over and propped himself up on one arm. 'What is it? What's wrong, Jayne?'

'I don't know,' she said, searching for her clothes. 'This just doesn't feel right.'

'But I thought you wanted it,' Didier said, watching as she retrieved her underwear.

'I do!' she said. 'At least, I thought I did. I don't know! Don't take it the wrong way,' she added, seeing the hurt on his face. 'I just don't know where it would leave us. I mean, sex is the perfect way to ruin a friendship.'

'Maybe,' he shrugged. 'Or maybe it could be the start of something else.'

Jayne frowned. 'I don't know what you mean by that, but I'd be very careful about making promises you can't keep.'

'But—'

'Look, let's not talk now.' Jayne zipped up her jeans and sat down beside him. 'I'm going to stay in a hotel—'

'You don't have to do that.'

'No, I will. I mean, you've still got things to sort out with Nou, remember?'

Didier groaned. '*Merde*! Jayne, I'm sorry. What can I

say? My life's a mess at the moment.' He took her hand. 'Just tell me I haven't damaged our relationship.'

She shook her head and squeezed his hand. 'It's OK. And I'm sorry, too. Let's talk tomorrow.'

Didier kissed her palm, reaching up with his free hand to trace the scar above her elbow.

'You still haven't told me how it happened,' he said softly.

'It was an error of judgment,' she said.

The body in the bar was mutilated beyond recognition, but the wallet identifying him had been left on a nearby table as if out of courtesy to the police. For Officer Komet Plungkham it was a relief to examine its contents, even though it was a job for a rookie cop. The lieutenant colonel's condescending smile implied as much as he issued the order. Komet didn't care.

He chalked around the black leather wallet so forensics could place it, and extracted an identification card with latex-clad fingers. He stared at a head-and-shoulders photo of a boyish-looking young man, as if he might transpose the image onto the body. Instead, the photograph mutated before him, triangular gashes appearing on the broad forehead and each of the smooth cheeks. But that was not the worst of it. At first, Komet thought what lay beside the bloodied corpse was a rat and took a closer look. Clutching his stomach and retching, he staggered over to an open drain to vomit. The young man had been castrated.

By the time his colleagues had responded to his radio call, Komet had cleaned himself up, tightening his belt one notch to keep his shirt tucked in and restoring his hat, pressing it down hard over his thick mane of hair.

'He was Sanga Siamprakorn,' Komet said now, making an effort to keep his voice steady. 'Age twenty-four. Born in Ayuthaya. Lives in the Hang Dong district.'

'I believe he hangs out more often round Loh Kroh,' offered Sergeant Pornsak.

Pornsak Boonyavivat had the swagger of a man who believed himself irresistible to women. And it was true he turned a few heads, having inherited his Chinese father's fair skin and bone structure, and his Thai mother's generous lips and lean physique. But on closer inspection, something made women inclined to walk on. Pornsak had joined the force a year before Komet and acted ten years his senior, though at twenty-five—both born in the Year of the Pig— they were the same age. It was typical of him to mention a choice piece of information—prior knowledge of the victim and his habits, no less—to highlight Komet's inexperience.

'And what would lead you to believe that?' A steely-eyed look from the lieutenant colonel and Pornsak's smirk faded.

'Encountered the victim in an official capacity, Sir.' He straightened his shoulders. 'Interviewed him on suspicion of soliciting. No arrest made at the time, Sir.'

Lieutenant Colonel Ratratarn nodded. 'Anyone else care to share something they might know about Khun Sanga?'

'Ah, Sir, I h-heard he has a farang b-boyfriend.'

It was Officer Tanin's turn to impress the commander. Tanin had been in the same intake of recruits as Komet. A native of Chiang Rai province, he was a short, stocky man, the buttons of his chocolate-brown uniform straining over his barrel chest. His bug-eyes gave him a look of continual astonishment, and his grey teeth indicated he'd been over-dosed with anti-malarial medicine as a child. Unlike Komet, he looked up to Pornsak. But lacking his arrogance and having a tendency to stutter, Tanin came across more as a parody than protégé of the sergeant.

'Really?' Ratratarn said, turning to him with exaggerated interest. 'And just how did you hear that?'

'Ah, ah…' Tanin frantically scanned the scene. 'H-he—sh-he—he told me.' He gestured towards the small crowd in an adjacent bar.

Among the gawping collection of scruffy street kids, bleary-eyed young men and a couple of bargirls Komet recognised from his beat, he spotted Tanin's target: a striking figure in full make-up and blond wig, pantyhose shimmering beneath the split of a pearl-grey evening gown and feet squeezed into silver stilettos. If not for the pronounced Adam's apple, which the kratoey instinctively covered with one hand, Komet could have sworn he was a woman.

'Over here,' Ratratarn barked.

Panic flashed across the kratoey's face.

'I said come here!'

He shuffled forward, a handkerchief held to his mouth.

'Name?'

'My professional name is Marilyn—*aie!*'

The honeyed tones evaporated in a cry as Ratratarn grabbed him roughly by the wrist and twisted his arm behind his back.

'I don't give a shit about your professional name, arsehole!'

The kratoey's body went limp for a moment, then Ratratarn yanked him back upright, eliciting another cry.

'I-it's P-Pairoj,' he whimpered, 'Pairoj Ni-Nilmongkol.'

'That's better. Man's body, man's name. Or are you one of those sick bastards who's had the operation?'

He put his hand between the man's legs and squeezed. Pairoj yelped, and his free hand fluttered from his face to his crotch.

'Obviously not,' Ratratarn sniggered, swinging Pairoj around so he faced the corpse. 'The thing is, someone has given our friend Khun Sanga here the operation. But I don't think they used any anaesthetic, do you?'

The groin of the corpse was black with semi-congealed blood. And blood lay in the palm of the outstretched right hand where Komet had found the severed penis. The kratoey turned his face away, tears making his mascara run.

'I-I don't know what happened,' he sobbed. 'I was doing a show at the Lotus. I was on my way home and saw the p-police car…'

'You told Officer Tanin here the deceased had a foreign boyfriend.'

'N-no, I—*aie*!'

Ratratarn twisted the man's arm further.

'You told Officer Tanin the deceased had a foreign boyfriend.'

'Th-that's right,' Pairoj whimpered.

'Good boy,' Ratratarn said. 'Now go and give your contact details to Officer Tanin so we can keep in touch, OK?'

Ratratarn released his grip. Pairoj lost his balance and reeled forward, almost falling on the corpse. With a choked scream he backed into Komet who gently steered him over to Tanin. He felt sympathy for the transvestite: at least he'd shown some emotion, whereas there was no sign of his colleagues being affected by the grisly murder. Komet was grateful no one had witnessed his own reaction.

The Scientific Crime Detection Division team arrived. With a glance from Ratratarn, Komet took the remaining papers from the wallet and carefully replaced it on the table. He shuffled through the items—motorbike licence, ATM card, a couple of withdrawal receipts, student ID—before coming across a business card, printed in English on one side, Thai on the other.

'Di Di Yah Der Mon Pahs,' he transliterated aloud.

'What's that?' Ratratarn materialised in front of him.

'Name card, Sir. It was in the deceased's wallet. Looks like it belongs to a foreigner.'

The lieutenant colonel snatched the card from Komet's fingers. '"Didier de Montpasse,"' he read in English. '"Research consultant, Rural Development and HIV/ AIDS." There's an address here…Komet, you're coming with me to check it out. Could be the farang boyfriend. Pornsak!'

His call interrupted the sergeant's interrogation of a young man in the crowd of onlookers.

'You and Tanin stay here until the SCDD boys are done.'

'Ah, Sir, here's something that might interest you. This guy—what did you say your name was?'

'Mana.'

The young man wore jeans torn at the knees and a pale

blue T-shirt, a thick fringe of hair shaded his eyes like a visor.

'Khun Mana was here a few hours ago, around ten,' Pornsak said. 'Says he witnessed an argument between the deceased and a foreigner.'

'The farang was very angry, Sir,' Mana piped up, licking his lips as he spoke. 'I'm not sure why. I think it had something to do with money.'

'Would you know this foreigner if you saw him again?'

'Oh, yes, Sir. We all know him.' He indicated the other young men in the group. 'He comes around here a lot. He helps us...' His voice trailed off.

'Helps you what?' Pornsak said, grabbing Mana by his T-shirt and eyeballing him.

Komet recognised the homage to their chief in the sergeant's action, but the gesture merely made Pornsak look like a thug.

'He helps us look after ourselves,' Mana said, more annoyed than frightened. 'You know, to look after our health, protect ourselves from getting AIDS—'

At the word AIDS, Pornsak let go of the young man as if he'd been stung.

'What's this foreigner's name?' Ratratarn said, toying with the business card.

Mana licked his lips again. 'We call him Khun Di, Sir.'

'*Cheu Khun Di proh wah pen kon dee, chai mai?*'

The young man nodded. 'We call him Mister Di because he's a good person. I think his real name is Didi, Didiyer—something like that.'

Ratratarn glanced at the card and smiled—or was it, Komet wondered, a grimace? His chief's smile was a lifeless tightening of the lips. Ratratarn was in his fifties, but his face was smooth, apart from two thin, crescent-shaped scars which enclosed his left eye like parentheses. Beneath his close-fitting uniform, his body had the strength of a much younger man.

The lieutenant colonel looked up sharply and Komet, fearing Ratratarn could read his thoughts, studied the serial number on the licence he'd taken from Sanga's wallet.

'Tanin, get a signed statement from this kid. Pornsak, interview everyone here and see if anyone else witnessed the argument between the victim and the foreigner. Komet, you come with me. We're going to pay a visit to this Mister Good.'

Didier was no stranger to insomnia, considering it an occupational hazard. But it wasn't his usual mantra of 'what more could I be doing?' that had him watching the luminous digits of his bedside clock change from 3:09 to 3:10. He looked at the empty space in the bed beside him, thinking about Jayne.

Had he damaged their relationship? The heat of the moment gave him an opportunity he couldn't pass up. Before that night, he wasn't even sure he could initiate sex with a woman—even one he loved as much as Jayne. But he had, and he felt proud. Part of him really wanted to fuck her.

But he shouldn't have come on so strong; he felt like he'd scared her off. Still, she'd agreed to come back in the morning to talk things through. Nou was usually at the gym by ten on a Saturday, and they'd have the house to themselves.

At the thought of Nou, Didier sighed. What would've happened if he'd walked in on him and Jayne? He suspected Nou wouldn't have been surprised, and doubted he'd even care. Didier couldn't say if it was a credit to their relationship or a sign of it failing.

He must have dozed off, because he dreamt that someone was pounding on his door in urgent need of his help. But he couldn't move—it was as if his limbs were made of lead. He could only lie there, listening to the sound, overcome with a terrible sense of failure and sadness. Then he realised someone *was* pounding on the front door. He looked at the clock: 3:45. He'd barely slept at all. Dragging himself up and pulling on a T-shirt over his shorts, he stumbled to the door, flicking a switch on the way. Blinded by the sudden light, it took him a moment to make out the figures standing on the balcony. Didier had the door open before he realised, with a wave of panic, that they were police.

'*Sawadee krup*,' he said. 'How can I help you, officers?'

'*Sawadee—*' a man whose nametag identified him as Officer Komet began, but the older of the two cut him off.

'Are you Didier de Montpasse?' There was steel in his voice.

Didier swallowed and glanced at the man's badge. 'Yes, Lieutenant Colonel.'

Ratratarn showed no surprise at Didier's ability to speak the language. 'Where were you between one and two this morning?'

'Excuse me, Lieutenant Colonel, what's this in regard to?'

'Just answer the question.' A muscle twitched in his forehead. To Didier, he looked like the sort of man who had control over every muscle in his body.

'I was here. Rather, I got back here around eleven. Before that, I was out with friends. Sir, perhaps if you told me what this is about I could be of some assistance.'

It galled him to have to be so polite, but he couldn't risk anything else. Not until he knew why they were there.

'We'll ask the questions,' Ratratarn said. 'And we'll do that inside if we may?'

It was a rhetorical question. No one invited the Chiang Mai police into their home.

Didier stepped back to allow the men to pass. The younger one, Komet, had a sweet face, the broad nose and thick lips of a native from northeast Isaan. He looked apologetic, ill at ease in his uniform. Didier guessed he hadn't been in the force long, and wondered how long it would take for Komet's face to lose its softness, how long before he would have the same contempt as his commanding officer.

'Komet, you look around.' Ratratarn issued the order with a tilt of the head and turned to Didier. 'Mister Good—I believe that's what they call you, isn't it? You work in Chiang Mai as a foreign academic. Research on rural development; AIDS education. You do—what's the expression?—"outreach work" in the clubs and bars.'

Despite the humidity, a chill ran down Didier's spine. Ratratarn spoke as if he'd had Didier under surveillance for some time. He should've seen this coming.

'So,' Ratratarn continued, 'exactly where were you earlier this evening?'

'I was in a bar behind the Night Bazaar called Man Date.'

'Who were you there with?'

'Friends. Thai friends.'

Ratratarn eyeballed him, a gesture Didier knew was disrespectful. 'What were the names of these friends?'

Before Didier could answer, the younger officer came back into the room.

'Excuse me, Sir,' he said, 'I thought you should see this.'

Komet handed over one of Didier's pamphlets. Ratratarn opened it, glanced at the contents, and folded it again. With his index finger, he slowly traced around the pink triangle on the cover.

Didier felt relief flood over him. So that's why they'd come! He opened his mouth to speak, but snapped it shut when he saw what Officer Komet held in his other hand. It was a framed photograph of himself and Nou, which he kept on the bedside table.

Ratratarn let the pamphlet fall to the floor. Taking the photo from Komet, Didier watched him trace the same shape, a triangle, onto Nou's forehead and cheeks.

'Was this man one of the friends you were with this evening, Mister Good?'

'Yes,' Didier whispered hoarsely. The sense of dread returned.

The lieutenant colonel placed the picture on the coffee

table and nodded to Komet. 'Check the back of the house, kitchen, garden, everywhere,' he said.

The junior officer bowed and walked out of the room. After a moment, Didier heard the back door bang shut.

'Khun Sanga Siamprakorn, native of Chiang Mai, age twenty-four. Worked for several years in Loh Kroh.' Ratratarn spoke as if reading from invisible notes. He paused and cocked his head. 'You don't think he was a bit young for you?'

There was a razor-thin smile on his face as his hand moved to the holster above his hip.

Didier understood. He gazed at Nou's photograph, feeling numb, almost calm. His thoughts were so far away, he didn't register that Ratratarn had spoken again.

'I said, walk towards the door.'

Didier faced the policeman and looked at him hard. 'I want you to realise,' he said in English, 'I know what's going on here.' And because he didn't want the last face he saw to be that of his executioner, he glanced back at the photo of Nou, and one of Jayne on the wall beyond it.

He whispered as he walked towards the door. 'Though I walk through the valley of the shadow of death...' He stopped and reached for the handle. '...I will fear no evil.' The door opened and he passed through it. 'For though art with me. Thy rod and thy staff they comfort me.'

Why should those words come back to him now? It had been years since he'd set foot in a church.

'Surely goodness and mercy shall follow me...' Was that a trigger being cocked, or the squeaking of the hinge? '...All the days of my life.'

He crossed the balcony, paused at the top of the stairs and inhaled deeply. The night air smelled of jasmine, over-ripe mangoes, wet earth and a subtle note of human sweat. It was a scent he'd come to think of as Thailand.

'And I will dwell in the house of the Lord…'

He stepped forward to take the first stair.

'…forever—'

His foot never reached the ground.

Jayne woke up frowning. She was baffled both by Didier's behaviour the night before and her reaction to it. What had possessed him to try and seduce her? And why, when it was what she'd always wanted, had it left her feeling so uneasy?

It was all mixed up in her head with Nou's talk of marriage and babies. Jayne had left Australia because she baulked at getting on the marriage-mortgage-multiply treadmill, but five years on it worried her that she no longer had the choice. Perhaps she should consider a marriage of convenience with Didier since the normal route to parenthood seemed unlikely.

But was that what she really wanted? Despite Didier's suggestion that this could be 'the start of something else', Jayne didn't believe he could turn for her. It was unfair for him even to imply it. And she didn't think she could accommodate his needs, let alone his relationship with Nou: a ménage à trois in which she was the only party not having sex held no appeal at all. Perhaps her desires were more conventional than she wanted to admit.

She splashed cold water on her face and looked at herself in the mirror. Her hair was a mess of rained-on curls, exposing her forehead where the first, faint lines of ageing had started to appear. Purple crescents beneath her eyes made them look more yellow than amber. And due to lack of sleep, her heart-shaped face was paler than usual, making her freckles stand out.

'You're getting ahead of yourself, Keeney,' she told her reflection.

She rearranged her hair with a wide-toothed comb, and pinched her cheeks to put colour in them. As anxious as she was to sort things out with Didier, she needed coffee first.

Jayne found a cafe near her hotel with tables on the street. She ordered coffee and, taking out her wallet, left her day-pack on a chair to reserve her place while she scanned the headlines of the Thai papers at an adjacent newsstand.

'Local Boy Murdered'. She snatched a copy of *Thai Rath* and stared at the gruesome front-page photograph. A jacket covered the dead body's face, though the mutilated groin was clearly visible in the picture. A policeman pointed to the corpse, as if to allay any doubts that the victim might still be alive. The image of the pointing policeman was a feature of Thai press photography that usually amused Jayne, but not now. There was something familiar about the setting, the coasters on the walls, the fountain in the background.

In a sidebar was a small head-shot like a passport photograph with the caption 'Sanga Siamprakorn: body found mutilated'. There was no mistaking it. Sanga—or Nou—was dead.

She leaned against the counter and tried reading the small print for details, but although she spoke Thai with near fluency, the written language was another matter. It was taking too long and she had to get to Didier's place. She couldn't begin to imagine the state he'd be in.

As she folded the paper, her eyes landed on a smaller headline near the bottom of the page, attracted by a single word she recognised easily. Farang. Foreigner. Jayne felt her stomach sink as she forced herself to translate the remaining words. She read 'Foreign Suspect Killed Trying to Resist Arrest', before the characters blurred on the page.

Feeling a hand on her arm, she raised her head. The shopkeeper was staring pointedly at the newspaper in Jayne's hand, her angular black eyebrows so close together it looked as if the letter M was painted on her forehead.

'*Kor thort na ka*,' Jayne stammered, wiping her eyes and fumbling for some change. 'I'm sorry…'

The woman looked up and the black M split apart. '*Mai pen rai*,' she said, patting Jayne's arm and giggling in the embarrassed way Thai people did in the face of grief. It was a custom Jayne had never been able to fathom, least of all now.

She staggered back to her table where her coffee was waiting. The glare of the sun on the white tabletop hurt her eyes and she put on her sunglasses with shaky hands. Then she smoothed the paper out in front of her to translate the Thai script. It was easier to treat it as an academic exercise, consulting her pocket dictionary, detaching herself from the meaning of the English words as she wrote them in a note-book. She even managed to order a second coffee.

Most of the front-page report was dedicated to graphic descriptions of Nou's injuries. His body had been found, disfigured and dismembered, in a bar behind the Night Bazaar around 2.15 that morning. 'Triangular shapes were carved into Khun Sanga's face with what Scientific Crime

Detection Division experts believe was a razor,' Jayne wrote in her notebook. 'Police believe the same weapon, which has yet to be found, was used to castrate the body. The male sex organ'—the paper used a formal term for penis that she'd never heard before—'was found on the ground some distance from the corpse…'

Jayne closed her eyes and rubbed her temples. She knew the explicit detail, like the gruesome photography, was as an object lesson to remind Thai Buddhist readers of the impermanence of the flesh, but it was hard for her to take.

Most of information about Didier was on page three.

> Tipped off by eyewitness accounts of a heated argument that took place between Khun Sanga and a foreign man, police proceeded to a house near the Muang Mai Market where they confronted the farang. When he tried to resist arrest, police opened fire, killing the suspect during his attempted escape. Sources say the man, Canadian expatriate Didier de Montpasse, was a known homosexual who was jealous of Khun Sanga.

There were no photos of Didier, which suggested the news of his death hadn't reached the paper until it was about to go to press. She'd left him just before midnight. Nou's body had been discovered around two. What time had the police gone to Didier's place?

An image flashed into Jayne's mind: Didier kissing her neck. Would he still be alive if she'd stayed with him last night? Or would she—?

Jayne shook her head. She double-checked her translation, folded the paper and placed both in her backpack. Leaving a fifty baht note under her coffee cup, she began walking in the direction of the river, crushing mango rind and withered frangipani blossoms beneath her feet. She waved away tuk-tuk drivers who crawled along beside her, and there must have been something in her demeanour that made the beggars leave her alone. As she passed a temple, its mirrored mosaic shattered her reflection into pieces.

When she looked up and saw the Rama IX Bridge, she realised she was on auto-pilot, walking to Didier's house to keep their appointment. But Didier wouldn't be there.

Jayne sat down on the riverbank with her back against a tree and her head in her hands. It couldn't be true. Not him—not Didier. Not dead.

Hot, angry tears rolled down her face. How was it possible? Didier was a good man who tried to make the world a better place—unlike herself, who was content to profit from its flaws. It wasn't fair.

And what about her? How could he kiss her—almost make love to her—and then die? How was she supposed to make sense of what happened between them now? Guilt mingled with anger in her tears.

When she finally raised her head, the sun was sliding towards the horizon. She had lost an entire day.

The Ping River looked like molten bronze and the gilt-tipped spires of Chiang Mai's temples sparkled in the dusky light. Such beauty seemed a travesty in the face of Didier's death, and Jayne's anger found a new target: she hated Chiang Mai.

She scowled as she walked from the embankment to the road and waved down a tuk-tuk. To avoid conversation with the driver she pretended she couldn't speak Thai, directing him in broken English back to the guesthouse.

Komet frowned as he read over his report. Paperwork was arduous at the best of times. Not having slept in more than twenty hours made it more so. Most difficult was recording events he hadn't actually witnessed. Still, Lieutenant Colonel Ratratarn didn't see it as a problem.

'As soon as we get back to the station, you're to write up what I've told you,' he'd said as they waited for back-up to arrive. 'It's imperative we get it down quickly.'

Komet complied, writing what he was told happened while he was searching the garden. Ratratarn said when he'd questioned the foreigner further the suspect admitted to being in the Man Date bar with the victim and confirmed they'd argued. When Ratratarn probed him as to the cause of the argument, the suspect became agitated and aggressive. Pointing to the photograph of the victim, he shouted that Khun Sanga was a bad person. *Chua meuan mah* was the exact phrase he'd used.

The lieutenant colonel asked the suspect if Khun Sanga was 'as bad as a dog', did he deserve to die like one. The foreigner replied in the affirmative. The lieutenant colonel then suggested that the suspect had killed Khun Sanga.

The suspect responded by rushing at Lieutenant Colonel Ratratarn with raised fists. Caught unawares, the lieutenant colonel, though unhurt, was thrown off balance. By the time he righted himself, the suspect had run out the front door, clearly intending to avoid capture.

Ratratarn said he called out for the man to stop as he was under arrest. When that failed to have an impact—by which point, the suspect had reached the top of the stairs—the lieutenant colonel fired a warning shot into the air. The suspect failed to stop and, as a last resort, Lieutenant Colonel Ratratarn fired his pistol again, aiming to wound him in the leg. The foreigner stumbled on the stairs, however, and the shot caught him in the back. He was dead by the time Officer Komet, on hearing gunfire, rushed from the garden to the front of the house.

Komet dutifully recorded this account of the events. His commander checked the draft and added a paragraph at the end.

'It's important we include all facts,' Ratratarn said, handing the document back. 'Since the case involves the death of a farang, we must anticipate some kind of inquiry. It's a regrettable business, but since there were only two of us present, here's hoping they'll get through it quickly.'

Komet returned to his desk and read Ratratarn's amended conclusion: 'Later asked by journalists at the scene whether he thought the suspect had committed the murder, Lieutenant Colonel Ratratarn replied there was no doubt as to the foreigner's guilt. "An innocent man would have done everything in his power to defend his innocence," he said. He added that he regretted that the suspect's death would not enable him to be brought to justice through the correct channels.'

Komet typed up the changes, unable to shake the feeling that the lieutenant colonel didn't regret the foreigner's death nearly so much as he regretted the prospect of an inquiry.

It was almost lunchtime when he submitted the finished report and stumbled home. With barely enough energy to greet his anxious wife, Komet fell into bed.

He woke several hours later to the sound of the television. Arunee was sitting on the end of the bed, eyes glued to the screen. Komet reached for the remote and turned up the volume to hear the news presenter on Channel 4.

'A Scientific Crime Detection Division representative has confirmed that a cut-throat razor found by police at the home of Canadian murder suspect Khun Didier de Montpasse bore traces of blood matching the type of murder victim, local boy Khun Sanga Siamprakorn. Police say they found the murder weapon wrapped in a plastic bag behind a water trough in the foreigner's backyard.'

'But that's not—' Komet began.

'Hush,' his wife stopped him. 'I want to hear this.'

At the next ad break, Komet staggered outside to the toilet, directing a stream of urine into the hole in the floor. He flushed with a scoop of water from the adjacent tub and poured a second ladleful over his head. Rubbing his face, he tossed the dipper back, watching it bob on the surface.

He could have sworn he'd checked the area behind the water trough at the foreigner's house. Not only that: though Ratratarn said he'd fired twice and forensics found two spent cartridges at the scene, Komet remembered hearing only one gunshot.

In hotel lobbies throughout Chiang Mai it was not unusual to see receptionists, bellboys, waiters and cleaners comatose in front of television soap operas and quiz shows, but it surprised Jayne to see the staff at the Silver Star transfixed by the local news. Glancing at the screen, she saw with a pang that it was an item about Nou and Didier. She removed her sunglasses.

'Police say they found the murder weapon wrapped in a plastic bag behind a water trough in the foreigner's backyard,' a silver-haired anchorman in a brown suit said.

The scene cut to a press conference at Police Bureau 5. A taut, hard-faced man in a skin-tight uniform, red braid coiled around one arm and fastened under an epaulet with a patchwork of coloured medals on his breast pocket, was surrounded by microphones. A caption identified him as Police Lieutenant Colonel Ratratarn Rattakul in charge of the murder investigation. Jayne listened as he droned on about the results of forensic tests, before an off-screen journalist asked if the foreign suspect had committed the murder.

'All the evidence points in that direction,' Ratratarn said.

'Have the police located any eyewitnesses?' another asked.

'Interviews are still under way.'

'You've said you regret accidentally killing the suspect. Is this because there's some doubt in your mind regarding the foreigner's guilt?'

Jayne stared at the man responsible for Didier's death. When Ratratarn looked into the camera, it seemed as if he were staring right back at her.

'There is no doubt in my mind as to the foreigner's guilt,' he said in a tone that defied anyone to question his judgment. 'I regret only that the opportunity has been lost to punish the offender with the full force of the law.'

'And in news just through,' the anchorman said, 'sources reveal that murder suspect, Didier de Montpasse, previously faced assault charges in his home town of Sainte Romauld in the Canadian province of Quebec. Police say the foreigner's history of violent crime is significant.'

'What the fuck—?' Jayne swore out loud, attracting anxious looks from the hotel staff. She mumbled an apology and retrieved her key.

Back in her room, she took a couple of painkillers, and lit a cigarette. There was a desk against one wall with a large mirror over it and she sat down and stared at her reflection. Her eyes were puffy and glazed, and her face was drained of colour. Her skin was chafed from using toilet paper to blow her nose, and her lips seemed swollen, as if bruised by kisses.

The man she had kissed the previous evening—her best friend, whom she loved—was the same person they were talking about on the news. The idea that Didier could commit a criminal act of violence was so at odds with his character, she was convinced there must be some mistake.

She picked up the phone, placed a call to Bangkok and had just lit a second cigarette when the connection came through.

'Your call to Bangkok, Ma'am,' the operator said. 'Go ahead, please.'

'Hello?'

'Jayne, is that you? Where are you?'

'Max!' She paused to swallow the lump that rose in her throat at the sound of her friend's voice. 'I'm in Chiang Mai.'

'Oh, God! So you know about—'

'Yes, I know about Didier. I…I was with him last night, just before…'

'Oh, Jayne, I'm so sorry,' Max said, his own voice shaking.

'Hang on.' She put down the receiver, wiped her nose, took a deep breath and picked it up again.

'Last night, we went to this bar—it was part of Didier's work—and Nou turned up. They had an argument because Nou's been gambling again, working the beat to pay off his debts. It got pretty heated, but things seemed to have calmed down by the time I left.'

'Have you—?' Max hesitated. 'The news reports mentioned eyewitnesses to the argument. Has anyone talked with you?'

Jayne frowned. 'What do you mean?'

'Have the police interviewed you?'

'Not yet,' she said, her mind ticking over. 'Shit! I should have thought of that.'

'Hang on a minute. I didn't mean to imply you should talk to the police. On the contrary, I think it's best if you get back here as soon as you can and—'

'But I can explain it,' she said quickly. 'I mean, you and I both know there's no way Didier could've killed Nou.'

It took so long for Max to reply that Jayne thought they'd lost the connection.

'Do we really know that?' he said finally. 'I mean, there

is the matter of what happened in Canada.'

Jayne felt her face flush. 'The assault charges,' she said. 'I saw it on the news. But that's got to be bullshit! I can't believe that.'

'Oh, Jayne, I didn't want to be the one to tell you this but it's true. Didier beat up a man, beat him senseless. The charges were dropped, but that doesn't change what happened.'

'But Didier would never—'

'Broken nose, lacerations to the face and arms, three broken ribs, severe concussion—'

'What the hell are you doing?' she snapped. 'Reading from the guy's bloody medical report?'

'Well, yes.'

Jayne flushed again. As second secretary to the Australian Embassy, Max would have access to such a document.

'But it must have been an accident or…or an act of self-defence. I mean, we don't know anything about the circumstances, do we?'

'The victim was sixty years old,' Max said. 'There was no evidence that a struggle took place. Nor was there any prior history of violence in the relationship between the victim and his assailant.'

'But—'

'The victim's name was Jean-Clément de Montpasse. He was Didier's father.'

'Oh shit!'

'I'm sorry, Jayne,' Max said. 'Believe me, I'm as shocked as you are. I mean, you think you know a person well…but sometimes you have to admit you didn't know them nearly as well as you thought.'

'But you can't honestly believe Didier killed Nou!' Her voice was barely audible above the static on the line.

'I'm not saying that,' Max said carefully. 'All I'm saying is there's evidence to suggest he was capable of killing Nou. The bottom line is it doesn't look good.'

'No,' she whispered, 'I guess it doesn't.'

'The Canadian Embassy will be organising an official inquiry. Forget going to the police. Just come back to Bangkok as soon as you can.'

She said she'd call him back when she had her travel details and replaced the receiver in its cradle. Her cigarette had burnt itself out, leaving behind a perfect cylinder of ash.

Jayne stared at the remains in the ashtray. With each new development the evidence against Didier was mounting. She'd witnessed the argument between him and Nou, and saw that Didier was unusually angry. There was also the matter of the murder weapon. Jayne had seen Didier use a cut-throat razor, and had accused him of being pretentious when he said it was the only way to get a really close shave.

But what really shocked her was the assault. Even though Didier hadn't been in Canada since the late seventies, it proved he was capable of violence. And there was a link between Nou's death and the assault on his father: in both cases the violence was directed at men close to him.

Jayne looked in the mirror. She was a private investigator! Could she have been so wrong about him?

Max supposed he only had himself to blame for bringing them together. Although Jayne was his friend first, once she met Didier, Max knew he'd been passed over. He long suspected her of having fallen in love with Didier, though Jayne scoffed at the idea.

'Really, Max!' she had said. 'There's nothing more pathetic than a straight woman pining for a gay man.'

Whatever the case, there was no mistaking Jayne's deep affection for Didier nor, for that matter, his for her.

Max had met Didier in his capacity as the international liaison officer at Chiang Mai University, and found him likeable, if serious. As for Jayne, he'd responded to her ad and hired her to spy on his boyfriend.

'You did what?' Didier said when Max told him.

'I hired a private detective. I knew Boun was up to something. And within forty-eight hours, I had evidence that the little prick was seeing the secretary to the defence attaché on the sly—a photo of them at the Sphinx bar with their hands so far down each other's pants you'd think they were examining each other for prostate cancer.'

Didier was intrigued and during his next visit to Bangkok, Max invited both him and Jayne to one of his soirées, a premier networking event. A plush apartment in Bangkok's embassy district was one of the perks of diplomatic life, and the monthly soirées took place in what Max referred to as his salon, a room modelled on the Long Bar at Raffles Hotel in Singapore, boasting marble floors, dark wood panelling, cane furniture and slow ceiling fans. Authentic Singapore slings were served from five o'clock. The night Jayne and Didier met there were around twenty people there, but Max couldn't recall either of them speaking to anyone but each other.

He watched them exchange business cards on arrival, a ritual greeting throughout southeast Asia.

'"Discreet Private Investigator, speaks English, French and Thai,"' Didier read aloud from Jayne's card. 'I've never met an Australian francophone before. "Experienced in both private and criminal investigations." What sort of criminal investigations?'

'Oh, petty theft, fraud, missing persons—that kind of thing.'

'She's too modest to tell you,' Max had interrupted, 'but one of those missing persons was murdered. And in the process of uncovering that information, Jayne busted a wildlife smuggling racket.'

'I'm putting Max on the payroll as my PR agent.' She smiled at him with exaggerated sweetness, then glanced at Didier's card. 'And you're an academic researcher based in Chiang Mai. You'd have your work cut out for you.'

'Yes—'

'He also does outreach work in the clubs and bars,' Max piped up again, 'and uses his own money to pay for the condoms he distributes.'

'An academic with a conscience,' she said, smiling at Didier. 'They must be as rare as Australian francophones.'

Max left them at that point to attend to other guests — the German ambassador's wife needed distracting, lest she complain again about her Thai domestic staff — and it was an hour before he had the chance to check in on their conversation.

'My career is a case of life imitating art,' Jayne was saying. 'All the PIs I read about were savvy and streetwise, flexible and resourceful. Having developed these skills just to survive in Bangkok, I figured I might as well get paid for it.'

'Why not!' Didier laughed. 'Drink?'

She nodded and he signalled for the waiter to bring them another round of cocktails.

'So what kind of detective novels do you read?' he said, handing her a glass.

'I like women writers mostly — Sara Paretsky, Val McDermid, Donna Leon — but not the forensic psychologists. I don't buy all that stuff about violence being purely pathological.'

'What about Agatha Christie?'

'Agatha Christie?' Jayne pulled a face. 'It's a bit old-fashioned. I mean, I read her when I was in my teens.'

'I like Christie,' Didier said. 'Her plots are intricate and you're always kept guessing whodunit until the very end.'

'I like Agatha Christie,' Max offered.

'The stories aren't exactly realistic,' Jayne said, barely glancing at their host. 'Not like the modern writers. Take James Ellroy, for example. His accounts of police corruption are based on historical events.'

'All form and no substance!'

'How can you say that?' she said, her indignant tone

belied by a smile. 'He's an amazing writer!'

'I'll bet nothing Ellroy ever wrote influenced the way policing is done. Whereas if you take the work of Sir Arthur Conan Doyle...'

She rolled her eyes. 'I don't believe you!'

'It's true! Conan Doyle created new methods of detective work through the Sherlock Holmes stories. He invented the use of plaster moulds to preserve clues, the technique of dusting for fibres and ashes, not to mention his influence on the science of deduction. I guarantee if you read the Sherlock Holmes stories, you'll pick up a few tips.'

With Jayne's laughter in his ears and a conversation clearly closed to him, Max moved on to his other guests. He didn't see Jayne and Didier again until they were leaving. Together.

'Gotta go, Max,' Jayne said. 'I've got a surveillance job.' She stood on her toes to kiss him on the cheek. 'Thanks for a lovely evening.'

'I'm walking her out,' Didier said. 'Thanks, Max. Great night.'

Still within earshot, Max heard Jayne say, 'Shame I don't have a Sherlock Holmes novel to take along and study, *n'est-ce pas*?'

'*Absolument*!' Didier laughed.

Max could have sworn they were flirting.

On returning to Chiang Mai, Didier sent Jayne a copy of *A Study in Scarlet* with an inscription: *To Jayne Keeney, Discreet Private Investigator. May the solutions to all your cases be elementary.*

Jayne reciprocated with Sara Paretsky's *Tunnel Vision*

and the note: *I'll let you know if Holmes comes in handy. Meanwhile, here's one for you. I figure the title sums up your taste in crime fiction.*

They corresponded often after that, sending books and reading lists, visiting each other in Bangkok and Chiang Mai, and their relationship remained flirtatious. Max couldn't blame Jayne for her part, but he disapproved when Didier played along. It wasn't fair on Jayne.

Max felt it would be more appropriate if Didier had flirted with him.

She was in a coastal village where the houses were made from disused bomb shelters. Turning a corner, she came face to face with a cow. It lowered its head and, using one of its horns as a prod, steered her out of the village along a path. Then she was on the edge of a cliff, the cow's horn still digging into her back, staring at the sea, baffled to think it had come to this.

Jayne switched on the lamp, got up and lit a cigarette. Disoriented by the dream, it took her a moment to locate the ashtray. It was on a side-table next to a copy of *The Adventures of Sherlock Holmes*, an early gift from Didier that she often carried with her. Not that she'd ever admit it, but Didier was right about picking up tips from Holmes.

The book reminded her of the night she took him to Baker Street, a Bangkok bar designed to look like a gentlemen's club. In keeping with the local talent for forgery, the bar's wood panelling was synthetic, the armchairs vinyl, and the books on the shelves facades of moulded plastic. But with a large movie poster above the bar for *The Hound of the Baskervilles* starring Basil Rathbone, and cocktails named for characters in the Sherlock Holmes stories, it seemed perfect for their first book club meeting. They'd spent the afternoon scouring secondhand bookshops along Khao San Road, buying a dozen books between them, which lay in plastic bags at their feet as they drank Moriarty and Doctor Watson cocktails and swapped life stories.

Jayne cast her mind back over their conversation, searching for any clues on what happened between Didier and his father. It was the night she figured out he was gay — that penny dropped when he talked about first arriving in Chiang Mai as a twenty-one-year-old student.

'Back then I thought anything was possible,' he said. 'I'd come from a small town where the greatest faux pas was to stand out in a crowd. So imagine how I felt the first time I saw a kratoey. With long hair, painted nails and wearing what looked like a miniskirt, I didn't pick that he was a boy. The skirt turned out to be flared shorts — part of his school uniform, no less — and he was standing with a group of school kids at a bus stop, laughing. A boy like that would've been crucified where I'd come from. But in Thailand, it seemed perfectly acceptable.'

Jayne's face must have betrayed her scepticism as Didier hastened to add, 'I was young and naive, Jayne. I've learned since then. I know being a kratoey is seen as punishment for sexual indiscretions committed in a past life — that they are tolerated rather than accepted. But back then, it was all new to me. I couldn't believe it when my first Thai boyfriend turned around after a year together and announced that he was leaving me to get married. He even invited me to the wedding!'

Jayne laughed and shook her head, amused by her own wishful thinking as much as Didier's story.

'That, one of my older Thai friends told me, was a case of falling for "a fish in the wrong pond".' He drew inverted commas in the air. 'What I needed to find was "a tree in the same forest". So I did. I found a guy who swore he'd never give in to family pressure to get married. Trouble was I made the mistake of telling him I had no intention of ever returning to Canada and he left me for a Swedish tourist.'

Still laughing, Jayne flashed him a guilty smile. 'I'm sorry, Didier. I shouldn't laugh. But it's comforting to know I'm not the only one who gets taken for a ride in relationships.'

'Give me an example—make me feel like less of an idiot.'

'OK.' She took a swig from her cocktail and figured she had nothing to lose. 'When I was starting out as a private investigator I was employed by this Australian guy, Richard Goodman, who'd been ripped off in a card scam. You know the sort of thing. Well-heeled tourist meets friendly local who turns out to be a croupier at the casino. Local says he can teach tourist how to play and win, and tourist agrees to participate in a private game for practice, a wealthy punter having conveniently turned up in the meantime. Then—lo and behold—tourist ends up losing hundreds of dollars.'

'People keep falling for stunts like that.'

'Yeah, well, that's what I thought,' she said. 'See, I did end up tracking down the people behind the racket—a group of Filipinos with a history of that sort of thing—and Richard was grateful. He not only paid my fee, but insisted on wining and dining me as well. One thing led to another and I ended up spending the night with him, only to wake up the next morning and read in the papers that the Filipinos arrested the previous day on fraud charges claimed they'd been set up. The real brains behind the operation, they said, was an Australian man called Ralph Godsell.

'Needless to say, Richard Goodman aka Ralph Godsell had done a runner in the night. And to really add insult to injury, he left me to pay the hotel bill.'

Didier laughed aloud. 'Oh, that makes me feel much better.'

'You'd think I'd have more sense,' she said with a wry smile, 'but I get so few offers in this place. Thai men seem to disapprove of me—I'm too loud, I guess—and most farang men prefer the local fare. Not that I blame them. Thai women are beautiful.' She gestured towards the window overlooking the street. 'Out there, I feel about as attractive as a sow's ear in a sea of silk purses.'

'Hardly an appropriate metaphor,' Didier smiled.

Jayne blushed. 'Take no notice, I'm just feeling sorry for myself. Another Moriarty and I'll be fine.' She signalled to the waiter. 'What about you? Has your love life improved?'

'I do have a partner,' he said slowly. 'We've been living together for nearly a year. He's Thai. I guess that makes me one of those farang men who prefer the local fare.'

'Sorry. That was out of line.'

'Not at all. I know how it looks. Sanga's more than ten years younger than me and an ex-bar boy. I'm a thirty-something expatriate who should know better. To be honest, I have no idea if it will last. But Nou—that's Sanga's nickname—has always been direct with me.'

Jayne raised her hand. 'Mate, I'm the last person to criticise anyone else's choices when it comes to relationships. I was going to say that I trust your judgment, but given your dodgy taste in crime fiction, I'm not so sure.'

'Oh, that's a low blow,' he grinned. 'Why don't you come and visit us in Chiang Mai.'

'You mean it?'

'Absolutely. It's my turn to host the next book club meeting anyway.'

'I'll drink to that.' She drained the last of her cocktail.

Jayne had enjoyed the night. It was a relief to make light of the Richard/Ralph saga, which had bruised her both personally and professionally. She'd been too embarrassed to talk about it with anyone else, but Didier had given her the freedom to fess up. That night set the tone for their friendship: they could tell each other anything. Or so Jayne thought.

But why hadn't Didier told her about the assault on his father? She wondered if that was why he'd left Quebec in the first place, and had never gone back.

'You could have told me, Didi,' Jayne said.

With a lump in her throat, she stubbed out her cigarette and picked up the Sherlock Holmes book, stopping at a passage marked in pencil in the margin:

> 'Circumstantial evidence is a very tricky thing,'
> answered Holmes thoughtfully; 'it may seem to
> point very straight to one thing, but if you shift
> your point of view a little, you may find it pointing
> in an equally uncompromising manner to something
> entirely different...'

Was Didier sending her a message? She recalled the Police Lieutenant Colonel's response when asked if Didier had killed Nou: 'All evidence points in that direction.'

'And what if you shift your point of view a little?' she said aloud.

Jayne returned to the desk and reread her notes from the paper. She added points from the Channel 4 report, together with what Max had told her. The TV stations would still be closed, so she switched on the radio, jotting down more information as it came through.

She watched the first news bulletins before taking a shower and washing her hair. The bathroom mirror showed the colour had returned to her face. There was determination in her mouth and jaw—an expression Jayne's mother said made her look stubborn as a child—and her eyes were clear. She dressed quickly, slung a Do Not Disturb sign on her door and sprinted to a nearby 7-Eleven for the morning papers and coffee.

By 9am, Jayne had mapped out the case against Didier. She considered each piece of evidence on its own then examined how it all fitted together, coming up with as many holes in the case as police claimed to have leads. Jayne was no lawyer, but she knew that in the absence of either eye-witnesses to the murder or a full confession, everything became circumstantial, even the alleged discovery of the murder weapon at Didier's house. As for the previous assault record, Max was wrong: while it might not look good, the bottom line was the charges were never substantiated.

If she assumed her friend was not guilty—not even of resisting arrest, let alone murdering his lover—Jayne could conclude Didier had been killed either by accident, the police fabricating a case to cover their own arses, or through some kind of conspiracy.

She thought of the steely-eyed lieutenant colonel. He didn't come across as the sort of person who made mistakes. To her mind, the police blunder theory only held if the lieutenant colonel was covering up for someone else—a nervous rookie, for example. But it didn't explain Nou's death, which was why the police went to interview Didier in the first place. It all happened too fast and was too seamless to look like damage control.

That left her with the conspiracy theory: that Didier was set up to get him out of the way. But why not simply kill him? With Chiang Mai a hub for heroin trafficking in the region, it was not unprecedented for foreigners to be killed in drug-related attacks. A few years earlier, three US Drug Enforcement Agency officials had been executed, Mafia-style, in the area. Why go to the trouble of killing Nou as well and framing Didier for the murder?

Didier must have been considered so dangerous, it wasn't enough to kill him: his character and his credibility had to be destroyed as well. But how could he have posed such a threat? His friends used to joke that he was more Thai than Thai because he was so respectful of local culture. To Jayne's knowledge, Didier's willingness to rock the boat didn't extend beyond covertly distributing explicit pamphlets on AIDS prevention.

She picked up the phone and placed another call to Bangkok.

Max fumbled with the receiver, still groggy after a dose of Valium the night before. A strange voice said something in Thai, before a familiar one took its place.

'Max, it's Jayne.'

'Uh-huh.'

'Sorry, did I wake you?'

'Yeah, it's OK.' He propped himself up on one elbow and checked his clock. 10.30am. He felt guilty for having overslept, even if it was a Sunday. 'When did you get in?'

'Ah, actually...'

Max recognised the tone in her voice and prayed he was still dreaming.

'I've decided to stay on here,' she said. 'So I was wondering if you could arrange for me to participate in the official inquiry into Didier's death.'

'Are you mad?' he spluttered, suddenly wide awake. 'A Canadian has been accused of murdering a Thai national, for heaven's sake. The Canadian Embassy isn't about to let an amateur in on the investigation.'

'I may be an amateur,' she said tersely, 'but I know a set-up when I see it. You know as well as I do that Didier couldn't have killed Nou.'

'Which brings me to the second point.' His head throbbed with the effort of remaining calm. 'You're too involved. And I'm not just talking about your desire to see riend exonerated. I want that as much as you do. But it's Chiang Mai, Jayne. Normal rules don't apply. If there's something going on—and I'm not saying there is—then you could be in danger. It's fortunate no one's made a connection between you and Didier yet. And you should get out before someone does.'

She said nothing, though Max heard papers being shuffled.

'Look,' he added gently, 'you're probably still in shock. Come back to Bangkok. At least then we can help each other get through this.'

It was an appeal for her support, but Jayne chose to ignore it.

'You know, there was a report in today's paper claiming police found amphetamines at Didier's place.'

'But that's ridiculous—' He stopped short, realising he'd played right into her hands. They both knew Didier was puritanical about drugs. It was absurd to think he'd have any in the house.

'Listen, Max,' she said quickly, 'Didier was my best friend. I can't sit back and let him be remembered as a murderer. You know you're wasting your time trying to talk me out of it. So do I do it on my own, or are you going to help me?'

'Help you?' he cried. 'It's bad enough losing one friend. Why should I help another who's hell-bent on ignoring my advice and putting herself in danger?'

'Because I'm going to do it either way.'

Max hesitated. 'There's something you should know.'

'What?'

'It's about Didier's attack on his father.'

'What about it?'

'I've known about it for some time,' Max said, pausing for effect. 'Didier told me.'

'Oh?'

He'd caught her by surprise and it took her a moment to take this in.

'So why did it happen?' she said.

So sure she was of a reason behind Didier's actions that Max felt ashamed for trying to pull rank on her.

'Didier told his father he thought he might be gay,' he spoke softly, 'and the old man took it badly. Cursed the day he was born, called him a depraved sodomite and damned him to hell. Didier knew it would be tough—the old man was a staunch Catholic—but he hadn't expected that level of contempt. I don't think he'd have hit him if the old man hadn't spat in his face.'

Jayne inhaled sharply. 'Didier lost it?'

'Sounded like blind rage. Says he doesn't remember a thing until his father was lying unconscious on the floor.

'The police pressed the father to lay assault charges but he wouldn't hear of it, desperate to avoid the publicity of a trial. Needless to say, Didier was wracked with guilt and felt he had to do something to punish himself. So he chose exile.'

'Exile?' Jayne said.

'He even had criteria to make it as hard as possible,' Max said. 'It had to be a Third World country where neither French nor English was spoken, the weather had to be hot and he wouldn't permit himself to live in the capital—it had to be a remote area. That's how he ended up in Chiang Mai.'

'But I thought Didier loved Chiang Mai,' she said.

'He did, and he felt bad about it.'

There was another pause on the line. 'Thanks for telling me, Max. I appreciate it.'

'That's OK,' he said.

'Now can we get back to the inquiry?'

He didn't have the energy to fight her.

'OK,' he sighed. 'My Canadian counterpart, David Freeman, will be in Chiang Mai in the next couple of days. I'll arrange for you to meet—'

'Max, you're the best!'

'—if you promise to return to Bangkok immediately afterwards.'

'What's Freeman like?'

'He's a by-the-book bureaucrat. And don't try to change the topic. Promise to come home once you've spoken with David.'

'OK, OK,' she said. 'I promise. I'll call again soon.'

Head aching more than ever, Max hung up the phone and stumbled into the ensuite in search of painkillers.

He'd feared Jayne would want to investigate Didier's death and thought it might take the wind out of her sails to know Didier had confided in him and not her about the assault against his father. But it seemed nothing could tarnish her image of Didier.

And Max knew something else about Didier. He'd longed to have children and for Jayne to have children with him. But he'd never got as far as asking her because Max had talked him out of it.

Max had told himself he was doing the right thing by Jayne. But now that Didier was dead, he felt guilty for having sabotaged the idea. More gay men were raising children with female friends—or 'entering co-parenting arrangements' as his Sydney friends called it—and there was no reason why Didier and Jayne couldn't have made a go of it.

Didier had never seemed entirely comfortable with being gay and Max wondered if this, coupled with his desire to become a father, had become too much for him. Could Didier's frustration have turned into violent rage like it did with his father, this time directed at Nou? Internalised homophobia, the psychologists called it. Could Max have been so blinded by jealousy that he'd failed to see the signs?

As he waited for his aspirin to dissolve, Max realised he didn't want to stop Jayne from conducting her investigation. One of them had to be wrong about Didier. Max could only hope the error of judgment was on his part.

It was a muggy evening, the kind of night that years before would have seen Komet out in the rice paddies with his brothers and sisters hunting for frogs. His family had tried raising fish in the irrigation canals, but kept losing their stock to the speckled herons that speared the fingerlings with their blade-like beaks. Komet's mother would have willingly trapped the herons to eat or sell, but his father refused to allow it. He'd seen villages overrun with flies and other pests once the birds were gone. So Komet's mother raised a few chickens and, when there was rain in the air, the children would hunt for frogs, armed with special baskets that prevented their catch from jumping away. The promise of rain made the frogs sing, and the children would follow the sound, mud oozing between their toes as they waded through the paddy fields. If the frogs stopped singing, the children knew the rain would pass them by. They also knew there was no point in continuing the hunt; when the frogs went silent, it was as if they became invisible.

The frogs in the garden of the foreigner's house were still counting on a downpour and their chorus grew louder with each passing moment. Komet checked his watch. Nearly 1.30am—ten minutes since he'd last checked it. He thought he'd been let off lightly for his recent mistakes. Now he wasn't so sure.

Komet had dreaded returning to work. The new

reports about amphetamines being found in the foreigner's house made him worry he could be stood down from the force. If he lost his job, he'd have to go back to farming. He'd have no choice, not with the baby coming.

He arrived at the City Police Station just in time to begin his shift, but his hopes of signing in and slipping off on patrol without being noticed were disappointed as he was summoned to the Lieutenant Colonel's office.

'Come in, Komet,' Ratratarn said. 'We have some serious matters to discuss.'

Closing the door, Komet stood, eyes downcast, in front of his commanding officer.

'I've decided to suspend you from your regular patrol duties,' Ratratarn began.

'But Sir, I—'

'I want you to work full-time on the investigation into the deaths of Khun Sanga and his foreign murderer.'

Komet was stunned. Surely he was on the verge of a dishonourable discharge? He almost missed the significance of Ratratarn's use of the term 'murderer' rather than 'suspect'.

'...and Pornsak and Tanin will continue with their inquiries,' the commander was saying. 'We can expect a delegation from the Canadian Embassy soon, and you're to ensure the information they receive is consistent with what's in the report. Understand?'

'Yes, Sir.'

'I will see to the material we took from the foreigner's house. The place is already under surveillance during the day, but I want a man there at night, too. You'll guard the house. No one is to go inside without my authorisation. If anyone approaches, you're to take down their details and report back to me. But before you go, you're to familiarise yourself with the official report, which has been brought up-to-date in light of the new evidence.'

He paused, eyeing Komet squarely. Komet politely lowered his own gaze, but not before he saw the look Ratratarn gave him; not the censure he was expecting, something more conspiratorial.

'Memorise this report,' Ratratarn added, handing him the document, 'so if you're questioned by members of the foreign delegation, you know exactly how to respond.'

Quivering with relief as he leafed through the pages, Komet could scarcely believe what he read about the discovery of the murder weapon.

> In his search of the rear yard behind the suspect's house, Officer Komet located a plastic bag behind the water trough. Opened by the senior officer at the scene, Lieutenant Colonel Ratratarn, the contents revealed a cut-throat razor with traces of a dark substance on the blade. The bag and its contents were handed over to the Scientific Crime Detection Division for analysis...

Komet didn't know how to react. The report was clearly inaccurate, but it was signed by Ratratarn himself. Ratratarn had been there on the night and knew Komet hadn't found the murder weapon. Why, then, would he allow Komet to take the credit?

He should've been grateful for being spared the loss of

face, but he couldn't help feeling uneasy. Ratratarn had done him a favour and Komet owed him for it.

It didn't help that guard duty gave him so much time to think about it. At first, it was just dull. After checking the doors and windows, he'd assumed a lookout position on the front balcony.

He watched the people passing by in the street. A small boy dragged his brother by the hand. A woman with a pushcart—a vendor of sweets—trundled home for the evening. A group of teenagers laughed at a joke that was out of Komet's earshot. And an old man sifted through piles of rubbish, putting anything worth salvaging into a hessian sack. No one came anywhere near the house. Only one or two even glanced in his direction.

He shifted his focus to the yard. The ground was thick with ferns, liana vines encircled tree-trunks like snakes, and large blood-red and flesh-coloured flowers that looked like body parts were scattered among the greenery. To Komet, the garden was wild, almost frightening.

As the street emptied, with no sound other than the frogs, Komet's imagination started to get the better of him. He imagined the *phii*—the ghost of the foreigner—was lurking somewhere in the jungle-garden, waiting to exact its revenge. That was why none of the passersby lingered, he thought, why none of the neighbours even looked over their fences.

Komet allowed his gaze to wander down the staircase where the foreigner died and immediately regretted it. The dark stain on the wooden step was unmistakable.

He began pacing the balcony, desperately wishing

someone else was with him. He'd even settle for Sergeant Pornsak. Better to be on the receiving end of his sarcastic jibes than the victim of a vengeful phii farang.

A noise towards the front of the garden stopped him. Heart racing, Komet strained to hear it over the frogs, releasing his breath as he made out two male voices in the street. Careful not to tread on the bloodstained step, he walked through the yard to take a closer look.

'I saw you with her!' one of the men was saying. 'Don't try and deny it.'

'Well, she asked me to meet her,' the other said.

'But she's my girlfriend!'

Komet cleared his throat. The men looked about his age. Both wore jeans, T-shirts and rubber sandals, one with a baseball cap facing backwards on his head.

'*Sawadee krup*,' he greeted them. 'Is there a problem?'

'He's trying to steal my girlfriend,' the boy in the cap said, jerking his head towards the other man.

'I'm not trying to steal her. Officer, my friend here is upset because his girlfriend asked me to take her on a date.'

Komet studied them for signs of intoxication.

'That's not true! Officer, he's been trying to steal her for months now. She's very beautiful, you see, and so sweet.'

'Oh, yes, she's sweet all right!'

'What do you mean by that?' the first boy growled.

'Nothing.'

'Yeah, and nothing's what you'll get from her.'

'I'm telling you, she's in love with me!' the second boy said.

'You're a liar!'

'*Jai yen-yen*—' Komet began, but the first man had already taken a swing at the other and knocked him to the ground. Komet called for them to stop, but the second man leapt to his feet and responded with a punch of his own. Then they were wrestling on the ground, churning up a cloud of dust.

Komet tried to separate them, but as soon as he managed to drag one away, the other would go on the offensive. He looked up and down the street, but there was no help in sight. Finally, he pulled out his police baton.

'If you don't stop this instant,' he said loudly, 'I will be forced to arrest you for creating a public disturbance.'

To his relief, the two men sprung apart. Sprawled on the ground, they glared at one another. Komet stood between them, still holding his baton,

'Have you boys been drinking?' he said.

'N-no, Officer,' the first one panted.

'Then there's no excuse for your behaviour. Look at yourselves, rolling around on the ground like a pair of dogs. Get up and go home!'

The young men slowly got to their feet and dusted off their clothes.

'I'm sorry, Officer,' the first one said, retrieving his baseball cap from the ground.

'Me, too, Officer,' said the second.

Both looked suitably humbled and Komet nodded to show he accepted their apologies.

As he backed away, the man with the cap raised his fingers to his lips and gave a loud whistle.

'Come on then, Deh,' he said, slapping his companion on the back. 'Let's go!'

'OK, Bom. *Mai pen rai*, hey!'

Komet watched them go, satisfied by how quickly their dispute had settled, and envying them each other's company. He checked his watch and sighed, replaced his baton in its belt-loop and turned back to the house.

Bom's whistle was Jayne's signal to get out, fast. There was no point continuing her search anyway, since the house had been ransacked. Didier's computer and all the files from his study were gone, drawers of the desk were left open and empty, contents scattered. There were large gaps in the bookshelves lining the walls of the main room, and Didier's beloved books lay strewn all over the floor. The wardrobes in both bedrooms were empty, bathroom cupboards also plundered.

The house was built in the northeast style, the stilts forming a space underneath where Thai women typically worked on their looms during the heat of the day and tethered their animals at night. In Didier's case, there was only enough room for motorbikes as the land sloped upwards. Anticipating the back door would be locked, Jayne had broken in through the bathroom window overlooking the back garden. She'd chosen it in advance, knowing it didn't close properly.

Passing by the place in daylight, she easily spotted the surveillance team of two and decided to wait in a nearby cafe to see what happened.

Didier lived in a residential neighbourhood where it

was hard for Jayne to look inconspicuous. She might pass herself off as a lost tourist, but it was a difficult act to sustain. Not so the 'World Traveller', a particularly earnest type of backpacker—the kind for whom Thai-English phrase-books were invented.

Smiling sweetly at the cafe owner and using her dictionary to communicate, Jayne ordered food and opened her notebook. For the rest of the afternoon, she pretended to be writing a journal, all the while watching the house across the street.

At ten that night, Jayne saw a young cop arrive on a motorbike. He nodded to the surveillance duo, which didn't even wait for him to dismount before driving away. Leaving a tip twice the size of her bill, Jayne waited outside the cafe in the shadow cast by an awning and watched the cop enter the house. She lost sight of him from time to time, but he re-emerged on the balcony whenever anyone came close. After waiting twenty minutes and satisfied the man was alone, Jayne walked to a public phone, called Bom, then flagged down a tuk-tuk to take her to his place.

She'd met Bom through Didier, the weekend they scheduled their book club meeting to coincide with the Yi Peng festival. They had joined a crowd on the banks of the Mae Ping to place small floats—traditionally woven from banana leaves—containing flowers, candles, incense and coins on the river. Thais believed all the misdeeds that might bring them bad karma in the next life would float away. Unique to Chiang Mai, and as a kind of karmic back-up, people also launched paper lanterns like hot-air balloons into the night sky.

Bom learned that Jayne had once been a drama teacher and grilled her for ideas to liven up the lessons he taught at a local high school. They'd met several times since and got along well; Jayne had even made a guest appearance at one of his classes. In the Thai scheme of things, this put Bom in her debt. But when she explained what she wanted, he was more concerned with helping her clear Didier's name—an indication of how much he was affected by their friend's death.

Recruiting his housemate, Deh, they came up with the idea of having a fight over an imaginary girlfriend. While Jayne made coffee, the two men worked on a routine and a signal for when to get out of the place.

Jayne hesitated when she heard Bom's whistle, reluctant to leave Didier's books, until she heard the cop's footsteps on the front stairs. She snatched those closest to her and tucked them into the waistband of her jeans. But she'd lingered too long to get back out through the bathroom window. She ducked into the kitchen, released the catch on the back door and dashed across the backyard. She scaled the back fence and ran to the lane where Bom and Deh were waiting on their motorbikes.

Jayne was more convinced than ever that Didier had been onto something—something in which the police were implicated. Why else would they have cleaned the house out so thoroughly? But she'd found no leads, no clues. All she had were a few paperbacks. Squirming in her seat on Bom's bike, she plucked them out from beneath her clothing.

'Are you OK?' Bom asked over his shoulder.

'Yeah,' she replied. 'How about you?'

'*Sanouk mark-mark*!' he said with a laugh.

'I'm glad you enjoyed it.'

Jayne managed to keep it together until the boys dropped her back at the Silver Star. But once she retreated to the sanctuary of her room, with the door closed behind her and finally alone, she started crying.

These were not the angry tears of the day before, but thick, wet tears of grief. The tension left her throat as her sorrow found its voice and she howled with the pain of losing the man she loved. She rocked her body back and forth with a sadness that came in waves. By the time her tears subsided, her chair was surrounded in soggy tissues and the box was empty.

She caught sight of the paperbacks she'd rescued from Didier's place. Two were Agatha Christie novels, *Nemesis* and *Death on the Nile*. But it was the third book, by Raymond Chandler, that set her off again: *Farewell, My Lovely*.

She searched her purse for another tissue and came across a business card she didn't recognise. On one side was the address and phone number of the Chiang Mai Plaza Hotel. On the other, in Didier's handwriting, was *Mtg. Moira O'Halloran, Room 1228. 6/5, 17.00.*

A flash of lightning outside her window followed by a whip-cracking thunderbolt signalled the storm that had been building all evening. Jayne checked her watch. The meeting was scheduled in twelve hours' time. And Jayne intended to keep the appointment with Moira O'Halloran on Didier's behalf.

With gentle prompting, the receptionist at the Chiang Mai Plaza Hotel revealed that Moira O'Halloran was an *ajarn* from Australia. Given the reverence accorded to teachers in Thailand, she could be anything from a primary school teacher to chancellor of a university. Jayne knew Didier had worked with Australian researchers and asked to be put through to room 1228.

To resist the urge for a cigarette, Jayne translated the health warning in Thai on the packet while she waited for the connection. 'Smoking impairs your sexual ability.' No real disincentive there. Marginally more cautionary were the messages, 'Smoking is like dying on the instalment plan' and 'Smoking causes your blood vessels and brain to burst'. Thinking her own brain would burst if she were forced to listen much longer to an electronic version of 'Für Elise', the phone was answered.

'Ms O'Halloran?'

'It's Professor O'Halloran, actually.'

'My apologies, Professor. My name's Jayne Keeney. I'm calling on behalf of Didier de Montpasse. I was wondering if—'

'Didier's not going to cancel on me, is he?' the woman said. 'He promised to get me an interpreter for the interview. We arranged it before I left for Chiang Rai. I told him Souk wouldn't be able to make it tonight.'

Moira O'Halloran didn't know Didier was dead. In a split-second decision Jayne elected not to enlighten her.

'I have Didier's calendar in front of me,' she said, shuffling papers. 'I'm sorry, Professor. Can you remind me of the time and location of the interview?'

'Half past six at The Nice Place. I need one more session to complete my field work before I return to Melbourne tomorrow and—'

'Oh, yes! Here it is. He's got me scheduled to do that one.'

'You?'

'You need a Thai speaker, don't you?'

'Yes,' the woman replied cautiously. 'But the subjects of my study are CSWs. All the other interpreters have been Thais.'

Jayne cringed at the acronym for 'commercial sex worker'. Though Moira O'Halloran was paid for the work she did, too, Jayne doubted she'd introduce herself as a 'commercial academic'.

'I can assure you, I have extensive experience conducting interviews in Thailand's clubs and bars,' she said, 'and I've found the women often feel more at ease talking to an outsider.'

There was a pause on the line.

'I mean, if you'd rather not use me, I can try to find someone else. Though at such short notice, I can't guarantee anyone with as much experience...'

'Look, Miss—?'

'Jayne.'

'Right, Jayne. To be frank, it's not ideal. Where is

Didier, anyway? I can't get hold of him.'

'Ah, he's been called away. He wanted me to apologise on his behalf.'

The woman snorted. 'That doesn't bode well for our proposed collaboration, especially on top of the differences we've been having.'

'Ah yes, the collaboration. Didier wanted to brief me on that but we ran out of time. Perhaps we could…Well, perhaps I could do your interpreting this evening in exchange for ten minutes to brief me on the project?'

Unable to resist a free interpreting service, Professor— 'Call me Moira'—O'Halloran gave her the address of The Nice Place and suggested they meet at six.

Jayne arrived early, spotting Moira as she approached. She looked like an up-market tourist—boutique haircut, white linen pants, sleeveless orange top, chunky silver brace-lets on both wrists, large leather tote bag—but she lacked the relaxed air of a holidaymaker. She barrelled through the crowd without lifting her head, shoulders hunched, until she reached the club. Up close, Jayne saw she had the leathery skin of an older woman and a tightness around the mouth that suggested an eating disorder. Once introductions were out of the way, Moira got down to business. 'I don't know how much Didier told you, but I've been conducting field work in northern Thailand for two weeks,' she said as they entered the bar. 'I'm collecting stories that demonstrate processes of gender-related discrimination and alienation resulting in women having to sell sex for survival.'

Jayne murmured noncommittally and glanced around the room. The Nice Place struggled to live up to its name.

Tables draped in pink polyester cloth, chintz curtains drawn over the windows, and smoke-stained prints of European landscapes on the wall only made it look dingy. The waitresses wore pink bikinis, rabbit ears fixed to headbands and white pom-poms on their backsides. Up-beat dance music in the background failed to charge the torpid atmosphere.

'I'll be presenting my findings at a conference in Sydney later this year,' Moira continued, gesturing to a corner booth, parallel bench seats of brown vinyl.

Jayne accepted her business card, exchanging it for one she'd had made near her hotel.

'You're based at Chulalongkorn University,' Moira observed.

'Yes, as I said on the phone, I'm hoping to work on a project with Didier. I—I mean, he was thinking you could brief me on it.'

A waitress appeared at their table, her bunny ears like antennae.

'Would you like me to order you a drink?' Jayne asked.

'Yes. Lemonade, please. And could you tell her,' she nodded at the Thai woman, 'that we're expecting Nalissa?'

Jayne relayed the information and ordered herself a lemon juice. She turned back to Moira, keen to pursue Didier's research topic, but the academic had other ideas.

'Now,' she said, moving a vase of plastic daisies to one side and taking a legal pad from her bag, 'I simply need you to translate my questions and the responses as we go along. I'll be taking notes, but there's no need for you to pause on my account. It's more important we maintain the natural flow of conversation. You should translate my questions precisely as I ask them,' she added, testing a pen.

'Don't you have them written down?'

'No, I'm using an open-ended interview technique.'

It was on the tip of Jayne's tongue to ask what distinguished that from a conversation, when a different waitress appeared with a tray of drinks. Like the others, she wore a pink bikini and bunny ears, plus a plastic badge with the number 11 on it. The pale make-up on her long face contrasted with the coffee-colour of her throat. Her eyes were close set and smeared with pink glitter, her nose flat with slightly flared nostrils—features that enhanced her rabbit-like appearance.

'Ah, Nalissa!' Moira said, beaming at the woman. 'Jayne, please invite Nalissa to join us on my behalf.'

'*Sawadee ka, Khun Nalissa*,' Jayne began in Thai. 'I'm Jayne. I'm interpreting this evening as—' she turned to Moira, breaking into English, 'what was your previous interpreter's name again?'

'Souk.'

'Souk is unable to be here,' Jayne said, reverting to Thai. 'Please have a seat.'

Nalissa sat so Jayne was between her and the academic.

'Right,' Moira said, 'now, please start by thanking Nalissa for her time.'

'She is going to pay me, isn't she?' Nalissa asked. 'Souk said she would.'

Jayne relayed this to Moira who flushed slightly and patted her bag. This seemed to satisfy the Thai woman who nodded for them to continue.

'So, Nalissa,' Moira asked, 'how did you come to be forced into sex work?'

Jayne hesitated. 'Do you want me to translate that literally?'

'Why not?'

'Well, in Thai, you'd use euphemisms like "bar work", "the service industry" or even "your current line of work" rather than ask directly about sex work.'

'Yes, well,' Moira frowned, 'for the sake of my research, the meaning must be very clear and specific.'

'Okay,' Jayne said slowly. 'But the question's a bit loaded, isn't it? I mean, you're assuming Nalissa was forced into sex work. Maybe she chose to—'

'Look, to be frank, I'm not interested in your opinions. I've been doing this research for two weeks without any problems. Just translate the question.'

With a shrug, Jayne turned, catching an amused look on Nalissa's face. 'Khun Nalissa,' she said in Thai, 'Khun Moira would like to know how you came to be forced into your current line of work.'

'*Dichan khao jai*,' Nalissa said. 'I understand a little English. You're right. I wasn't forced to do this kind of work. It was my choice. But Souk said the farang—' she tilted her head in Moira's direction '—doesn't want to hear that. So we make up stories to please her.'

She smiled sweetly and Jayne fought the urge to laugh. 'So what do you want me to say?' she whispered in Thai.

'Oh, make up some sad story,' Nalissa said. 'That's what Souk did for the other girls. Tell her my father was an opium addict or something.' She sipped a bottle of lemonade through a straw, fluttering glittery eyelids.

Jayne turned to Moira. 'Nalissa says her father was an opium addict,' she said deadpan.

Moira, brows knitted, wrote it down in her notebook. 'Hmm, yes, go on.'

'What do I say next?' Jayne asked in Thai.

'*Arai godai*,' Nalissa said. 'Make it up—tell her I was sold to pay for my father's addiction.'

'The family was very poor,' Jayne said in English. 'Nalissa was the eldest child and the most beautiful of the daughters.'

'*Dee mark*,' Nalissa said. 'I like that. You know, I came here on my own to find work. I studied up to middle school, but there was no senior school in our area. When I got to Chiang Mai, I could earn one hundred baht for working twelve hours a day in a garment factory—and those places are so hot—or I could make the same money just by sitting down in an air-con bar like this and drinking with a customer. That's for ten minutes! And if I want to make more money, that's up to me. It wasn't a hard decision.'

'Nalissa says her father sold all he could to support his opium addiction,' Jayne said, 'until the family had nothing left but their small plot of land and the house on it. At this point, Nalissa's mother, frightened they would lose their home, invited a man to come, a person known to arrange work for young women in the provincial capital.'

'I knew it!' Moira said, scribbling furiously. 'There's going to be a whole section in my paper about internalised patriarchy and the complicity of mothers in young women's oppression…Please, ask her to continue.'

'She wants you to continue,' Jayne said in Thai. 'What should I say next?'

'You're doing fine so far,' Nalissa said. 'I mean, this is easy money for me. She pays a thousand baht just to sit around talking!'

'Nalissa's not sure her mother knew she'd be sold to a brothel owner,' Jayne said to Moira. 'Such men tell parents they'll find jobs for their daughters as maids or waitresses. The man gave Nalissa's mother a thousand baht and took her away. It wasn't until she arrived in Chiang Mai that Nalissa understood her real fate.'

Moira raised her head, a concerned look on her face. 'Please, Jayne, tell Nalissa I know this must be painful, but it would be helpful if she could provide as much detail as possible.'

Jayne turned back to Nalissa. 'She's asking for details now. And I suppose you're going to tell me to keep making it up.'

'*Nae norn*,' Nalissa said. 'I'm enjoying the story myself. By the way, do you think this farang knows what her name means? You know, *moi ra*.'

With certain tones, *moi* sounded like the Thai word for 'pubic hair' and *ra* as 'mouldy'. Jayne bit her lip and glanced sideways at the academic whose head was buried in her notes.

'Anyway, Jayne, what do you do?' Nalissa said. 'Do you work here in Chiang Mai? How come you speak Thai so well?'

'Nalissa says the middleman expected her to repay the money he'd given her mother,' Jayne said. 'In effect, she became a slave to the brothel owner. He kept everything she earned to pay off her debt.'

'Ask her how many customers she serviced in a day,' Moira said.

'I live in Bangkok,' Jayne returned to the conversation with Nalissa. 'I came here to visit a farang friend—the one killed by the police three days ago. Maybe you've heard about it? They say he murdered his boyfriend, but I don't believe it.'

'Oh, yes!' Nalissa said. 'It was in the papers. I saw the boy, Khun Sanga, the night he was killed.'

'What?'

'Yes, it was around one o'clock.'

That was close to the time of Nou's death. Jayne wanted to press Nalissa for details, but feared blowing their cover.

'Nalissa cannot say how many men she was forced to service in a day,' she said quickly. 'To be honest, Moira, I think the memories are too painful.'

'Oh?' The academic couldn't hide her disappointment. 'Well, ask her to tell me as much as she can.'

'Can we meet again?' Jayne asked Nalissa. 'I'd really like to talk with you.'

'Sure. How about tomorrow morning? Somphet Cafe near the Tha Pae Gate, around ten? In the meantime, could you bring this story to a close?' She glanced around the room. 'I really should get going.'

'Nalissa paid off her debt last year,' Jayne said. 'But she's a ruined woman and can no longer go back to her village. That's why she works here. She still sends money to her mother, but she's too ashamed to return home.'

'Of course.' Looking up from her notes, Moira assumed her concerned expression again. 'Please, tell her I understand.'

Jayne turned back to the Thai woman. 'I'll see you tomorrow, OK?'

'Sure. Thanks for your help with the story.'

'Nalissa would like to thank you for the opportunity to tell her story,' Jayne said to Moira, nodding at her tote bag. 'She needs to go now…'

'Right.' Moira handed Jayne an envelope. 'Please thank her again.'

'The mouldy pubic hair says thanks,' Jayne said, 'And I'll see you in the morning.'

Nalissa took the envelope, pressed it between her hands and bowed in a wai—a gesture Moira emulated, unaware of any intended irony. As the Thai woman walked towards the bar, Jayne turned back to Moira.

'Maybe we could have that briefing now.'

The academic, absorbed in her notes, looked up frowning.

'You were going to tell me about the work you and Didier are doing.' The music got louder as Jayne spoke.

'What about Didier?' Moira was forced to shout.

Jayne leaned closer. 'Perhaps we should go somewhere quiet?'

In response, Moira stood up and moved towards the door.

'What about the bill?' Jayne called after her, but she was out of earshot.

Annoyed, she checked the drinks invoice and slipped some money beneath the table marker. She saw Nalissa sidle up to a blond man at the bar and grab his crotch in greeting. Jayne wondered what the academic would make of that.

'I haven't got long,' Moira said as Jayne joined her. 'I still have to finish writing up these notes before I pack.'

Jayne smiled through clenched teeth. 'Perhaps we could talk on the way back to your hotel.'

'Fine.' Moira raised her hand and flagged down a tuk-tuk. 'We—go—hotel—Chiang—Mai—Plaza?' she said to the driver in a loud voice.

The elderly man nodded.

Moira's bag between them made for a tight fit on the bench seat. Jayne ignored the clasp digging into her hip and cut to the chase. 'So the proposed collaboration, what's it about?'

'We're hoping to use my research findings as the basis for a much larger study on the sex industry in northern Thailand,' Moira said. 'We've proposed a joint project between the University of Melbourne and Chiang Mai University.'

She re-positioned herself as if making a formal presentation. 'Didier and his assistants will map out patterns in the procurement and trafficking of women into the sex industry, both within Thailand and from neighbouring countries, as a starting-point for identifying how culturally specific notions of gender, age and ethnicity make women vulnerable to sexual exploitation. The team in Australia will be responsible for survey design and data analysis.'

The jargon left Jayne cold but she pricked up her ears ~tion of trafficking. Chiang Mai was a centre for human trafficking as well as drugs, and it was assumed both police and border patrol were complicit in the trade.

'Sounds interesting,' she said. 'You mentioned some difference of opinion between you and Didier over the project?'

'Yes, well…' Moira cleared her throat. 'He's suggested we include child prostitution in the study. But as I told him, it's beyond the scope of the research. Paedophilia is a political minefield in Australia at the moment, what with the new laws coming in and everything.'

Jayne remembered reading that the Australian government recently introduced legislation to enable child sex offenders to be prosecuted under Australian law for crimes committed overseas.

'Besides,' Moira added, 'it wouldn't look good to have someone like Didier involved in a study like that.'

'What do you mean?'

'Well, he's a single man in his thirties who's lived in Thailand for fifteen years. And…well…it just wouldn't look good. I mean, he *is* gay.'

Jayne turned away so Moira couldn't see the look on her face. The tuk-tuk pulled up at the entrance to the hotel and she got out.

'How much should I give him?' Moira called after her.

'Oh, two hundred baht should be enough.'

The driver looked at her with raised eyebrows—the figure was four times the regular price; Jayne smiled and allowed the academic to pay.

'I think it's a good sign that Didier asked you to see me for a briefing,' Moira said as they ascended the stairs. '

makes me think he's come back on board.'

'I'm sure he'll be pleased we've had the chance to talk,' Jayne said. 'Before I go, though, Didier said something about a background paper he'd prepared. He didn't have time to give it to me. Do you have a copy?'

It was a long shot, but it hit the mark.

'There *is* something…' Moira took a folder from her bag and leafed through it. 'Not so much a background paper as notes. But…oh, it's a bit dated. It still mentions children and—'

'That's OK,' Jayne said quickly. 'It'd be good to have something to start with. And I'll take our discussion into account.'

'Well, in that case, I suppose it's all right.'

It was all Jayne could do to resist snatching the document from Moira's hand. If nothing else, it had escaped the clutches of the Chiang Mai police. She offered to make a photocopy and leave the original at the reception desk.

While the copying was done, Jayne wandered around the lobby, typical of the excesses of Thai interior design. A huge, bronze temple bell dominated the main entrance, while larger-than-life statues of warriors guarded the stairs and elevator doors. The cavernous ceiling was augmented with recesses, each housing enormous, multi-tiered light-fittings like sprays of inverted parasols. The staff wore Lan Na period costumes, evoking Chiang Mai's golden age as the kingdom of One Million Rice Fields: the men in tailored arongs swept up between their knees; the tching silk jackets and long skirts, elaborate ikling like wind-chimes when they moved.

Distracted by the back of one woman's head, it took Jayne a moment to notice the receptionist gesturing at her.

'It's the blue colour,' she said, shaking her head.

Jayne looked at the documents. Not even this grand hotel could resist turning down the settings on the photocopier to make the toner last longer. As a result, notes in biro on the front page of the original hadn't come out in the duplicate. She glanced at the woman and pushed the copy back across the desk.

'Older sister,' she said in her most polite Thai, 'please make sure Khun Moira gets this.'

'*Mai pen rai*,' the woman replied with the hint of a smile.

Before another night's guard duty at the farang's house, Komet fortified himself with a visit to the mor phii. The shaman, much revered for his ability to appease ghosts, gave him an amulet of herbs in a pouch of snakeskin, which Komet tucked beneath his dark-brown shirt. At the station, to his dismay, he was again summoned to Ratratarn's office. And this time there was no mistaking the Lieutenant Colonel's displeasure.

'The deputy sergeant on the surveillance team that relieved you this morning says he found the back door unlocked. What do you have to say about that?'

'But Sir,' he said, thinking aloud, 'I checked all the doors and windows. One window in the bathroom didn't shut properly. But everything else was locked.'

'So you have no idea how the back door came to be unlocked this morning?'

'No, Sir.'

'Well,' Ratratarn clapped his hands, 'it must have been the phii come to haunt his old house, right?'

Komet blushed, aware of the amulet scratching against his skin. 'Sir, I'm not sure—'

'Oh, spare me these idiots from the *ban nok*!' he banged his fist on the desk.

Komet flushed again and bowed his head so low his chin touched his chest.

The lieutenant colonel sat forward in his chair. 'There must be a rational explanation,' he said. 'Think, Officer Komet. Think back and tell me everything that happened last night.'

'Sir, I arrived at the farang's house as ordered at 22.00. The surveillance team left and I entered the property. That's when I checked the windows and doors. After that, I maintained a watch on the street from the front balcony.'

'Did anyone approach the house?'

'No, Sir. Though there were a few passersby, no one came near the place, except—'

'Except what?'

'Well, there were a couple of young guys—this was around 2am. They got into a fight in the street. I broke it up then returned to my post.'

Ratratarn narrowed his eyes. 'Did you get the names of these young guys?'

'No, Sir. They were just two guys arguing over a girl. I threatened to arrest them if they didn't stop fighting, and when did, I let them go.'

'You let them go,' Ratratarn repeated. 'And would you recognise these men again?'

'Ah, I'm not sure, Sir. It was quite dark, not long before the storm. One of them wore a baseball cap…' He hesitated. 'Oh, I remember! Their names were Bom and Deh.'

'Bom and Deh,' Ratratarn said, 'that should narrow the field. Idiot! There'd be hundreds men in Chiang Mai who go by those nicknames. Now think again, Officer. Is there anything else you can tell me, anything out of the ordinary you saw last night?'

Komet mulled over it for a moment. 'Well, I did see a farang woman near the foreigner's house when I first went on duty.'

'What farang woman?' Ratratarn's tone was no longer sarcastic.

'I don't know, Sir. She had white skin. She was standing outside a cafe across the street.'

'What time was this?'

'When I arrived, Sir. She might have looked at the house once or twice. But she went away after that.'

'Think harder, Officer Komet,' Ratratarn said as he leafed through a pile of documents. 'What did the farang woman look like?'

Komet took a deep breath. 'She had dark hair, like a Thai person, but curly.'

'And was this farang woman's curly hair short or long?' Ratratarn said, finger poised on a document.

'Long enough to touch her shoulders.'

'Gotcha!' Ratratarn punched the page in front of him. 'It's in the interviews Pornsak and Tanin conducted at the Night Bazaar. Several witnesses reported seeing a farang woman with long, dark, curly hair in the bar that evening.'

'Oh?'

Ratratarn looked up as if he'd forgotten Komet was in the room. 'You can go, Officer. But when you resume your post this evening, your orders are to take down the names of all pedestrians—even the damn garbage collectors—and report back on any activity in the area surrounding the foreigner's house.'

'Yes, Sir.'

'One more question. Did you check the locks on the doors and windows after those boys got into a fight in the street?'

'I'm not sure, Sir.'

Komet regretted the words as soon as he'd said them.

'Damn it, Komet! Did you or did you not check the doors and windows after the boys had left?'

'I checked the front door, Sir. But maybe not the back...'

'Just get out of here!'

Ratratarn picked up the phone and began making a call before Komet had even closed the door.

The young officer resolved to be more diligent. He would check the doors and windows every hour. He would take down the names of everyone who even glanced in his direction. And he would not let his imagination run away with him. As Ratratarn said, phii were things peasants believed in, not members of the Chiang Mai police. Komet had a job to do. And with a baby due in the cool season, it was vital he kept doing it.

The line was busy. Ratratarn smoked a cigarette before trying again. It was risky, calling from his office. But his mobile phone battery was flat and it couldn't wait. He had to talk to Kelly.

Ratratarn didn't like dealing with farangs; but the building that housed Kelly's venture was owned by the *jao por* whose business interests Ratratarn protected. And it wasn't a task he could delegate—despite years in the country, Kelly hadn't learned Thai, whereas Ratratarn spoke reasonable English, a result of being posted as a young officer to the US Air Force base in Udon Thani.

He tried the number again. The phone was answered with a gruff '*kup*'. It was Kelly's bouncer, Mongkol, a man with the face of a bullfrog and charm to match.

'Get Kelly,' Ratratarn said.

'G'day Lieutenant Colonel,' Kelly came on the line almost immediately. 'What's up?'

Ratratarn cleared his throat. 'Looks like the foreign woman resurfaced last night.'

'Are you serious? This is bad.'

It irked Ratratarn that Kelly only considered the situation serious when another foreigner was involved. He'd tied up loose ends within his own ranks, even allowing that imbecile Komet to take the credit for locating the murder weapon. Yet Kelly showed no sign of feeling under threat from the Thai side.

'Who is this woman?' Kelly continued. 'Is she Australian?'

'That's what we're trying to find out,' Ratratarn said. 'In the meantime, keep your eyes open. We can't let anything slip at this point.'

'For sure,' Kelly said. 'You'll keep me posted?'

'Excuse me?' Sometimes Kelly's vernacular was beyond him.

'You'll let me know, right?'

'Of course.' He paused for a moment. 'You do realise this latest development affects our agreement.'

'Oh, come on—'

'I have to dedicate additional manpower to finding the farang woman. Such services cost time and money.'

Ratratarn wanted him to understand how the system worked: everybody served somebody. Ratratarn served the local mafia boss, while the jao por's underlings served him. Pornsak, Tanin and Komet served Ratratarn, too, as did Kelly, although the Australian failed to appreciate this. Kelly laboured under the delusion that if he paid enough money he could buy himself out of the hierarchy. He thought the issue was price when, in fact, it was all about order and respect.

'Listen, mate,' Kelly said. 'Can we meet in the next day or so? I agree, this changes things.'

Ratratarn smiled. 'I'll come tomorrow at midnight.'

He hung up and returned to the files on his desk. When Pornsak interviewed the owner of Man Date, he'd mentioned meeting a farang woman on the night of the murder. He said she'd accompanied the Canadian to the bar, witnessed the argument between him and Khun Sanga and left soon after. He couldn't recall her name but said she spoke Thai.

One of the kids there also mentioned a farang woman. But Officer Tanin, who conducted that interview, hadn't thought it warranted further questioning; he hadn't even bothered taking down a physical description.

He read over the particulars in Pornsak's report:

Name: Unknown
Height: approx. 1.6 metres
Race: European (white skin)
Appearance: Black-brown, curly, shoulder-length hair
Nationality: Unknown
Address in Thailand: Unknown

Other: Can speak Thai

He pressed the intercom button on his desk. 'Send Sergeant Pornsak to me.'

'He's on patrol, Sir,' the receptionist said.

'Then put through a call to his *meu teu*, will you?'

The department did not distribute mobile phones to officers of Pornsak's rank but he'd bought his own. Ratratarn picked up the receiver after the first ring and heard Pornsak's voice through the static.

'You wanted to speak to me, Sir?'

'Yes. Pornsak, I want you to go back to the bar behind the Night Bazaar and question the owner again. See if he remembers anything else about the farang woman who was there on the night of the murder.'

'Sir?'

'Any details at all, especially where she might be staying in Chiang Mai. I want you to track down the kid whose statement Tanin took, too...' he leafed through the file, 'Khun Mana Traisophon. Lives at 4/17 Soi Wat Chiang Yeun. Ask him for the same information. I need a name.'

'Yes, Sir.'

'And Pornsak, you are to report back directly to me on this. Understand?'

'Perfectly, Sir.'

Ratratarn terminated the call. His key chain was by the phone and he picked it up, weighing it in the palm of his hand. He walked across the room and unlocked a large filing cupboard.

The door opened on the material he'd taken from the

dead foreigner's house: computer, disks, files, folders full of documents and a bundle of personal effects, including letters. Ratratarn had checked all of the computer stuff and while he'd found plenty relating to the foreigner's work on AIDS and prostitution, there was nothing that fingered him or Kelly in any way. Either Kelly got it wrong, in which case there'd been no point getting the Canadian out of the way, or the guy had seen them coming and passed on the evidence to someone else. Ratratarn was confident the foreigner's Thai colleagues weren't in on it, which suggested that information had been leaked to another farang. He found colleagues' names among the computer files, but nothing that raised his suspicions.

He picked up the bundle of letters. Although the foreigner was Canadian, none of the envelopes bore stamps from Canada. There were a few from Australia, some from European countries and a large number from within Thailand.

Closing the cupboard, Ratratarn took the letters to his desk. He dreaded going through them, but it was another task he couldn't delegate. Sorting them into piles by country, he lit another Krung Thep, inhaled deeply and opened the first of the envelopes.

Jayne patted the document on her desk — lovingly, as if she could touch Didier by association — and looked at the familiar handwriting at the top of the page. Didier's impatient scrawl was at odds with his nature. It made his letters difficult to read, though it pleased Jayne that he never resorted to typing them.

She shook her head and focused. The document was printed from a computer file. Didier had written in the top margin: *Background notes as requested: will discuss on 6/5.*

The paper, 'The Impacts of the AIDS Epidemic on the Demographics of the Sex Industry in Northern Thailand', was dated April 1996. It opened with a brief history of how AIDS, once a disease of injecting drug users and homosexuals in Bangkok in the mid-1980s, exploded into a national epidemic affecting one per cent of the Thai population — some 500,000 people — by 1992. HIV had quickly spread through the community via the sex industry, with rural areas the worst affected, particularly those in the north.

'A survey of nearly 3000 sex workers in Chiang Mai last year found 40 per cent infected,' Jayne read. 'Infection rates are even higher among the city's poorest sex workers: an estimated 72 per cent of women who charge fifty baht or less per customer are HIV-positive. Such women average ten to twenty clients per day, the majority of whom do not use condoms.'

Jayne shook her head at the implications: for a sex worker to service twenty clients per day meant, somewhere in the town, women were being fucked by a different man more than once every hour for less than two dollars a time.

Most of the sex workers Jayne had met were like Nalissa, working in up-market establishments catering to foreigners. There was no way she could get inside a brothel patronised by the poorest locals.

She rubbed her temples and returned to the report. It described how the successful implementation of public health activities such as a '100 per cent condom campaign' was complicated by the fact that prostitution remained illegal in Thailand—a perplexing situation, given the industry's high profile, and a testament to the Thai capacity for polite disregard.

'Last year, as part of the national AIDS response, the government introduced a bill proposing to decriminalise prostitution,' Jayne read, 'arguing that if prostitution were no longer illegal, more sex workers would be encouraged to come forward for testing and counselling and the industry would be easier to regulate. However, the bill is yet to be enacted—'

The remainder of the sentence had been scribbled out, possibly by Moira O'Halloran, the lines in black ink rather than the blue Didier had used. Scowling, Jayne held the page up to the light and gradually made out the words beneath the lines: 'nor is it ever likely to be enacted, so long as the military and police continue to profit as they do from the illegal trade.' The words were significant and Jayne wondered why anyone would delete them.

She found the answer under a subheading 'Shifts in Procurement Patterns' in the local sex industry. In the north in particular, men were demanding greater access to non-Thai sex workers—such as women from the hill tribes and from neighbouring countries Burma and Laos. Demand had also increased for 'virgins' (younger women and children) in the belief that they were more likely to be 'AIDS-free'. But in fact, the paper said these groups were at great risk of HIV infection, especially the children. And because of their status as minors, lack of family support and inability to speak Thai, most did not know how to access health services.

'These shifts in demand have been well documented by the Zero Tolerance for Child Prostitution (ZTCP) Agency,' Jayne read, 'and are noted among both Thais and foreign sex tourists. Thai patrons favour underage, albeit post-pubescent girls. However, at least one expatriate entrepreneur in Chiang Mai is known to offer foreigners pre-pubescent children—a situation that could not exist without the collusion of the local police.'

Jayne paused to light a cigarette. Echoes of a conversation with Didier came back to her from a couple of months ago. They'd met to talk books, but Didier was preoccupied, his mood bleak. He told her that in villages around Chiang Mai where he worked, not a week went by without a funeral for someone who'd died of AIDS.

'Last week, it was a sixteen-year-old girl,' he told Jayne. 'Given how long it takes AIDS to develop, she couldn't have been more than eleven or twelve when she got infected.'

Jayne flicked the ash from her cigarette, kicking herself for not having thought of it before. Didier was looking into a child sex racket—possibly involving the 'expatriate entrepreneur' referred to in his notes. An operation like that would be worth a fortune, both to whoever ran it and to the cops paid to turn a blind eye. He must have found out who was behind it, and they'd killed him to keep it quiet. That would explain why he'd been framed for Nou's murder, too: if his findings surfaced after his death, they could be dismissed as the ravings of a man unhinged, the amphetamines further evidence of an unbalanced mind.

Jayne forced herself to finish reading the document. 'The conditions of vulnerability are clear,' Didier had written. 'They consist of poverty, gender, youth, ethnicity and illegality of status as a prostitute and/or illegal immigrant. The key is to enact legislation and develop projects that will have a real impact on changing such conditions.'

Jayne assumed it was Moira O'Halloran who'd put a single, black line through the text, from the subheading to the end of the document. Moira had told Jayne that her proposed study would 'identify conditions of vulnerability'. Didier believed the conditions of vulnerability were already clear.

Her cigarette still smouldering in the ashtray, Jayne rose to her feet and started pacing the room. Didier had given Moira highly sensitive information—information that may have cost him his life—and she intended to do nothing with it. Jayne cursed again, searching for a way to both exonerate Didier and show the bitch up.

An awful thought stopped her in her tracks. Didier had entrusted this material not to Jayne, but to Moira. He'd brought that stupid academic into his confidence—a woman with no understanding of Thailand—over a close friend who lived there.

Jayne slumped back into her chair, angry tears stinging her eyes. Why would Didier do this to her? She thought he admired her intelligence.

'Shit!' she groaned, pressing her palms into her eye sockets. Surely he knew Jayne wasn't the gung-ho type. Despite her predilection for hard-boiled crime fiction, she preferred her real-life cases to be challenging rather than deadly—like the heroes of the 'cosy' books Didier read.

If the knife wound had opened Jayne's eyes to the dangers of her work, learning of Didier's lack of trust had now shaken her confidence. Max was right to warn her against staying in Chiang Mai. Perhaps Moira was right to erase the incriminating passages. Paedophile rackets, police corruption, cold-blooded murder—it was as if the whole mess had a sign over it saying DO NOT ENTER in luminous, red letters.

But how could she abandon her investigation? Of all people, Didier would have known what he was up against, yet he was prepared to take the risk. There was nothing reckless in his motivation; it was there in his paper. Those children mattered to Didier. And it mattered to Jayne that her friend had been killed and vilified for trying to do something to help them.

'So, what would you have me do, Didi?' she said aloud.

She reached to butt out her cigarette, knocking his document to the floor. It fell face down, revealing a note on the reverse side of the back page. It resembled a shopping list, written in French: *jus de citron, allumettes, bougie.*

Why would Didier write a shopping list on the back of an official document? And why lemon juice, matches and a candle? It didn't make sense. It sounded more like the sort of implausible clue someone like Sherlock Holmes or Miss Marple would stumble across—

'Oh, shit!'

She put the paper back on the desk and opened the drawer beneath it. Room service menu, hotel stationery, tourist magazine. She searched the bedside cupboards and, alongside the Gideon Bible, found what she was looking for. Chiang Mai's hotels weren't immune to power failures and provided their guests with candles. Jayne melted the end of one, emptied the ashtray into the bin, and converted it into a candleholder. She lit the wick and picked up the document again.

If her instincts were correct, Didier's shopping list was a set of instructions for reading and writing in invisible ink. It was a plot device in one of the novels he'd loaned her: Holmes, detecting the scent of citrus fruit and knowing what he did about ciphers, applied the heat of a naked flame to reveal the hidden message.

Jayne scrutinised the three-page document until she found an area where the texture of the paper was slightly irregular as if liquid had dried on its surface. Holding the page in both hands, she passed it slowly back and forth over the flame.

Just as she was beginning to feel stupid, the flame leapt up and as she snatched the page away, Jayne noticed a distinctive, dark-brown line against a smudge left by the candle. Trembling, she lowered it again, closer this time, allowing the flame to lick the paper. One by one, the letters appeared. D-O-U-G-K-E-L-L-Y. She blew out the candle and sat back in her chair.

Doug Kelly. The name meant nothing to her. But there was no mistaking what Didier meant by it: he'd written it alongside the mention of the expatriate entrepreneur in Chiang Mai known to offer pre-pubescent children to foreigners.

Jayne hugged the piece of paper to her chest. Didier *had* trusted her. He must have known he was in danger and slipped the Chiang Mai Plaza Hotel card into her handbag to pass on the details of his appointment with Moira O'Halloran. He knew he could rely on Jayne to ask the right questions and follow the trail of clues he'd left. And there was no doubt those clues were intended for her.

Heart racing, she used the hotel stationery to rush off an urgent, confidential fax to her friend Gavan at the *Bangkok Post*, asking him to send whatever he could find on Doug Kelly. She waited downstairs to ensure it went through, then shredded it into the bin once back in her room.

By the time she slid between the sheets, her heart rate had returned to normal, allowing a sense of dread to return. Hoisting herself back out of bed, she grabbed the copy of *Nemesis* she'd rescued from Didier's place, hoping to take her mind off what lay ahead. Instead, in a case that rang with eerie familiarity, she found Miss Marple confronted by an entreaty in a letter from a deceased friend:

> You, my dear, if I may call you that, have a natural flair for justice, and that had led to your having a natural flair for crime. I want you to investigate a certain crime...

Lieutenant Colonel Ratratarn was back in his office six hours after leaving it. He glanced at the paperwork that had appeared on his desk, a report from Komet on top of the pile. Ratratarn scanned the account of the officer's observations during his watch. It was written in excruciating detail, but contained nothing significant. Ratratarn snorted and as he tossed it into the filing tray, saw a fax from the Canadian Embassy advising him to expect a delegation that afternoon.

There was a knock on the door. Ratratarn lit his sixth Krung Thep for the morning. 'Enter!' he barked.

Sergeant Pornsak strode towards his commander. 'Reporting directly to you as instructed, Sir.'

Ratratarn knew Pornsak looked up to him as a mentor, and he was reliable, but the young man's vanity riled him.

'What do you have for me?' he said.

'Sir, I conducted those interviews you ordered,' Pornsak said. 'The bar owner couldn't shed much light on the identity of the farang woman. To the best of my knowledge, the subject had never met the woman before that night and knew nothing of her background. By that, Sir, I mean I interrogated him thoroughly and I'm confident he was telling the truth.'

Ratratarn nodded for him to continue.

'As for my interview with Khun Mana, I obtained a

physical description matching the one given by Khun Deng and ascertained that the farang is an Australian who lives in Bangkok.'

'There must be hundreds of Australian women in Bangkok,' Ratratarn said. 'What about a name, Sergeant, or an address?'

Pornsak straightened his stance. 'No one could remember her name, but I was able to jog Khun Deng's memory sufficiently for him to recall that the dead Canadian was friendly with the manager at the Chiang Mai Plaza Hotel. She might have stayed there. But...'

'But?'

'I went to the hotel and they have five Australian women registered: three elderly women on a package tour, one on her honeymoon and a professor. None of them fit the description of the woman we're looking for.' He paused. 'Perhaps she's already left town, Sir.'

Ratratarn inhaled thoughtfully on his cigarette. 'What about the professor?'

Pornsak extracted a notepad from his shirt pocket. 'She's older, Sir, nearly fifty according to her registration details. Address in Menbon.'

Ratratarn snatched the sergeant's notebook. Moira O'Halloran had listed her address as the University of Melbourne. He walked to the cupboard containing the dead foreigner's files. Rummaging through a folder marked Correspondence, he extracted a fax with the University of Melbourne letterhead.

'Sergeant, the dead Canadian also worked as a university professor. Did it occur to you there might be a connection?'

'Ah, Sir, I—'

'Here is a fax addressed to Khun Didier and signed by Professor Moira O'Halloran,' Ratratarn said, waving the piece of paper in the man's face. 'Didn't you even think to interview her?'

'Sir, I—' Pornsak swallowed hard, all smugness gone. 'Sir, the receptionist said the woman doesn't speak Thai.'

Still holding the fax, Ratratarn sighed. 'Right, fine, I guess I'll have to interview her myself.'

'Ah, Sir, sh-she was due to check out this morning.'

'Damn it, Pornsak!' The lieutenant colonel picked up his cap. 'Why the hell didn't you say so?'

It was 9.45 by the time Jayne got out of the shower. She dressed quickly, only noticing the envelope slipped under the door as she left. She didn't open the message until she was in the back of a tuk-tuk on her way to the Somphet cafe. It contained a return fax from Gavan.

> Dear Jayne,
> Lucky you caught me on night shift. The guy who does the entertainment column here says Douglas Kelly was a well-known Bangkok (and Pattaya) identity before he left for Chiang Mai two years ago. He's a fellow Aussie who used to run a bar in Soi Cowboy, co-owned another in Pattaya, and had interests in a tour company that ferried clients between the two. Rumour has it he worked as a mercenary for the Americans in Laos in the early 70s, but it's likely he spread the story himself. More

reliable sources say he fled a financial scandal in Australia in the 80s. He's maintained a low profile in Chiang Mai, but if you do get wind of anything nasty (i.e. newsworthy) going on, I know I don't have to remind you that you owe me.

Yours,

Gavan

P.S. Don't know if the photo will fax through. I pulled it out of the archives at the Post from an article on tourism in Pattaya. GB.

Jayne flattened the lower half of the page. The man identified as Doug Kelly was standing behind a bar, his hands raised in a gesture of welcome. In front of the bar, perched on stools, were three Thai women in bikinis holding elaborately garnished cocktails. Kelly looked broad-shouldered and didn't have much hair, but the fax wasn't clear enough to show his face.

As the tuk-tuk approached the Tha Pae Gate in the remains of the old citadel wall, Jayne stuffed the pieces of paper into her day-pack and directed the driver to stop. She checked her watch. She'd made the appointment with two minutes to spare.

She almost didn't recognise Nalissa. The woman's oval-shaped face was clean, making her look several years younger. She wore a modest floral print dress with a lace collar and white rubber sandals.

Jayne greeted her with a wai and took a seat. 'I really appreciate you meeting me like this.'

'*Mai pen rai*,' Nalissa smiled. 'Somphet makes the best

khao soi in Chiang Mai. You want to try it?'

She gestured to the cafe's eponymous Somphet who was plunging a wire basket full of dried noodles into a steaming cauldron of water the size of a kettledrum. Beneath the pot, a terracotta brazier glowed with hot coals. A moment later, Somphet removed the basket and dumped the noodles into a bowl with one hand, ladling curry soup on top with the other. Garnishing the khao soi with a handful of beansprouts and a sprinkle of chopped shallots, he tapped loudly on the countertop to attract a waitress. Jayne nodded eagerly for Nalissa to place their order.

The soup came with the usual condiments, small caddies of dried chilli, sugar, vinegar and MSG, and Nalissa added a generous scoop of the latter to her bowl. It was only when they finished eating that Jayne got down to business.

'Nalissa, you mentioned yesterday you'd seen Khun Sanga at around one o'clock on the morning he was...that he died.'

The Thai woman rested her chopsticks across her bowl and blotted her lips with a serviette.

'Yes. I'd gone to Loh Kroh to meet a friend. While I was waiting, I saw Khun Sanga. He was with a farang man, but I don't think it was your friend.'

'Why's that?'

'The papers said the farang who killed Khun Sanga was from Canada. But the man I saw him with was Australian.'

'How do you know?'

The Thai woman smiled. 'Sometimes when we're bored at work, we play a game to guess the country of the different customers. For the Asian men, it's easy. You start with the face and you can tell if he's Chinese, Japanese, Korean, and so on. Then you look closer.'

She started counting on her fingers. 'Chinese face with bad haircut and cheap shoes means mainland China. Chinese face with brand-name clothes, good shoes and meu teu means Singapore or maybe Malaysia. You have to guess.'

'What about farangs?'

'Ah!' Nalissa started counting on the other hand. 'Germany, he drinks a lot of beer, has a loud voice and big shoes. England, drinks a lot of beer, too, but not so loud. And the skin is pink.'

Jayne laughed.

'As for Australia,' the Thai woman said, 'he also drinks a lot of beer. Wears big shoes like the German, but is not pink like the English. But you know he's Australian when he talks because he doesn't move his lips very much. Like this.'

Her impersonation of an Aussie drawl was impeccable.

'How old would this man have been?' she said.

'Much older than Khun Sanga. Maybe more than fifty. He had lines on his face and not much hair.'

'Was he big, medium, small?'

'Tall,' Nalissa nodded firmly. 'That's why I remember. I couldn't hear them talking, but it looked funny because this tall man was almost carrying Khun Sanga.'

'What do you mean, "carrying"?'

'I don't know…as if Khun Sanga was too tired to walk by himself.'

Jayne thought about it for a moment. 'Did you tell any of this to the police?'

'Oh, no!' Nalissa moved her soup bowl to one side and leaned across the table. 'If I see police I run away because if they catch me I have to give them all my money. Otherwise they'll put me in prison because of…because of my job.'

Jayne nodded and checked her watch, wondering if she'd catch Deng at Man Date. She needed to find out more about what happened at the bar after she left.

She reached into her bag for some money to pay for lunch and caught sight of Gavan's fax. On impulse, she took it out and spread it on the table. 'Nalissa, I don't suppose this was the man you saw with Khun Sanga?'

The Thai woman studied the picture, a crease forming between the fine arcs of her eyebrows. 'It could be, but…I can't be sure.'

Jayne wasn't surprised as the image wasn't clear enough for a positive ID. 'Thanks anyway,' she said. 'You've helped me a lot.'

'*Mai pen rai*,' Nalissa said, rising to her feet. 'You helped me last night. *Kam sanong kam.*'

Jayne smiled gratefully, paid Somphet and farewelled Nalissa with a wai.

Moira O'Halloran stared in horror at the tight-lipped man in the chocolate-brown uniform. She was checking out when he'd turned up and insisted on asking her a few questions. Anxious not to miss her flight, she'd kept her answers brief. Yes, she knew Didier de Montpasse. No, she didn't know a Sanga Siamprakorn. Yes, she was working with Didier. Yes, their research was about AIDS and the sex industry in Chiang Mai. Yes, she had a paper he'd written on the topic. Yes, well, she supposed the policeman could have a copy, though it was highly inconvenient as she'd have to re-open her suitcase. Unpacking would be no small effort, given the amount of stuff—hill tribe silverware and baskets—she'd hidden in layers of clothing to avoid a delay at Customs.

'Are you aware,' Ratratarn said, 'that Mr Didier was shot dead four days ago when attempting to resist arrest for murder?'

'Dead?' she gasped. 'Didier, dead?'

'You haven't heard about it? It's been all over the news.'

'I-I've been in Chiang Rai,' she stammered. 'I haven't seen...Oh my God! What happened?'

'His death was accidental. But he was wanted at the time for murder.'

'I don't believe this.' She put her head in her hands and slumped against the reception desk. 'This is dreadful,' she whimpered, 'just dreadful.'

'I sympathise, Ma'am,' Ratratarn said. 'It must be highly unpleasant to discover something like this about a good friend.'

'Good friend?' She raised her head abruptly. 'Believe me, Officer, Mr de Montpasse is no friend of mine. I've had my doubts about his involvement in this project all along.'

'What do you mean?'

'Quite frankly, I can't imagine why I agreed to the collaboration in the first place,' she said, thinking it wise to put as much distance between her and Didier as possible. 'We've never really seen eye to eye on the issues.'

She unlocked her suitcase as she spoke. 'Take this paper you asked about. I've had to do a significant amount of editing. I'm still not convinced I should use it at all...'

Her voice trailed off as the policeman scanned the document. He narrowed his eyes, but that was all.

'I see,' he said. 'You did quite a lot of editing.'

'Exactly!' She breathed a sigh of relief.

'You understand, Ma'am,' he said, rolling the paper into a tight tube, 'I'll need to retain this as evidence.'

'Oh?' She glanced at the document in the man's fist. 'Yes, well, of course.'

'I also need to know if anyone other than yourself has read this.'

'Only Didier's assistant. What was her name?' She rummaged through her tote bag. 'Keeney, that's it!' She pulled out Jayne's business card. 'Jayne Keeney. I gave her a copy after we'd—'

'After you what, Ma'am?'

'Jayne did some interpreting for me last night as part of my field research,' Moira said quickly. 'But she didn't say anything about Didier being dead.'

If Didier's death had been all over the news, why hadn't Jayne mentioned it? What if she was trying to elbow her way in on the research? After all, with Didier out of the way, there would be no one to accuse her of plagiarism. The idea of such shameless opportunism took Moira's breath away.

'Officer, I think you'd better contact this woman,' she said, handing over the card. 'She may be operating under a whole set of assumptions—' She saw the man frown and changed tack. 'You may need to break the news to her gently. I got the impression she was close to the deceased.'

Ratratarn looked at the card. 'Any idea where she's staying?'

'She said her hotel was near the footbridge.'

'Anything else that might help us find her—a physical description?'

'She'd be around thirty,' Moira said. 'Smaller than me. Long, curly hair—dark. And she's Australian.'

She gave the policeman her sweetest smile, the one she'd rehearsed for working in Asia. 'I do hope, Officer, this affair won't negatively impact on my ability to work here in Chiang Mai?'

'We don't want to delay your departure any longer,' the policeman said, ignoring the question.

Moira nodded. That suited her just fine. She had a plane to catch and a conference paper to write. The sooner she started the better, if she was to outwit Jayne Keeney's attempt to steal her data.

It was disgraceful what some people would do to make a name for themselves as academics.

The Night Bazaar was open for business, but the same goods that seemed exotic after dark looked cheap and tawdry in the daylight. Several large cockroaches scuttled out of Jayne's way as she stepped into the alley leading to the bars. She became aware of smells she hadn't noticed before: stale cigarette smoke, beer, rotting fruit, rising damp.

She was relieved to find Deng at Man Date, with a couple of other young guys. But the smile on her face froze when she saw that Deng was emptying the shelves, stacking CDs, photos and ornaments into a box. Another boy was emptying the water feature into a drain, the ceramic Chinese fisherman sitting forlorn on the bar. A third young man was taking the posters and beer coasters down from the walls, despite having one arm in a sling.

'Khun Deng,' Jayne said. 'What's happening?'

When he looked up, she saw the right side of his face was bruised purple from cheek to jaw. There was a cut above his eye, and the index finger on his left hand was bandaged as if it'd been broken.

Deng groaned. 'Go away, Khun Jayne! It's not safe for you here.'

'What do you mean? Who did this to you?'

'It doesn't matter. You have to go.'

She recognised the boy with his arm in a sling—the one

who'd practised his English on her. He'd been beaten up, too, one eye reduced to a slit by the swelling around it.

'Deng, please!' she said. 'Tell me what's going on.'

'It's not safe,' he repeated. 'You're putting us all in danger.'

Jayne felt her hair stand on end. 'You mean someone did this to you because of me?'

'Look,' he spoke quickly, 'this guy came round asking about you. I told him we'd never met before the other night. Mana, too. But he didn't believe us. He wanted to know everything about you—your name, your nationality, your appearance, where you were staying. In the end I said I thought you went to the Plaza because Khun Di had a friend working there.' He resumed his packing. 'I'm sorry.'

'No,' Jayne said. 'I'm the one who's sorry. Who was it?'

'It doesn't matter,' Deng said. 'There's nothing you can do about it.'

'Pornsak,' Mana said, ripping a poster from the wall. 'Police Sergeant Pornsak.'

Jayne looked from him to Deng and back again. Mana screwed the damaged poster into a ball and threw it to the ground.

'We've got to get out of here,' Deng said, 'and you should, too. If the guy comes back and sees you, we're dead.'

'OK, OK.' She backed away. 'Just tell me, Deng, do you know a guy who runs a bar in Chiang Mai called Doug Kelly?'

Deng frowned. 'I know Mister Doug—' he pronounced

123

it 'duck'. 'He runs a place in Loh Kroh, the Kitten Club. Why do you want to know about Mister Duck?'

'No reason,' Jayne murmured. She turned to leave. 'By the way, I'm not staying at the Chiang Mai Plaza. It's OK, Deng. You didn't tell that cop anything.'

Jayne fought the impulse to run; the Thais slowed to a shuffle in the afternoon heat, and she'd only attract attention. She walked briskly back to her hotel, stopping short when she saw a police car parked nearby. She took a deep breath and told herself not to be paranoid. No one other than Max knew where she was staying. She hadn't even given the details to Moira O'Halloran.

But Moira *was* staying at the Chiang Mai Plaza. What if that cop, Pornsak, got on to her? What could she tell him? Enough for him to track her down?

Jayne couldn't risk it. She had to change hotels, fast. The receptionist handed her a message with her key, but she didn't stop to read it. Once in her room, she threw her belongings into her backpack and made her way out.

A light showed the lift paused on the fourteenth floor. Too impatient to wait, Jayne took the fire escape downstairs, her injured arm straining under the weight of her pack. She opened the exit door then closed it again. Reflected in a mirror on the wall of the lobby, she'd seen two policemen at the reception desk. One of them was the man on the television, the lieutenant colonel who shot Didier—she was sure of it.

Jayne was confident she hadn't been seen. She eased the door ajar and strained to hear what they were saying.

'*Ka, ka*,' the receptionist nodded. 'Yes, an Australian,

124

early thirties, with long dark curly hair. She's just come in, Sergeant Pornsak. Third floor, room 312.'

Jayne backed away as the cops headed for the lift, but left the door open a crack. She wanted to get a look at this Pornsak, the bastard who'd beaten Deng and Mana because of her. He wasn't what she'd expected. He was young and didn't look like a brute. If anything, he looked like a Chinese movie star.

She shut the door and ran along the corridor in search of a way out. She'd settle her account some other time, grateful the hotel hadn't kept her passport as security.

Outside the sunlight was almost blinding but she didn't stop to put on her sunglasses. She waved down a tuk-tuk and directed the driver to the Mai Pai Guesthouse, a quiet place across the river where she'd stayed years earlier as a tourist—before she cashed in the last leg of her return flight and decided to remain in Thailand. The Nawarat Bridge was decorated in honour of Coronation Day; a portrait of the Thais' beloved king, swathed in gold silk, hung from the central pylon, and pots of vivid yellow and orange mari-golds lined the railings. But Jayne was too distracted to appreciate it.

She didn't know how intensive the cops' search to find her would be, but she couldn't risk checking in under her own name. In the back of the tuk-tuk, she went through the fake identification cards she kept in her wallet. Forged by experts in Khao San Road, there was something for every occasion: a press card announcing her as a journalist with Agence France Presse; student ID that took five years off her age and listed her as a New Zealander; and a staff card for the British Council her friend Simone gave her when she left Thailand. Inspired by what she read of Sherlock Holmes' disguises, Jayne had replaced Simone's photo with one of herself in a blond wig and had even forged business cards to go with it. So far it had been an intellectual exercise: she hadn't used it yet, but given what the Chiang Mai police knew about her it now seemed appropriate.

Covering her hair with a scarf as the tuk-tuk pulled up to the guesthouse, she checked in under Simone's name and paid five days in advance on a room she didn't stop to inspect. She needed to find a hairdresser and buy some more clothes and a carton of cigarettes. There was something else nagging at her—something she was supposed to do—but she didn't pause to dwell on it.

It wasn't until she'd returned to the guesthouse and was shaking the stray hairs from her short, newly bleached locks, that she remembered the message left for her at the Silver Star. Searching through her backpack, she found the slip of paper.

> *Miss Jayne*
> *Mr David call to you. Phone 270099. Pornping*
> *Tower, Rm. #1527.*

Komet knew something was wrong when he saw Pornsak leave the lieutenant colonel's office. The man's cheeks burned red as if he'd been slapped and he shoved past Komet with enough force to push him into the wall. And there were none of his usual jibes.

An hour earlier, Komet had been summoned to attend a meeting with the Canadian Embassy delegation. What Pornsak was doing at the station outside of his shift, Komet didn't know, though he'd clearly angered their commander. When Komet finally entered the office, Ratratarn was pacing behind his desk, muttering something about Sergeant Pornsak's mother fornicating with dogs.

Komet cleared his throat.

'What?' Ratratarn barked.

'Officer Komet reporting for duty as ordered, Sir.'

Ratratarn scowled.

'The interview with the Canadian officials, Sir,' Komet said.

'Son of a bitch, the farangs.' The lieutenant colonel glanced at his watch. 'Come on.'

He put on his cap and picked up a pile of documents, issuing orders as he steered Komet along the corridor towards the meeting room. Ratratarn was to do all the talking, but if 'any of these smart-arse embassy types' insisted on asking Komet any questions, he was to answer yes, no or, 'It's all there in the report'. Under no circumstances was he to volunteer any information.

'Right,' Ratratarn concluded, 'let's get this shit over with.'

He turned the sign on the door to Interview in Progress and entered the windowless room. Its two occupants, a farang man and a Thai woman, rose to their feet. Empty teacups on the table indicated they'd been waiting for some time.

'Urgent police business,' Ratratarn said in lieu of an apology. 'Lieutenant Colonel Ratratarn in charge of the investigation. This is Officer Komet.'

'*Sawadee ka*,' the woman said with a wai. Her chic, short hair was dyed burgundy and she wore a raw silk suit to match. 'This is Mr David Freeman, Second Secretary of the Canadian Embassy. He is in charge of the inquiry.'

The farang had the pallid skin of someone who spent too long in an office. His jowls hung over his white shirt collar and his hand when Komet shook it felt like sponge. Ratratarn and the farang exchanged business cards.

'My name is Khun Israporn,' the woman continued, enunciating each tone like a schoolteacher addressing slow learners. 'Personal assistant to Khun David. I will be the interpreter.'

Komet shot a glance at Ratratarn, wondering whether the lieutenant colonel would let on that he could speak English. Ratratarn nodded for them to proceed.

Komet waited until everyone else was seated, before sitting behind Ratratarn. Not knowing what else to do, he opened a notebook and placed it on his lap. The farang spoke in a low voice to his interpreter, folded his hands on the desk in front of him, and faced the lieutenant colonel with a polite smile.

'Khun David thanks you for your time this afternoon,' Israporn said.

'It's a regrettable business,' Ratratarn said.

'Khun David would also like to thank you on behalf of the Canadian ambassador for your assistance with this investigation.'

'It is my duty,' Ratratarn said.

The farang nodded in response to Israporn's translation.

'Khun David says he, too, has a duty here. He'd like to add his personal thanks for your co-operation in helping him carry out his duty.'

'Good co-operation is important.'

'*Ka, ka*,' Israporn said, 'especially when the case is such a sensitive one—such a tragedy.'

'A tragedy,' Ratratarn nodded.

Komet looked down at his notebook to hide his confusion. Everyone was so polite, even the lieutenant colonel. There was no trace of the fury that had been in his voice minutes earlier.

'The fact that this tragedy involved a Canadian national is, of course, why Khun David is here,' Israporn said. 'As we know, Khun Didier de Montpasse lived in Thailand for many years.'

'So I believe.'

'Khun David says Khun Didier was not known in embassy circles for having a violent disposition.'

Ratratarn didn't miss a beat. 'Then it must have been a

shock to discover he had a record for violence in his own country.'

In the wake of Israporn's translation, the two men eyed each other squarely and Komet understood the meeting had moved on to new ground.

The farang broke away first to confer with his colleague.

'If it's convenient, Lieutenant Colonel, we would like to clarify one or two points in relation to the report you so kindly provided. It states that when you went to Khun Didier's house to question him about the death of Khun Sanga, he all but confessed to the murder. Did you find that unusual, Sir?'

'Not in my experience,' Ratratarn said.

The farang consulted Israporn again.

'We would also like to ask whether—' She paused as a ringing sound emanated from somewhere in the room. Ratratarn removed his mobile phone from his pocket and glanced at the screen.

'Excuse me a moment,' he said.

The Canadian stood as he left the room, the phone still ringing. Resuming his seat, he smiled blankly at Komet for a moment, before turning to say something to Israporn.

'Officer…Komet, wasn't it?' she said, as if noticing him for the first time. 'Perhaps you could assist us.'

Komet was sure they could see the panic on his face, but he swallowed hard and nodded.

'Khun David was about to ask your superior officer if there were any suspects other than Khun Didier in Khun Sanga's murder?'

'No.'

'So as far as the police are concerned Khun Didier was responsible for the murder of Khun Sanga?'

'Yes,' he said.

'Don't you think it was premature to close the murder investigation following Khun Didier's accidental death?'

'It's all there in the report,' he said.

Israporn conferred with the farang. 'The report says Lieutenant Colonel Ratratarn was convinced of Khun Didier's guilt,' she said. 'But we are interested in your opinion, Officer Komet. You were there on the night—you located the murder weapon, didn't you?'

'Yes.' Komet felt his cheeks burn.

'So, do *you* think Khun Didier murdered Khun Sanga?'

Many aspects of the case made Komet uneasy, but it wasn't his place to offer opinions. 'The f-farang's death was accidental,' he stammered. 'But it must've been his fate, because he was guilty!'

Israporn gave him a withering look before translating. David frowned and Israporn added something that made them both laugh. Komet scribbled in his notebook to hide his embarrassment.

'We assume there will be a full coronial inquest into Khun Didier's death?'

Komet looked up to see the translator waiting for his answer.

'That's a matter for the Lieutenant Colonel,' he said.

'What's that?' said Ratratarn, at the doorway.

'The official was asking about the—'

'The coronial inquest into Khun Didier's death.' Israporn cut him off, addressing Ratratarn as if Komet were no longer in the room.

'End of the week,' Ratratarn said brusquely. 'After the forensic report is completed, the body will be released to the family.'

'The family haven't claimed the body…' Israporn began, before the farang stopped her. '*Kor thort na ka*, Khun David will not be present at the inquest. But he'd be grateful if you would send a copy of the coroner's report to the Canadian Embassy.'

'Of course.'

The farang rose to his feet. 'Khun David would like to thank you again for your time,' Israporn said. 'On behalf of the ambassador, he'd like to add that he trusts the spirit of co-operation that exists between our two countries will not be adversely affected by this tragedy.'

As the officials left, Ratratarn's satisfied look faded. 'The sooner we get this business behind us the better,' he said. 'I've had it with farangs.'

Komet coughed nervously. 'Will that be all, Sir?'

'What? Yes, Komet. Go home. You're off surveillance tonight. I need you to accompany me on other business. Report back to me at eleven-thirty.'

He saluted and turned to leave, when Ratratarn grabbed him by the arm.

'You did OK today,' he said. 'I heard what the farang said to his translator and you didn't give anything away. It's time you were rewarded for your efforts.'

Komet was stunned. It was unprecedented for the

lieutenant colonel to pay him a compliment. And he could only imagine what reward Ratratarn had in mind. Komet knew certain policemen took kickbacks from various businesses—'direct taxes' some called it—payments made to the service provider instead of disappearing into government vaults in Bangkok. He knew what went on, but he wasn't sure he wanted to be a part of it.

At times like these, Komet missed his father. Khanthong Plungkham had been a village leader widely consulted for his advice. Though Komet's family was poor, his father had a reputation for fairness and wisdom. He'd studied with the monks as a boy and his understanding of the Buddhist precepts, coupled with his ability to make them relevant to people's daily lives, gave him a status at odds with how little land the family owned.

If Komet confided in Arunee about Ratratarn's proposal, she would rest her hand suggestively on her distended belly—the same way she did when he was choosing between the Honda Dream he'd wanted, and the cheaper Kawasaki motorbike he'd ended up with.

And he could equally well anticipate his father's response to the prospect of deriving wealth from dishonest means. '*Kam sanong kam*,' he would say. It was his standard response, whether Komet and his brothers were being chastised for stealing fruit from a neighbour's tree, or praised for helping their mother with the housework. 'What goes around, comes around.'

'So that's the case against him.' Jayne sighed and closed the folder. 'I wish I'd seen this earlier.'

David Freeman smiled at the young woman across the table. His colleague at the Australian Embassy had warned him she was a handful, but he hadn't mentioned how attractive she was.

Of her neat, even features, Jayne's eyes were the most striking: a piercing shade of green that reminded David of a cat. But the overall impression conveyed was one of fragility, skin so pale it was almost translucent. She seemed shy, almost deferential, yet she'd asked intelligent questions about the procedures involved in official inquiries and the jurisdiction of the Canadian Embassy. She'd also asked about the de Montpasse case and his interview with the police. Normally, David would refuse to discuss such information, but she appealed to him as a personal friend of the deceased, saying it would help her with 'the grieving process'.

And so he allowed her to read Israporn's translation of the police report. Painful as it might be, the young woman simply had to face the facts.

'I'm sorry, Jayne,' he said with a meaningful glance at the report. 'But I hope this clarifies things.'

She ran her fingers through her short, blond curls. 'So, you're convinced of Didier's guilt.'

'My personal opinion is irrelevant,' he replied. 'The fact is, the police are certain they've got their man. And you must admit the case against him is what one might call watertight.'

She bowed her head and David thought she might cry. He was on the verge of reaching over to take her hand when she flashed him a look that made him glad he hadn't.

'The police case is a sham,' she said.

He opened his mouth to disagree, but she held up her hand.

'David, please hear me out. Number one,' she counted on her fingers, 'according to the report, Didier told the officer in charge that Nou—I mean, Sanga—deserved to die like a dog. That exchange has got to be a fabrication. Didier would never speak like that—he loved Nou.'

David shifted in his seat, but Jayne pressed on.

'Two,' she said, 'and Max can vouch for this: there's no way Didier would've had amphetamines on the premises. He used to give me a hard time for smoking. The drugs had to be planted.'

'Max did mention something about that,' David said carefully.

'Well, did you ask the cops about it?'

'No, Jayne, I didn't ask the police about it,' he said, sounding more pompous than he intended. 'You see, Max also told me that Monsieur de Montpasse's...ah...companion was a known prostitute. It's therefore conceivable the young man had a history of drug abuse and brought the amphetamines into the house, albeit without the knowledge of Monsieur de Montpasse.'

'But Nou wasn't into drugs!' she said. 'Don't you see? It's all part of a plot to discredit Didier—'

She placed her elbows on the table and buried her face in her hands. This time David thought she really was crying.

'Jayne,' he said softly, 'I know this is hard for you. But your allegiance to your friend—admirable as it is—isn't enough to exonerate him. The police have a motive, a de facto confession *and* the murder weapon. All you've got is hearsay and loyalty.'

Her shoulders sagged, and for a moment David imagined her in his arms, allowing him to comfort her.

She mumbled something into her hands.

'What's that?' he said gently.

'I said you're right!' She raised her head. Her eyes were dry. 'I appreciate your time,' she added, reaching for her bag, 'and I won't keep you any longer. Shall we get the bill?'

Moments earlier she'd seemed crushed but now she was acting as if nothing had happened.

'Don't worry about the bill,' he said impatiently. 'Listen, Max suggested I might accompany you back to Bangkok.'

'Oh?' She raised her eyebrows. 'No, I won't be going back yet. Don't worry, I'll call Max and explain.'

'But...' He fumbled for something to say. 'Are you going to be OK?'

'I'll be fine. Really.' She leaned over and patted his hand. 'What you said tonight has been inspirational.'

David felt himself redden. 'W-well, is there anything else I can do to help?'

136

'Perhaps you'd order me a taxi.'

'Of course.'

'Thank you,' she said. 'That would be most kind of you.'

He walked into the hotel lobby and asked one of the bellboys to arrange a car, but when he returned to the table there was no sign of Jayne.

'Did you see where that woman went?' he asked a passing waitress.

'Excuse me?'

'The woman who was sitting here, the one who was sharing my table. Did you see where she went?'

The waitress smiled.

David sighed. 'Just bring me the cheque, will you please.'

Jayne cursed herself for having placed any faith in an official inquiry. As if a bureaucrat like David Freeman would give a damn about Didier! Still, she'd pilfered a copy of the police report so the meeting wasn't a complete waste of time.

Freeman maintained the case against Didier was watertight. His only doubts—and she presumed he was speaking on behalf of the Canadian Embassy—concerned the absence of other murder suspects and the speed with which the investigation had been closed. This gave Jayne an added incentive to build a case against Kelly.

She had a precedent, too. A year earlier, the Thai wife of an Australian expat in Bangkok was arrested for allegedly attempting to murder him. The man, drugged at the time of the assault, had been unable to finger his assailant. Adamant his wife couldn't have done it, he employed Jayne to come up with an alternative suspect.

'That should be enough to get Phet off,' he'd said. 'You know, reasonable doubt and all that.'

It had worked. Jayne managed to identify the woman responsible—the man's estranged German mistress—and Phet was acquitted.

Reasonable doubt. Such a loaded term. She'd had doubts about the case against Didier from the start, but these weren't 'reasonable' to Freeman. What was it he'd said—something about her needing more than hearsay and loyalty?

So be it! She'd find grounds for doubt so bloody reasonable even David Freeman would be swayed. And she'd do it by capitalising on his own uneasiness about the lack of alternative suspects in Nou's murder.

She needed to find out more about Doug Kelly and what had happened when Nalissa saw him with Nou. She'd start by checking out the Kitten Club. She wouldn't stand a chance of getting inside the place, but some surveillance might prove useful. At the very least, she could try for a photo of Kelly to get a positive ID on him from Nalissa.

But the Kitten Club was in Loh Kroh, and with her new-look blond hair and green eyes—courtesy of coloured contact lenses—she'd stand out like a beacon. A man in her situation might get away with posing as a sex tourist, but it wasn't going to work for her. There were only two reasons why a white Western woman might be seen wandering the streets of Loh Kroh: she'd have to be either a working girl or a nun.

There were stories in the papers about women from

former Soviet Union countries coming to Thailand on tourist visas and working in the sex industry. 'Economic refugees' the press called them. Blonds in particular could command high prices in Bangkok's exclusive gentlemen's clubs, but Jayne wasn't sure any of these women had found their way as far north as Chiang Mai. Besides, masquerading as a sex worker was risky. What would she do if someone approached her? Then again, how would she feel if no one did?

She sighed then changed into the most conservative outfit she'd bought that afternoon: a white blouse buttoned to the neck, black skirt and flat sandals. She toyed with the idea of wearing socks under the sandals—a fashion statement she associated exclusively with evangelical Christians—but couldn't bring herself to look that awful. She removed all but the barest traces of make-up and hung a large crucifix she'd bought at a street stall on a leather thong around her neck, making sure it sat over her blouse. As a final touch, she took the Gideon Bible from her bedside table.

'Jesus loves you,' she said to her reflection in the mirror.

Two tuk-tuk drivers refused to take Jayne to Loh Kroh no matter how much money she offered. A third agreed, drove in silence and deposited her at the end of a narrow, unsealed street. One side was lined with garment factories—sweatshops with names like Beauty Queen and Blissful Smile. On the other side, wooden shacks slumped against each other as if exhausted. It was a humid night and the street itself appeared to sweat, oily pools of water reflecting the glow of fairylights from the shacks. There were few people around apart from the brothel touts and bouncers who hovered in the doorways. Even food vendors steered clear of Loh Kroh after dark.

The factories were closed for the night, and Jayne headed down the street, picking her way around puddles and garbage, holding the Bible like a shield against her chest. A small, pink neon sign identified the Kitten Club as the only concrete building on the strip. The ground-floor windows were blacked out and the entrance partly concealed by an awning. There didn't appear to be anyone on the door, and as Jayne moved closer, she heard music and voices from inside.

A tuk-tuk rounded the corner and headed towards her. Jayne retraced her steps and ducked inside a low-walled shack opposite the club. She peered through slats in the wood, watching as two farang men paid the driver and entered the two-storey building. When the tuk-tuk pulled away, she saw she'd taken refuge inside an old police box, a wooden booth with a thatched roof once used as an information and sentry point. Most of the paintwork had peeled away, there was rubbish on the floor, and a thick layer of spiderwebs appeared to keep the ceiling from caving in.

The booth gave Jayne an excellent vantage point for watching the club and the irony of using a police box for surveillance was not lost on her. Putting the Bible aside, she took out her camera and rested it on a narrow bench that ran the length of one wall. She loosened the slats to poke the lens through, then checked the focus. She'd be able to watch the action through another hole in the wall while recording it on film. She took out a notebook and pen, allowed her eyes to adjust to the gloom and began taking notes.

> *Tues. 7 May 1996, 22.30. Two Caucasian men arrive by tuk-tuk. Both mid/late-50s. 1) Bald; long face, pronounced lines in cheeks, flabby neck; black-rimmed glasses, square frames. Approx. 1.8 m. Medium build. Red & white gingham shirt, white trousers, clean sneakers. 2) Silver-grey hair, thinning on top; stocky build, approx. 1.85 m. Didn't see face. Neat appearance, pale green shirt, possibly silk; grey trousers, shiny material—synthetic(?); grey canvas loafers, clean. Slight limp in right leg.*

The detail was inspired by Holmes stories—the difference between seeing and observing, as Conan Doyle put it—and as the hour dragged on, to stave off boredom, Jayne made her own deductions about the two men.

The whiteness of the first man's trousers suggested he was married to a woman whose fidelity he took for granted—only a doormat would be prepared to launder white trousers. Though lean, the loose skin on his face and neck implied he was once fatter. Since nothing in his appearance suggested vanity—his glasses ugly and old-fashioned—Jayne surmised he'd lost weight due to illness, or possibly on doctor's orders to reduce the risk of heart attack. His sneakers were clean, despite Chiang Mai's dusty streets, indicating he may have spent the day poolside at his hotel.

She didn't get as close a look at the second man, but from his clothing deduced that he spent most of his time in air-conditioning: silk and polyester were sweat traps, but his armpits were dry. She imagined the limp was a war wound—he might have fought in Vietnam. Both men looked ordinary: white, middle class, middle-aged, conservative—the type she'd pass in the street without a second glance. But she'd seen them enter a brothel, and try as she might, Jayne couldn't imagine the interest for these men in having sex with children.

A mangy dog wandered into view, sniffing around the booth. It had scratched itself hairless in patches, hips jutting through scabious grey hide, sores on its muzzle and eyes. The back streets were full of unloved dogs. Thais believed them incarnations of people who'd been bad in a previous life. Jayne reached down as if to pick up a stone: strays were so used to having things thrown at them that the gesture was enough to make the dog yelp as if it had been hit, and lope away.

A motorcycle taxi pulled up outside the club. Jayne got

a good look at the passenger as he moved into the bike's headlight to pay his fare. As the driver took off, the man looked over in Jayne's direction, allowing his gaze to linger so long she thought he'd seen her. But he turned away and, pausing to tuck in his T-shirt, went inside.

Jayne exhaled and picked up her notebook. She checked her watch and recorded the time—23.45—on a new page, but found it hard to continue. This man was younger than the other two, around her age. He was handsome: high cheekbones, strong jaw, broad forehead, aquiline nose. With olive skin and thick, dark short hair, Jayne guessed a Mediterranean background. He looked fit, a physique suggesting an outdoor job. A builder, perhaps, or a sports instructor. Why would a young, good-looking man go to a child sex brothel? Jayne knew it shouldn't matter, but he disturbed her more than the older men.

Before she could add further to her notes, another tuk-tuk pulled up and three drunk men, shouting in German and punching each other, fell out onto the street. Though their clothes were stylish, sweat discoloured the backs of their shirts and one had dirt stains on the knees of his pants. They were having a dispute over who should pay the driver, who waited anxiously. After a minute or two of their loud banter, the door to the club opened, casting a shaft of light across the step, and Jayne saw a man who matched the image in Gavan's fax.

Her heart racing, she crouched lower, releasing the shutter on the camera as a toad-like Thai man appeared beside Kelly and walked over to the Germans to remonstrate with them. One quickly shuffled over to pay the driver, who took off at once. The Germans and the bouncer disappeared beneath the awning, while Kelly paused to glance up and down the street before following them inside.

Jayne eased her finger from the camera button and slumped back against the wall of the booth. That pause had given her the shot she'd hoped for, a close-up of Kelly to show Nalissa.

She was on the verge of packing up when she heard a car engine. Through the gap she saw a brown vehicle with tinted widows stop outside the club. Camera still in position, she began shooting, almost losing her nerve when she saw who got out of the car.

Lieutenant Colonel Ratratarn closed the front passenger door, straightened his cap and marched over to the entrance, his gun holster visible over one hip. He was followed by two other police officers, one of whom Jayne recognised as Pornsak. The other—their driver—looked familiar, but she couldn't place him. She kept taking photos until an abrupt click signalled the end of the film.

She rummaged through her backpack, found a new roll and reloaded the camera. If the cops were planning a raid, she guessed there'd be more than three of them, which meant they were probably paying Doug Kelly a courtesy call. Catching up with an old friend. Sharing news. Collecting the rent.

She took up her notebook, recorded the time and made detailed notes, using her camera's zoom lens to take down the vehicle's registration details. She had just put the notebook away when a voice behind her made her freeze.

'What the fuck—?'

Hand resting on her camera, Jayne turned and gasped. It was the Mediterranean man. Before she could say a word, he ducked inside and crouched on the floor of the booth beside her.

'Who the fuck are you?' he whispered, his accent distinctly Australian.

Her back not just literally against the wall, Jayne considered whacking him over the head with her camera and making a run for it. But it was expensive equipment.

'S-Simone Whitfield,' she began. 'I, uh…'

He eyed the crucifix around her neck. 'Oh, Jesus, you're with one of those Christian organisations, aren't you. Shit, won't you people ever learn?'

'I don't know what you're talking about,' Jayne said, inching the camera towards her.

'Don't try playing the dumb blonde with me!' the man hissed. 'I can see your camera. You're doing surveillance, aren't you! Playing spot-the-high-profile-businessman-or-politician-among-the-paedophiles. A nice little scoop to raise your organisation's profile. Shit! I thought ZTCP had an agreement from you lot to back off and leave it to us now.'

Jayne had no idea who the guy was, but she relaxed at the reference to ZTCP, the anti-child prostitution agency mentioned in Didier's paper. Bristling from the 'dumb blonde' comment, she eyed him squarely.

'Listen, mate,' she said, her voice low but steady, 'I don't know who you are, but this isn't what you think. I'm working undercover as a private detective investigating a murder. What's your story?'

The man frowned. He looked her up and down slowly,

as if deciding whether or not to believe her. Then he gave her a wry smile and extended his hand. 'Mark d'Angelo,' he said, 'Australian Federal Police.'

'Mark,' she shook the proffered hand, hoping it was dark enough to hide the colour in her cheeks, 'I think we need to talk.'

Doug Kelly sat at the bar nursing a glass of single malt scotch. His upturned mouth, bald pate and patches of curly hair above his ears gave him a comical air at odds with his conservative clothing and bleak mood. He'd lost enough weight recently to need a belt for his khaki slacks, and his navy-blue shirt hung loose to conceal the bunched-up waist. Liver spots were appearing on the back of his hands. Checking his watch, he looked over the top of his glasses to scan the room.

Most of the tables were occupied and some patrons had already chosen a girl to sit with them. Other girls maintained a steady flow of traffic between the tables and the bar, placing orders for drinks while keeping an eye out for an offer. There was a spotlight over the stage at the end of the bar in anticipation of the evening's entertainment. The club was doing a roaring trade, but Kelly was distracted.

At times like this he missed Pattaya. The port town had been good to him, but there was too much competition there, and the product had been spoiled. The girls were jaded—most spoke American English and seemed to be studying for diplomas in business—and the customers weren't getting the service they'd come to expect from Thailand. Kelly blamed the collapse of the Soviet Union. Pattaya was fine when it was just the regular tourists and sailors on R&R. But then the Russians got in on the act and ran their operations like the mafia, undermining the accepted order of things and distorting the market.

The Russians undercut him in every respect but one: they increased the percentage paid in protection money to the Pattaya police. Up until then it had been like dealing with country cops in New South Wales where Kelly had grown up: provided he maintained regular payments things stayed civil, even friendly. After nearly ten years, Kelly thought he'd be exempt from any sudden price hikes. But he'd overestimated his own worth. As soon as the cops saw what the Russians were prepared to pay, they started leaning on Kelly; and in light of his already shrinking profit margins it wasn't smart to stay.

So he sent out feelers through his networks, and picked up the buzz about Chiang Mai. The girls were reputedly unsophisticated—many coming from hill tribes and neighbouring countries—and the overheads were much lower. He was able to lease a venue in a part of town previously considered off-limits to non-Thais, and although the place needed work—it had holes in the ground for toilets when he took it over—labour was cheap and easy to come by.

There was no shortage of girls, and there appeared to be almost no limit to what customers were prepared to pay for them—the younger, the better. The first time a customer asked Kelly if he could procure 'a virgin under thirteen', he baulked. But the man was prepared to pay as much for one night as Kelly made in a week.

He intended it to be a once-off, but when word got out, Kelly became inundated with requests, which placed him in a dilemma. Privately he thought you had to be a sick weirdo to get off on fucking kids, and he didn't see himself as the sort of man who'd run a child sex brothel. On the other hand, there was no denying the demand, and Chiang Mai was full of businessmen with fewer scruples than Kelly. At least he would ensure the girls got their fair percentage of the take.

He decided to compromise: once a night, the club would offer a younger girl to the highest bidder. The rest of the girls would be of legal age, albeit young-looking. He gave these specifications to his Thai agents and left the procurement to them, keeping his own dealings with the girls to a minimum. It wouldn't have surprised him to learn that more than a few were under sixteen. But as far as Kelly was concerned, he was doing the right thing by both his clients and his employees. Business was booming, he'd worked out a deal with the cops, and a comfortable retirement seemed assured. But that was before the Canadian started causing trouble.

He'd fronted up one night and accused Kelly of complicity in the death of some girl he could barely remember. The girl had died of AIDS, though what the link was with the Kitten Club, he didn't know. Kelly paid a doctor to conduct regular health checks and give condoms to the girls, and there were signs stating that the business abided by the '100 per cent condom use' policy. Maybe the kid was a junkie. While drug use was forbidden on the premises, Kelly explained he couldn't be held responsible for what his girls might get up to out of hours.

Unmoved, de Montpasse started mouthing off about his friends at the embassy. Kelly had read about the new laws that allowed Australian cops to override the locals, and there was a real risk that if de Montpasse did put the Federal Police on to him, he could lose everything. He had no choice. The Canadian had to go.

Kelly told Ratratarn that de Montpasse wasn't just out to get him, he was after the Chiang Mai police as well. Ratratarn's response was more than Kelly might have hoped for. And it seemed once again that things were back on track, but the business of the missing foreign woman made Kelly think again. Just the thought of her being out there unnerved him. It'd be canny of the AFP to use a female operative. And it'd be just like Ratratarn to assume a woman posed no threat. Kelly cursed the man's arrogance, wishing he could cut loose. But he'd bound Ratratarn to him—it was his own fault—and it was going to cost him.

Out of the corner of his eye, Kelly caught a signal from Mongkol. One of the punters wanted to go upstairs with Win Win, a Burmese girl. Kelly nodded for the customer to meet him at the bar where he'd accept payment in advance. The moment the punter stood up, the cops walked in.

Ratratarn nodded for the two junior officers to sit. Kelly liked to hold their meetings in the main part of the club, creating the impression the police were under his control, when the opposite was the case. He waved from behind the bar, pointing to his watch and holding up five fingers. A few minutes wait then. Ratratarn saw him take a bottle of scotch from the top shelf and order a waitress to bring it on a tray with ice and glasses. He allowed the young woman to pour out three shots, but waved her away when she made a move to join them. This whole business had become more trouble than it was worth, which was saying something, given what Kelly was prepared to pay. Not for the first time, Ratratarn suspected it was a serious mistake to have gotten in so deep with a farang.

Farangs were bad news in Ratratarn's experience. On returning to Chiang Mai in the 1970s, he was made police liaison officer on anti-drugs projects funded by international agencies. The intention was to eradicate opium production in the hill tribe villages and substitute it with cash crops. But the mountainous terrain, while ideal for growing opium poppies, was disastrous for cabbages. There was massive soil erosion, the crops failed, and pesticides poisoned the water supply. The hill tribes ended up poorer than they were to begin with and rather than compensate the villagers, the farang project directors paid their government counterparts in Bangkok to keep the whole thing hushed up.

Around this time Ratratarn was approached by the local mafia lord, who was responsible for organising opium production and trafficking around Chiang Mai. He also involved himself in building roads, schools and health centres to support the poppy growing villages. Ratratarn saw that more could be done for the local people by supporting drug production than by trying to eradicate it. He'd worked for the chao pao ever since.

'Sorry to keep you waiting, mate,' Kelly said, pulling up a chair and acknowledging the two officers with a nod. 'Busy night.' He helped himself to a drink from the table. 'So you don't think the Canadians are going to create any problems for us?'

'Well, they're not the only ones we have to worry about,' Ratratarn said. 'There's also the farang woman.'

Interested, Kelly leaned forward. 'So you reckon she's really a problem?'

'We can't afford to ignore her. That is, *you* can't afford to.' Ratratarn raised his voice to be heard above the noise. 'It's your country's laws you have to worry about. In the meantime, we're going to need more resources.'

'Look, mate,' he said carefully, 'you know I wanna do the right thing by you. But I've got other expenses and debts.'

'Tell me,' Ratratarn said, lighting a cigarette, 'who could you be more indebted to than the man who got rid of your enemies?'

Kelly's jaw tightened. 'We were ridding ourselves of mutual enemies. Remember, it was your idea to have the boyfriend killed.'

Ratratarn flicked the ash from his cigarette on the floor without taking his eyes off Kelly. 'That's not how I recall it.'

'You've got to be joking—'

Ratratarn stopped him by pointing a finger at what was taking place on the stage by the bar. The Australian muttered something and downed a second glass of whisky before regaining his composure.

'How much?'

'Around twenty thousand baht.'

'*What*? That's normally what I pay you guys for a month. I thought we'd had an understanding.'

'That was before these complications.'

'You act as if it's my fault. Why? Because the missing woman's Australian?'

Ratratarn said nothing, but stared at his cigarette as he rolled it between his thumb and index finger.

Kelly groaned. 'OK, OK. Fifteen thousand.'

'Twenty.'

'What happened to the fine Thai tradition of bartering?'

'Twenty.' Ratratarn stubbed out his cigarette. 'Fixed price.'

'OK,' Kelly said, 'but give me a week.'

'Three days.'

'Oh, so now it's OK to barter?'

Ratratarn paid no attention. 'I'll be back on Friday.'

'You drive a hard bargain, mate,' Kelly stood up and extended his hand.

Ratratarn ignored the hand, nodded for him to sit down again and lit another cigarette. He took his time, drawing back slowly, tossing away the dead match, and exhaling a large cloud of smoke over Kelly's head.

'You mentioned our regular fee,' he said. 'I've taken on a couple of young officers to help manage the workload,' Ratratarn inclined his head towards Pornsak and Komet, 'and they're looking forward to being rewarded for their efforts on your behalf.'

Kelly stared hard at Ratratarn. 'At the end of the show,' he hissed. 'You'll have your money then.'

A Thai man in a purple waistcoat skipped onto the stage.

'*Sawadee krup*,' he said into a microphone. 'Welcome to the Kitten Club where we take pride in catering to every taste!'

He spoke in Thai and English, punctuating each

sentence with theatrical laughter. Komet wondered why he bothered speaking Thai at all; apart from the staff, Pornsak, Ratratarn and himself were the only locals.

'Tonight we have a special item on the menu,' the emcee continued, 'a rare and exotic dish, native to the north-east of our country.'

'Hey, that's where you're from,' Pornsak said, nudging Komet.

'Please show your appreciation for Khun Malithong!'

The audience burst into applause as, to Komet's alarm, a young girl was ushered on stage. She wore the traditional wedding dress of Isaan: gold *pah sin* skirt and matching sash, hair piled into a bun and wrapped in gold beads, garlands of jasmine and marigold around her neck. Her face was heavily made-up like a bride, too, but there was no disguising her age. Small and flat-chested with the prominent belly of a child, she couldn't have been more than nine or ten.

'Her name means "golden jasmine flower",' the emcee said. 'And what an appropriate name it is, for she is precious like gold, and pure as a white flower.'

Several men whistled loudly and the emcee raised his hand.

'I see we have many eligible bachelors here tonight who recognise a precious jewel when they see one. But only one of you gets to enter the honeymoon suite tonight. Who will it be? Who'll start the bidding?'

Komet stared around the room in alarm as customers leapt to their feet.

'One thousand!' said one.

'Two thousand!' shouted another.

'I'll pay four thousand!' a third said, waving baht notes in the air.

'What's happening?' Komet gasped.

'It's an auction,' Pornsak said, cleaning his fingernails with a toothpick. 'Farangs pay top dollar for a virgin.'

'But this isn't right!'

'Oh, come on,' the sergeant said. 'We all like the young ones.'

Komet had been with a prostitute only twice. At the age of sixteen, he and some friends pooled their money to visit a woman in the neighbouring village. She was much older and, by accommodating the urges of randy, teenage boys, was seen as protecting the purity of young women in the area. Komet remembered little of the experience except that it was soon over. Several years later, drunk, he'd ended up at a brothel in Chiang Mai with a group of fellow recruits. The girl there was maybe eighteen and pretty, too, but she just wanted the money and Komet didn't enjoy himself. Since marrying Arunee, he'd never felt the urge to go out for sex. Though they were abstaining now she was pregnant according to the custom, for Komet it was worth the wait.

'Hey, isn't your wife expecting?' Pornsak said, reading his thoughts. 'Maybe you should get a girl for the evening.'

'But she's not a girl,' Komet said, gesturing at the stage. 'She's a child!'

'Yeah, well, you know, farangs aren't like Thai people,' the sergeant said, affecting an air of worldliness. 'They have strange tastes.'

But that doesn't make it right, Komet thought.

The bidding had reached 10,000 baht and was still rising. An old, bald farang with thick glasses was waving his hand in the air in front of the stage. At another table, the only other Asian man there—Japanese or Korean by the looks of him—was bidding by raising a single finger. A group of younger men argued amongst themselves, one trying to raise his hand while his friends held him back. The emcee appealed to a few others, who shook their heads. The bidding was down to two people.

'Come now, gentlemen, just look at this pearl, this unplucked lotus,' the emcee said. 'Surely you can make a better offer than that?'

Komet stared at Malithong, trying to meet her eyes. But her face was blank and he suspected she'd been drugged. He considered rushing over to rescue her, but knew they wouldn't have made it to the door.

Komet turned his attention to the table, anything to take his mind off the spectacle on the stage.

'What are they talking about, do you think?' he whispered to Pornsak.

'This farang, Kelly, reckons the lieutenant colonel owes him 'cause it was his idea to have Sanga taken care of,' Pornsak said. 'You know, to make it look bad for the Canadian.'

Komet felt a knot in the pit of his stomach. 'Kelly killed Sanga,' he said, a statement rather than a question.

'Yeah, of course, he didn't do the handiwork himself—hired a guy out of Mae Sai for that. Those *kha* from the mountains, they're savages. I mean, you saw the body.' Pornsak pulled a face. 'But it was Kelly's idea.'

It all became horribly clear to Komet. 'And the lieutenant colonel killed the farang.'

'Yeah, well, they had to get him out of the way and—' Pornsak hesitated, suddenly suspicious. 'Shit, Komet, don't tell me you didn't know? I figured that with you in on the investigation—'

'Yeah, I knew,' Komet lied. 'I'm just interested in the details.'

'Sure, like how much Kelly's going to pay us, right?' Pornsak grinned. 'I wouldn't have thought you had it in you, Komet, but there you go! You're a player now.'

For any other rookie in Komet's position, this would be a night of triumph, a turning point in his career when he became a 'player', as Pornsak put it. But Komet didn't want to play.

Aware that the crowd had gone quiet, he glanced up. The emcee was looking in the direction of his table.

'Sixteen thousand,' the Thai man said. He spoke into the microphone, but the message was clearly directed at Kelly. The farang nodded, said something to Ratratarn, and walked over to the stage.

'The matter has been settled!' the emcee said triumphantly. 'Khun Malithong is to wed Khun…?'

'Bob,' the old man with the glasses said.

Komet watched him step onto the stage with a broad grin on his face.

'A few more minutes,' Ratratarn said, nodding towards the farang. 'I'll get your reward and we'll be out of here.'

For Komet it was like being offered money from the sale of his own sister. He muttered something about a toilet.

'Left of the bar,' Pornsak said. 'Don't wander into the honeymoon suite by mistake, will you?'

The sergeant's laughter burned in Komet's ears as he crossed the room. Khun Bob reached the doorway at the same time, holding Malithong in the crook of his arm. Again Komet had to resist the urge to snatch her away.

'*Sabaidee, bor*?' he said as he came up alongside her.

The child frowned as if the sound of her native tongue were foreign to her. 'Am I OK?' she echoed.

It was only when she spoke that the farang seemed to notice Komet. He took in the police uniform and tightened his grasp on the girl. Komet met his gaze for a moment, the rheumy, opaque eyes of a man old enough to be the child's grandfather.

All farangs smell like white water buffalo, one of his school friends had told him years before they'd ever seen a foreigner. But Khun Bob lacked the earthy wholesome smell of a buffalo. Beneath the whisky, smoke and aftershave there was an odour like flowers left to rot in a vase.

They backed away from each other, the farang steering the child up a staircase, Komet stepping into the bathroom and locking the door behind him. He turned on a tap and doused his face. In the mirror above the basin his face looked haggard, as if the evening's events had suddenly aged him. For the first time he resembled his father.

Komet thought of him now: Khanthong Plungkham sitting cross-legged on a grass mat, preparing a tray of betel nut pan wrapped in lime leaves, one of the few pleasures he allowed himself.

'I have taught you about the Eight Precepts,' his father

had said, 'and how I followed them diligently as an acolyte. The young people of today see them as old-fashioned and impractical. "Why should we fast from midday to the following dawn?" they ask. "Why go out of our way to ensure a bad night's sleep by refusing comfortable bedding?" And so I tell them.'

He put the tray of betel nut to one side, tightened the *phakhama* around his waist and closed his eyes.

'Such disciplines remind us of what is and isn't important in this life. They remind us of our humanity and the ephemeral nature of our existence. But, my son, there are other ways we may be reminded of such things…'

His voice had trailed off, and Komet had wondered if the old man had fallen asleep.

'You shall not kill,' he said suddenly. 'You shall not steal. You shall not commit adultery. You shall not lie.'

His father was reciting the Precepts. Komet bowed his head in anticipation of the remaining four rules. No alcohol and drugs. No artificial scents and cosmetics. No attending performances and other forms of entertainment. And the rules about fasting and resting. But they did not come.

At the time, Komet had been puzzled. Why had his father only cited four of the Precepts? Now, however, seeing his likeness to the old man in the mirror, he understood. He knew what his father meant when he said there were other ways of being reminded of the vulnerability of humankind.

As he made his way back inside the club, Komet felt an inner strength that was new to him, as if he'd invoked his father's ghost. Or perhaps Khanthong Plungkham's spirit had been with him all along, just waiting to be recognised.

159

You shall not kill, Komet chanted silently as he approached the table where Kelly had joined Ratratarn again.

You shall not steal. He watched Kelly hand over a wad of cash.

You shall not commit adultery. The words echoed in Komet's mind as he followed Ratratarn and Pornsak through the crowd and saw a man fondle the immature breasts of a waitress as she leaned over his table.

'That's your cut,' the lieutenant colonel said as they got into the car.

Komet placed the folded bills in his shirt pocket without looking at them.

'There'll be more where that came from on Friday,' Ratratarn said. 'But we've got to find the Australian girl first.' He looked in the rear-view mirror to the back seat where Pornsak was counting out his share. 'Sergeant, I'm putting you on surveillance.'

'What?' Pornsak groaned. 'But, Sir, I mean—'

'Starting tonight,' he said. 'We know the farang girl was a close friend of the dead Canadian. We also know she's been to the house before. You're to keep watch and apprehend her if she approaches.'

Pornsak sighed audibly.

'Komet, I want you to spend the rest of your shift on the phone to all the hotels and guesthouses in Chiang Mai. Ask if anyone matching Jayne Keeney's description checked in this afternoon. Start with the places outside the main tourist precinct. My guess is she'll want to keep a low profile.'

'With all due respect, Sir,' Pornsak piped up, 'why are

we trying to track down this girl anyway? I mean, we've got nothing to worry about from the Canadian Embassy. You said so yourself. And we don't know if she's—'

'Precisely, Sergeant Pornsak,' Ratratarn cut him off. 'We don't know. But I'd say this Jayne Keeney is trying to avoid us, wouldn't you?' He paused for effect. 'And why would anyone go out of their way to avoid the Chiang Mai police?'

Pornsak shifted in his seat.

'Because, you stupid motherfucker, they've got something to hide!'

The sergeant flinched at the insult.

'This girl is a loose end, and I don't like loose ends. So I want you and Komet to tie this up so we can close this case. Is that clear?'

'Yes, Sir,' Pornsak mumbled.

'Komet?' Ratratarn said.

'Yes, Sir.'

Komet turned into the bureau carpark.

You shall not lie his father's ghost whispered.

Once he overheard the cop tell Kelly he'd make the pick-up on Friday, Mark d'Angelo left the Kitten Club. He couldn't trust himself to stay a moment longer and not blow his cover by storming the stage to rescue the girl.

Maybe the kid wasn't as pure as the driven snow. The mongrels who ran these kinds of clubs were known to recycle so-called virgins, smearing a girl's genitals with chicken's blood to fool the punters. But the thought that she might not technically be a virgin didn't make it any easier for Mark to walk away. He used to rescue kids like Malithong in raids on brothels in Cambodia. He'd even dodged bullets once. But that stuff was easy compared with undercover work.

Seven years with the Queensland Police and nearly three with the Feds had taught Mark to keep his emotions in check. He hated paedophiles as much as the next person, but he'd seen what happens when people let their hatred get the better of them. When he first started with the special squad in Brisbane, he was assigned to work with a Sergeant Thompson who'd been tracking a suspected paed for over a year. When they finally brought the guy in, they had something like thirty-two counts against him. During a recess in the interview, Mark left the room and Thommo simply lost it. Beat the absolute shit out of the guy. It not only ruined Thommo's career, it fucked up the case as well: they had to let the bastard go.

It was an object lesson for Mark. You've gotta keep a cool head on your shoulders, he told himself. His ZTCP trainer, Karen, said much the same thing, and stressed the importance of having some sort of outlet, such as playing a sport, to manage the emotional impact of the job.

Karen had taught Mark and his AFP colleagues a lot. She talked about ZTCP's work in public education, research and surveillance, and its legal reform agenda so child sex offenders and people who profited from child sex could be prosecuted in Australia for crimes committed overseas.

Most of the patrons in the Kitten Club were what Karen would call 'situational child sex offenders'. Not the type who would try this at home. Mark guessed most were blue-collar workers who'd chosen Thailand as a budget holiday destination. These guys were shit-kickers in the real world, but they'd get to Thailand and suddenly feel like kings. Every whim could be catered for, every desire met, at a price they could afford. Places such as Kelly's club gave them the impression it was OK to fuck young girls if they wanted. The rules were different in Thailand. It was a 'cultural' thing. Some even believed they were doing good by putting money into a poor country.

Mark hated them for their ignorance, but he hated Kelly more. According to AFP files, Kelly didn't screw children himself. His own tastes tended towards thirty-something Thai women. But he traded on other people's weakness. With the rural poor being the supply, and the ignorant, insecure and downright deviant creating the demand, Kelly was the worst sort of entrepreneur.

But Mark reserved special loathing for the Thai police.

They weren't just letting it happen, they were turning a profit in protection money and in protecting a scumbag like Kelly instead of the children—their own people.

So the AFP had mounted its own operation to get Kelly. The ZTCP people in Chiang Mai had collected more than enough evidence to bring a case against him. But as Ted Baxter told Mark during his briefing in Bangkok, they had nowhere to take it.

'To prosecute Kelly under Thai law, ZTCP would have to rely on the same cops who are protecting him. And they're not likely to bite the hand that feeds them, are they?'

Despite thinning hair and ill-fitting false teeth, the AFP's Overseas Liaison Officer had a fierceness that commanded respect.

'The good news for us is that Kelly has a company registered in Australia,' Baxter continued, 'which means we can get him on procurement and profiting, though it's gonna have to be handled delicately…' He shuffled through the papers on his desk. 'I've got a copy of the speech the minister gave recently in which he assures his Thai counterpart—and I quote—"the new Australian legislation on Child Sex Tourism is designed to act primarily as a deterrent, and the Australian government has no intention of usurping the Thai government's role in policing child sex offenders."

'We can't afford the diplomatic fall-out of a high-profile operation,' he said, waving the document in the air, 'but we've got to stop this arsehole. You're gonna have to do this as quickly and quietly as possible. When you get to Chiang Mai, all you need to do is confirm ZTCP's story and bring Kelly in.'

But Mark had been given the authority to call the shots and, though it meant a slight delay in moving against Kelly, he had a bigger and better plan.

Kelly would be up on indictable offences—his assets up for grabs once they brought in the charges against him—and this would cut off the Thai cops' source of income. But that wasn't enough. Mark wanted a positive ID on the officers involved and a shot of them accepting a pay-off. Then he'd go for broke.

His plan was to leak the photo to the Thai press with a note attributing it to 'an Australian source', which should protect the local ZTCP staff. The story was bound to make a big splash, paedophilia being such a hot topic, and he figured that with irrefutable evidence and enough pressure both at home and abroad, the Thai authorities would have no choice but to take punitive action against the cops.

So far he'd kept the plan to himself. For all Baxter's posturing, he wouldn't have got where he was without being careful and, in Mark's opinion, it was time someone rocked the boat.

Simone Whitfield seemed the sort of person who'd understand that. Anyone who'd break into a house under police guard and stake out a child sex brothel wasn't afraid of making waves. She had guts, but she didn't have a case. Mark took pains to explain this, anxious that in her drive to make a case, she didn't jeopardise his own.

'Look, I believe you, Simone,' he said when she finished her story. 'But what have you got? A possible motive, maybe, since Kelly's capable of having an innocent person whacked to cover his own arse—'

'Two innocent people,' she interrupted.

'Yeah, but you've got nothing substantial on the cops and all you've got on Kelly is a possible sighting on the night by an unreliable witness.' He held up his hand. 'I'm sorry, but that's how the courts would see it. Short of an eyewitness account of the murder by a reliable source or a full confession, I don't see how you can make it stick.'

She stared out across the river. 'You're the second person today who's tried to talk me out of it,' she said. 'At least you believe me.'

How could he not believe her? She was savvy, passionate—it felt like a lifetime since he'd been around such a woman. She'd blown away his first impressions of her by suggesting they talk over beers at a local pub and, without waiting for an answer, hailed a passing tuk-tuk with a loud whistle. On the way, she chatted with the driver in fluent Thai. And to top it all off, before he could even take out his wallet, she'd paid the fare.

Mark found them a table on the terrace and ordered drinks while she went to the bathroom. The pub had a surprisingly good house band and he was tapping his foot along to 'Mustang Sally' when Simone reappeared, without the crucifix but with crimson lipstick. She might have changed her clothes, too, as he noticed her cleavage for the first time. Then, lighting one cigarette after another and matching him beer for beer, she filled him in on the story that led to her stakeout at the Kitten Club.

Mark responded in kind, mentioning his recent stint with the paedophile unit in Cambodia, before explaining why he was in Chiang Mai. He described the case against

Kelly—giving her possibly more information than he should have, but he was on his fourth beer by then—and outlined his plan for dealing with the cops.

'You might not be able to get Kelly and the cops for murder,' he said, 'but we can get them for complicity in the child sex racket. Both our interests are served by bringing them down.'

Simone considered this. 'The problem is, getting them on complicity or racketeering or whatever still won't mean my friend Didier is exonerated for a murder he didn't commit.'

He loved the way she pronounced the guy's name with a French accent.

'Yeah, but I could leak your stuff about the murders to the press when I hand over the photos.'

'Maybe.' She didn't seem convinced. She held up her empty beer bottle. 'One for the road?'

'Sure.'

She summoned a waiter and placed the order in Thai, before lighting another cigarette. She even made smoking look good.

'I guess, Mark—and I say this with all due respect— I'm not convinced your plan will work. Thai police are a resilient mob. They're not all corrupt, of course, but the ones who are tend to get away with murder. Literally.'

'But—'

'Let me finish,' she held up her hand. 'Your strategy rests on the idea that exposing police complicity in an underage prostitution racket will generate a public outcry and force those in charge to do something about it, right?'

'More or less,' he said.

'The thing is, there's significant local demand for under-aged girls in the sex industry here. Up until a few years ago, it was perfectly acceptable for a girl to be married off as soon as she reached puberty.'

Mark frowned. The waiter arrived with their beers.

'Then there's the bigger picture,' Simone continued, exhaling smoke. 'The impact of poverty. When it comes to making ends meet among the poorer rural families, children are expected to pitch in. They're part of the labour force.'

She sounded as if she were reading from an academic paper on the subject.

'What's your point?'

'I think you're looking at the whole thing as an Australian. And I'm not convinced a strategy that would work in Australia will work in Thailand.'

Mark was offended. He was a Federal Police agent for Chrissake, and he'd got where he was on his ability to handle 'culturally sensitive' situations.

'Surely you're not suggesting the Thais think it's OK to fuck children?' He made little effort to conceal his anger.

'No, of course not—'

'In fact the Thai government's just passed a bill that'll pave the way for a huge crackdown on child prostitution.'

'Good luck to them,' she murmured, adding in a louder voice, 'Look, I want you to nail those bastards. It's just...' she hesitated. 'This is going to sound awful, but you need to put a spin on it to get the reaction you want. The fact that Kelly's a farang helps—'

'What if I told you I watched a nine-year-old girl's virginity being auctioned off at his club this evening?'

'That's perfect!' she said without missing a beat. 'If Kelly's dealing in pre-pubescent kids, that'll do it. The Thais like them young, but not that young—'

All of a sudden, she hid her face in her hands. When she raised her head again, there were tears in her eyes.

'Mark, I'm sorry. It must've been terrible for you to see that poor girl…That's what my friend Didier was trying to stop. That's why they killed him…' Her voice trailed off as she fumbled through her bag.

Her tears didn't alarm Mark. He'd dealt with plenty of 'recently bereaved' and he admired her for keeping it together as well as she did. And she was right about needing to put a spin on the story.

He watched her wipe her eyes and sip her beer.

'I want to help,' she said in a slightly unsteady voice. 'The Canadian Embassy isn't interested in what I've got to offer. I don't suppose there's any chance the AFP could use me?'

'I don't know,' Mark said. 'I mean, we've got a solid case against Kelly. All I really need now is an incriminating shot of the police officers involved, so we can identify them and release the details to the press. I know they'll be going to the Kitten Club Friday for a pick-up—'

'Ratratarn,' Simone said slowly. 'Lieutenant Colonel Ratratarn. The older, well-built one with the hard face. He's the one who killed my friend Didier.'

Mark stared at her.

'The one who looks Chinese is Sergeant Pornsak. He beat up some guys I know to get information out of them. Broke their fingers, that kind of thing.'

'But, how—?'

'I can't place the third one who was there tonight—the young one with the round face—but I know him from somewhere. I've got the number plate of the car they were driving and photos of them going into the club. I realise you'll need something more explicit for the press. But it might help.'

Mark was impressed. 'I could kiss you for that, Simone!'

To his surprise, she butted out her cigarette and leaned towards him. 'Be my guest,' she said.

They met half-way across the table and kissed as if it were a drunken joke. But it felt good and they kissed again, seriously.

'Let's get out of here,' Mark said.

It was disconcerting at first, the way he kept calling her Simone. Jayne had used the alias as a reflex action, never dreaming Mark would turn out to be a cop. By the time they ended up in his hotel room, it seemed too late to correct him.

Besides, there was something erotic about having him whisper Simone's name in her ear as he unbuttoned her blouse, cupped her breasts in his hands and kissed her throat. Her nipples hardened beneath her bra. Even at this point, Jayne Keeney might have baulked at going to bed with a virtual stranger, even one as gorgeous as Mark d'Angelo. But not Simone Whitfield. She had neither Jayne's inhibitions, nor disastrous track record with men. Best of all, by masquerading as Simone, Jayne could forget everything that had happened since she left Bangkok five days earlier. And from the moment Mark kissed her at the Riverside, that was all she wanted.

She ran her fingers through his hair and worked her way down his back, pulling at the hem of his T-shirt. Mark slipped it off over his head, exposing a thicket of black hair on his torso that tapered to a thin line down to his belt-buckle. A bulge was discernible through his jeans and he took her hands, put them around his neck and tilted his pelvis against hers so she felt his hard cock. His kisses were deep and hungry and she felt her desire take on a momentum of its own.

Still kissing his mouth, she moved her hands to the belt buckle, unfastened it, and unzipped his jeans. At the same time, he unhooked her bra and she let it slip off. Their semi-naked bodies pressed together, he encircled her with his arms and lifted her onto the bed, laying her down and kissing her breasts as his hands loosened the zip of her skirt.

Both naked now, they were all over each other, kissing, biting, touching. Mark turned her on to her tummy and slowly traced the line of her spine with his tongue. The hairs on her body stood on end and she groaned aloud as his fingers worked their way into her wet cunt. Still stroking her clitoris, he turned her back over and exchanged his fingers for his mouth. His hands moved to her breasts and she placed hers on top of them, pushing them hard against her nipples. His tongue brought her clitoris to its full height and she came in a rush, then burst into tears.

'Simone,' he whispered, 'sweetheart, are you OK?'

Mark was beside her, his face anxious. She could smell herself on his lips as he gently kissed the tears on her cheeks. 'I didn't hurt you, did I?'

'No, no.' She was laughing and crying at the same time. 'I always…that is…'

'What?' His concern gave way to a broad grin.

'It's just been a long time between drinks,' she laughed, wiping her eyes with the back of her hand.

'Mmm, me too,' he said, nuzzling her neck.

'Really?' She raised herself up to her elbows.

'Yeah,' he murmured, kissing her shoulders.

'I'd have thought—'

He looked up sharply and she left the sentence incomplete.

'Do you have any condoms?' she said. 'If you don't, I do.'

'I love these modern girls,' he laughed, reaching over to a drawer in the bedside table.

Mark pulled out a condom and opened the packet, but she took it from him and, without taking her eyes off him, transferred it to her mouth. He raised his eyebrows in an unasked question, but she placed her hand on his chest and pushed him to lie back down.

Several months earlier, Jayne got drunk with a group of Bangkok bargirls she played pool with and they showed her how to put on a condom with her mouth. It was a technique they'd developed in the age of AIDS to deal with recalcitrant clients, and which they practised on peeled cucumbers.

Jayne would never have had the guts to try it out on a

real penis but as Simone, she felt she could do anything. She fumbled at first to make sure the condom was the right way around, but once in place she unrolled it deftly with her lips and took Mark's hard cock deep into her mouth. She massaged the shaft with her lips, then ran the tip of her tongue around the ridge, before working her way back down again. Stroking his balls, she felt them tighten beneath her touch. Finally, he groaned aloud, grabbed her by the shoulders and pulled her on top of him.

His cock slipped inside her and they rocked in and out of one another before Mark pushed her upright, her weight resting against his hands on her breasts, and she felt him deep inside her.

The second orgasm took her by surprise, but Mark seemed to have been waiting for it as, moments later, she felt his body shudder beneath hers. She lay there for a few minutes, catching her breath and kissing wherever her mouth touched skin, before easing herself away to lie beside him in a tangle of sheets, sweat and hair.

He moved one arm around her, head resting against his shoulder. Their legs entwined and his free hand rested lightly on her waist.

'Wow!' she whispered, not even loudly enough to be heard over the hum of the airconditioner. Then she fell into a profound sleep.

Komet phoned every hotel and guesthouse within seven kilometres of Chiang Mai and took down the names of all farang women in their late twenties to early thirties who had registered since midday Tuesday.

It was one thing to call four- and five-star hotels where reception was staffed twenty-four hours a day, but he felt awful rousing people at the cheaper places, even if it was official police business. Over and over, Komet explained that the matter was of utmost importance. And it was: he had to get to Jayne Keeney before Ratratarn, Pornsak or Kelly did.

'We know the farang girl was a close friend of the dead Canadian,' Ratratarn had said. If that was true, Jayne would believe what Komet had to say about the deaths that night.

'Any progress?' Ratratarn stuck his head around the door.

'Nothing yet, Sir,' he said.

Ratratarn sneered and withdrew, leaving Komet to his telephone books and tourist guides. There was a distinct advantage in being taken for an idiot by the lieutenant colonel. If, by the end of his shift, Komet had nothing to report, Ratratarn would put it down to incompetence, never dreaming he might have something to hide. But after nearly five hours on the phone, Komet feared the task was beyond him.

No one had registered any Australian woman fitting Jayne Keeney's description. She might be staying with friends, but Komet thought it unlikely or she'd have done so in the first place. He was on the verge of reporting, quite truthfully, that he thought the woman had left town, when he remembered something Ratratarn had said in the car.

'Why would anyone go out of their way to avoid the Chiang Mai police? Because they've got something to hide.'

Jayne Keeney had managed to outsmart the lieutenant colonel, and a smart person who knew the police were on to her would do more than change hotels and register under a different name. She'd change her identity, her nationality, even her physical appearance.

Komet went back over his notes; there were forty-five places where women the right age had checked in the previous afternoon. Trembling at his own daring, he made a bogus copy of the notes and, keeping the original, entered Ratratarn's office.

'S-sir,' he said, 'there's no record of the farang woman or anyone matching her description. I'm sorry, Sir.'

'Not half as sorry as I am, Officer Komet. Have you got anything useful?'

Komet handed him a piece of paper. 'These are the places that registered farang women in the same age group.'

Ratratarn scanned the list. 'What a good thing for us it's not high tourist season,' he said, tossing it aside. 'Sergeant Pornsak hasn't anything to report either. What about those kids you saw at the dead farang's house? Any chance you'd recognise them again?'

'I don't know, Sir.'

'Shit! How difficult can it be to find one foreigner in this town!'

Komet shifted his weight nervously. 'Ah, I could try to find the boys, Sir, maybe on my shift this evening?'

Ratratarn snorted and waved him away.

Komet checked his watch as he started his motorbike. He had enough time to visit a few places on his list before Arunee would start to worry. He'd begin with the more up-market hotels, go home, grab a few hours' sleep, and resume the search in the afternoon.

Jayne rolled over and glanced at the time. Rather, she glanced at the empty space on the bedside table where her clock should have been. Frowning, she propped herself up on her elbows and surveyed the room: the sheets were in disarray and the floor was strewn with clothes. She heard the sound of running water from the bathroom.

She sat bolt upright as the events of the previous evening flooded back to her. Wrapping herself in a sheet, she started searching for her clothes, when she heard a noise behind her. She looked up and saw Mark framed in the doorway of the bathroom, white towel slung low on his hips accentuating his bronze skin and black hair. Cheeks burning, she turned her back to him. A moment later, his arms encircled her.

'Good morning, Simone,' he said.

'Hi,' she said, as casually as she could manage. 'Sleep well?'

'Hmm.' He kissed the back of her neck, his whiskers tickling her skin. 'Best I've slept in a long, long time.'

Jayne flushed with the pleasure of the moment and what it triggered in her memory of the night before. She turned in his arms and kissed him.

'I could stay like this all day,' Mark murmured, nuzzling her neck.

'Me too,' she said. 'But I should go, change my clothes—'

'And the photos,' Mark said. 'Don't forget about them.'

'Of course not.' She took a step back.

'I could get them developed for you.'

Jayne wasn't sure why, but the offer made her uneasy.

Mumbling something about having to pick up more film, she resumed the hunt for her clothes, until she felt Mark's arms around her again.

'Isn't there something you should be doing?' she said.

'Not much I can do before Friday night,' he said. 'Nothing that can't wait.' He released the sheet around her.

'Mark, you don't think I'm...that is, in spite of everything that's happened—'

'I want this as much as you do,' he said, before dropping to his knees and putting his mouth on her crotch.

Jayne groaned, wondering whether it was some kind of karmic reward to be sent a lover who liked giving head, or if she just got lucky.

Komet had eliminated four possibilities from his list before going home. As he slipped off his shoes and entered the house, Arunee was seasoning a pot of the rice porridge they ate for breakfast.

'*Sabaidee bor*?' she said as he washed his hands.

'Yes, I'm fine. I was given a bonus last night,' he added. 'I thought you might want to buy some new clothes or something for the baby.'

He wiped his hands, then fished into his shirt pocket for the money Ratratarn had given him. Short of burning it, Komet felt the only thing to do was to give it to his wife. She'd never know where it came from.

Arunee raised her eyebrows. 'A bonus, you say?'

He nodded.

'It's twice as much as your usual pay.'

'For all the overtime, I suppose.'

She looked from the wad of notes to Komet and back again. With a shrug to suggest she accepted the explanation, she put the money in her purse and joined him on the floor.

'I was wondering,' Komet said, helping himself to some fried shallots, 'shouldn't you be thinking of going to your mother's place soon?'

'Why?' she said in a tight voice.

'It's just, well, you seem to be getting…big, that's all. And I thought—'

'Husband, is this your way of telling me you've taken a *mia noi*?'

'A minor wife?' Komet made no attempt to conceal the hurt in his voice. 'Arunee, how could you even suggest it?'

'First, you come in here, waving money around and telling me to take myself shopping for new clothes. Then you tell me I'm getting fat—'

'No!' he protested. 'Not fat! I said big. I meant the baby's getting big.'

'You must have a mia noi!' she said, ignoring the interruption. 'That's why you want to get rid of me and—' She burst into tears.

Putting his bowl to one side, Komet leaned over and patted her arm. 'Oh, don't cry little one. I didn't mean to upset you. I'm only thinking of what's best for you and the baby. There could never be anyone else for me. You know that.'

'Husband, I want to believe you,' Arunee sniffed. 'But I hear stories…'

'What? Stories about me?'

'No, about other policemen. The wives, they say their husbands get money and…and favours from…from concubines.'

The old-fashioned word made Komet stifle a smile. 'Wife, you mustn't trouble yourself with such stories. If I have any mia noi, it's my job. And it's because work is so busy right now that I suggested you go to your mother's place.'

'Are you sure that's all?' she said timidly.

'I promise.'

She patted her eyes with her skirt and nudged him affectionately. 'Come on, eat before it gets cold!'

Komet smiled, but his heart was heavy. Arunee had far more to fear from the implications of his work than from him taking a mistress.

'Actually, I was thinking of going to Mae's place soon,' she said between mouthfuls. 'Wiangwilai's cousin is driving to Nakhon Phanom tomorrow and I could get a lift with him. I'll write and tell you when you should come—when the baby's coming.'

The sudden prospect of her leaving filled Komet with dread.

'OK.' He forced himself to return her smile.

'And you still don't mind if it's a boy or a girl?'

'Not at all.'

This time his smile was genuine.

Jayne crept back to her room, relieved to have kept her key. Though the staff wouldn't be shocked to learn that a female farang guest had spent the night elsewhere, she didn't want to make a bad impression. She messed up the bed to make it look slept in, put her clothes in the laundry basket and ran a bath.

The hot water was soothing, though she welcomed the novelty of the mild aches in her body. She had assumed Mark, like most transient expats, would prefer the 'local fare' and couldn't believe her luck. After a year's drought, to have great sex like that twice in less than twelve hours—

But she was forgetting Didier and what had happened between them only a few days earlier. She felt guilty—as if she'd been unfaithful to him by sleeping with Mark.

Prior to Friday night, it had been a long time since anyone had held her and kissed her at all. Didier knew it, too—she'd confided in him about all her lousy love affairs. She'd even told him about Anthony, her fiancé who ended up marrying the woman he was having an affair with. Though Jayne had suspected him of cheating, Anthony denied it, refusing to give her a reason to break off their engagement on the grounds it would 'destroy' his mother. In the end, Jayne fled to Paris with her share of the house deposit they'd saved. And just so Anthony's mother wouldn't miss her, she scandalously left with a Frenchman she'd met at the high school where they both taught.

'Touché!' Didier had clapped in response to the story. 'And what happened to the Frenchman?'

'Turned out Étienne wasn't over his previous girlfriend,' she said, 'but there were no hard feelings; he got me out of Melbourne.'

'I don't understand,' Didier said. 'Why didn't you just leave this Anthony?'

'I was in love with him,' Jayne said. 'And he was very manipulative. He made me feel like I was being paranoid when I knew he was screwing around.'

'So how long before you learned to trust your instincts again?'

'What is this, Didi?' she frowned. 'The third degree?'

'I'm curious,' he said. 'You've ended up in a job where you have to rely on your instincts, and you spend a lot of time spying on unfaithful lovers. Don't you think there's a connection?'

'What are you implying?' she said.

'Nothing,' he shrugged. 'I just can't figure out how a good detective can make such bad choices when it comes to love.'

Jayne hadn't wanted to admit it, but Didier was right. She steered away from relationships and put her energy into friendships instead. But expatriate friends came and went, and her Thai friends' family responsibilities prevented them from socialising as freely as she did. So Jayne came to depend on Didier. He'd seemed a safe bet.

But even in that she'd been mistaken. What the hell had Didier been thinking? Of all people, he knew how vulnerable she was. Had he taken advantage of her? Or was there something else going on? She didn't know. She'd never know now that he was dead.

Jayne got out of the tepid bath, wrapped herself in a towel, and stared in the bathroom mirror, asking herself how much her lust for Mark had to do with her unresolved night with Didier. Her eyes were bloodshot from having slept in her contact lenses, the skin around her mouth was blotchy with whisker rash, and the blond hair made her look washed out. She wondered what on earth Mark saw in her. Perhaps he was just sleeping with her to keep her on side and prevent her from interfering in his investigation.

But then she remembered about how he'd held her in his arms that morning after they'd had sex on the floor of the hotel room, how he kissed her and murmured, 'You turn me on.' She thought of the confidence with which he made love, the pleasure he took in her body. While she wasn't sure about Mark's motives, she didn't doubt his desire was real. And it was mutual.

But she needed to maintain her distance—for Didier's sake. Getting dressed, she told herself it wasn't personal. Even if Mark's offer to kill two birds with one stone was genuine, working in Thailand had taught Jayne always to have a fall-back position.

She wanted to show Nalissa the photo she'd taken of

Doug Kelly to confirm if he was the man she saw with Nou on the night he was killed. While it might not stand up in court, it was worth something to her.

She handed in her key to Ornsri, the receptionist.

'*Norn lap, mai?*' she asked.

Jayne started but the question seemed like an innocent one. 'Yes, I slept very well, thank you,' she said in Thai.

The clouds were swollen and bloated, the air sluggish, as if the atmosphere itself had PMT. 'Pre-Monsoon Tension.' Jayne had concocted the phrase, even before learning that the colloquial Thai for menstruation—*pen reudoo*—means 'to be in season'. She made a mental note to buy an umbrella.

Mark was conscious of the swagger in his step as he made his way to the ZTCP office. He felt better than he had in ages. Meeting Simone had lifted a weight from his shoulders. They'd agreed to meet for dinner that evening and it would be like going on a date back home.

It wasn't just the sex. If that was all it took, he could have got that easily enough. But Mark wasn't interested in getting into bed with the locals.

Truth was he could never be sure in this part of the world that when a woman came on to him, it wasn't for his money. Other guys didn't seem to have a problem with that. An embassy colleague—a fat, old, ugly bastard called Whitehead who wouldn't stand a chance of scoring back home—told Mark with a straight face that the nubile, Cambodian woman on his arm was crazy about him. They were drinking at the Foreign Correspondents Club at the time, a French colonial building overlooking the Tonlé Sap river, where the walls crawled with geckoes feasting on insects attracted to the lights. The young woman—half the guy's age and stunning—sat between them at the bar, sipping a bottle of green lemonade through a straw.

'Is that true?' Mark asked her. 'You really like this guy?'

The woman giggled.

'Ah, Touk doesn't speak much English, do you sweetie?' Whitehead said, patting her thigh.

'I didn't realise you spoke Cambodian,' Mark ventured.

'I don't,' he said, signalling for another beer. 'Not a bloody word of it!'

Cambodia had been full of guys like Whitehead, anxious to believe that what made them attractive to local women had nothing to do with money and the prospect of a visa out of there.

And paying for sex was out of the question. Although prostitution was illegal—not that you'd know it in Phnom Penh or Chiang Mai—it was pride that stopped him. No matter what the experts said, Mark reckoned you had to be desperate to pay for it. And he wasn't that kind of man.

Still, despite his attraction to Simone, Mark had a job to do. He needed Baxter's source at ZTCP to verify her ID on the cops. He had no reason to believe Simone would lie to him, but her grief over her friend's death might have clouded her judgment. If not, there was no harm done. It would simply give him one thing less to do in between getting a photo of Friday's pay-off, and arresting Kelly the following morning.

Mark knew the action at the Kitten Club wound down around two, the place all but empty by three. Kelly had an apartment upstairs, which he shared with his Thai girlfriend. Security was minimal—a concertina-style metal gate dragged across the entrance and fastened with a padlock—but Kelly didn't bother employing a night guard. With half the Chiang Mai police force on his payroll, he figured he had the best security money could buy. This made it easier for Mark to move against him without involving anyone from Bangkok. He'd call Baxter for approval after seeing the ZTCP people, but was confident of getting the official OK.

The sound of distant thunder caused him to glance up. He hoped the rain would hold off until early Saturday morning. It wouldn't hurt to have the extra cover.

Among the strip of guesthouses inside the old city walls, there were more signs in farang languages than in Thai. Nestled between a 'Bier Garten' and a travel agency, Komet found the next place on his list. Leaving his shoes at the door, he introduced himself to the receptionist and pointed to one of the names on his list.

'*Farang kon nee put Thai dai, mai?*' he said.

The woman peered at the piece of paper. 'Why on earth would that foreigner speak Thai? She's one of those dirty backpackers.'

'Are you sure?'

'Oh, she says "hello" and "thank you" and wais everybody, even the cleaning ladies,' the woman laughed. 'But can she speak Thai? No.'

She handed back the paper and glanced towards the door. 'Look, she's coming now.'

Komet raised his eyebrows as a young, ginger-haired woman entered the foyer. She wore the baggy pants typical of Isaan farmers, but instead of the normal blue colour, hers were bright orange, with grass stains on the knees. There were safety pins on her blouse where buttons should have been, and her hair was matted together with strings of beads. Her bare feet left a dusty trail on the white-tiled floor of the lobby.

'*Sawadee ka*,' the receptionist beamed as the farang approached the desk.

'*Sawadee ka*,' the girl said, her hands together in a wai.

'Just how long is it since you've washed your clothes?' the receptionist asked in Thai.

'Sorry?' the farang said.

'Look at you, you're filthy!' she said, still smiling sweetly.

The farang smiled and gestured to the board on which the room keys were hung.

'See what I mean,' the receptionist said.

Komet crossed the name off his list. This was all taking a lot longer than he'd anticipated. He was only halfway through his list, and although his shift didn't start for a few hours, he wanted to spend some time with Arunee before she left the next day. He would have to invent a lead on the boys he'd seen outside Khun Di's house. It wasn't as if Ratratarn could send anyone else to follow it up.

Outside, he slipped his notebook into his shirt pocket and kicked his motorbike into life.

Nalissa looked around the empty lounge of The Nice Place before sliding into the booth beside Jayne. She was wearing her work clothes—pink bikini and ridiculous rabbit ears—but hadn't finished applying her make-up; her one painted eye made her face look lopsided.

'I'm sorry to disturb you,' Jayne said. 'I only need a moment.'

'That's OK,' the Thai woman said, looking over her shoulder.

'Is anything the matter?' Jayne said.

'Not really. It's just, you know, it looks strange, the two of us here like this...'

Jayne leaned forward and lowered her voice. 'Has anyone spoken to you about what happened last weekend?'

Nalissa's eyes widened. 'No! Why would anyone—?'

'*Mai pen rai*,' Jayne said quickly, sitting back again. 'I'll keep this brief. But could you look at this—' she took out her photo of Doug Kelly '—and tell me if this is the man you saw with Khun Sanga last Friday in Loh Kroh.' She handed Nalissa the photograph.

'Yes,' she responded firmly. 'That's the man who was with Khun Sanga.'

'You're absolutely certain?'

Nalissa looked up sharply. 'What? You think I'm only saying it to please you, like a polite Thai girl?'

'No, I didn't mean to imply—'

'I recognise him and the building, too. That's the Kitten Club. That's where I saw them.'

Jayne smiled to herself. 'And will you sign a piece of paper to confirm it?'

'What?' Nalissa held one hand to her mouth. 'Oh, no, Khun Jayne, I couldn't do that.'

'Why not?'

'Because, I just couldn't.'

'But I need written confirmation,' Jayne said, struggling to keep her voice down. 'Otherwise, this man gets away with murder.'

'And what if he finds out about it?' Nalissa said. 'Then he'd know my name. And I could end up dead, like poor Khun Sanga.'

Jayne kicked herself. She should never have suggested someone else might want to speak to Nalissa about Nou's death. Now she'd spooked the woman.

'Listen,' she said, 'I can guarantee nothing will happen to you and—'

The look of misery on Nalissa's face stopped her. Jayne's promises sounded hollow, even to herself. She couldn't guarantee Nalissa's safety and the Thai woman knew it.

'*Mai pen rai*,' she said softly. 'It's OK. I'm sorry. I really appreciate what you've done for me.'

Nalissa nodded and stood up to leave.

'Is there anything I can do,' Jayne said, 'to thank you for your time?'

'Buy me a drink!' Nalissa said, tension dissolving in a broad grin. 'There's a bonus for the girl who brings in the first paying customer of the night.'

Komet reached the Mai Pai guesthouse around 11pm and parked his motorbike beneath a banana palm in the driveway. The reception area looked deserted but then he saw the bluish glow of a television screen and a woman sprawled on a pile of cushions. She looked more curious than startled when he tapped on the glass, and rose slowly to her feet, tightening the cotton *pah sin* around her waist and smoothing down her hair.

'Excuse me, older sister,' Komet said, removing his cap, 'I wonder if I might have a moment of your time.'

'Of course, Officer,' the woman smiled, ushering him in. 'But I'm hardly your older sister. Younger sister will do. Call me Nong Ornsri.'

Komet nodded politely. With her crow's feet and traces of grey in her hair, Ornsri definitely had a few years on him.

'Fine, Nong,' he said, taking out his notes. 'I called your guesthouse last night and spoke with your husband—'

'No,' she interrupted him, 'I'm not married any more. My husband was a lousy drunk, Officer. I got rid of him. You must've talked with my son. He's out tonight.

'Hmm,' he said neutrally. 'Well then, old—, I mean, younger sister, I was asking about farang women who'd checked in on Tuesday afternoon or evening and was given two names.' He held out a piece of paper.

'Ai Leen Run Den,' Ornsri transliterated aloud, 'See Mon Wid Feed.' Gesturing for Komet to follow, she took the registry, tilted it towards the light from the TV, and scanned the list of names.

'Yes, Officer, both those women are staying here.'

'Can you tell me anything about them?'

'Khun Aileen, she's American and Khun Simone, she's from England,' she said, reading from the ledger.

She looked up and narrowed her eyes. 'Why? Are these women in trouble with the police? Because, you know, Officer...?'

'Komet,' he said.

'Officer Komet, I run a very respectable business here. I tell my guests, no drugs, no girls. And if there's any idea that these women—'

'No, no,' Komet reassured her. 'It's nothing like that. I just need to talk with them.'

The smile returned. '*Mai pen rai*,' she said, squinting at the pigeonholes on the wall where the room keys were kept. 'Khun Aileen is in. She came back hours ago. Chances are she's already asleep. Do you want me to wake her?'

'Ah, that may not be necessary,' Komet said. 'Tell me, Nong Ornsri, does Khun Aileen speak Thai?'

The woman frowned. 'No.'

'What about Khun Simone?'

'Oh, yes, she speaks Thai very well,' Ornsri said. 'Krung Thep accent, but otherwise very good.'

Komet inhaled sharply. A Bangkok accent was a good sign. 'I know it's late, but would it be possible for me to speak with her?'

Ornsri glanced over her shoulder again. 'She's not in, Officer Komet.' She leaned forward and nudged him. 'She didn't come in at all last night.'

'Oh? Well, when did you last see her?'

'It was around seven. She said she was going out for dinner.'

Komet looked at his watch; she'd been gone four hours.

'Perhaps you'd like to wait here for her?' Ornsri added, glancing at the pile of cushions on the floor. 'You can sit with me and watch television. And I have some *lao Kwang Thong*...'

Komet suddenly became aware of how it looked, the two of them in the dimly lit reception area, the woman offering him rice whisky.

'Ah, younger sister, thank you for your kind offer,' he said carefully, 'but I can't drink on duty. And since the farang didn't come back at all last night...Well, I have other police business. It'd be best if I try again tomorrow morning.'

'Up to you,' the woman shrugged.

'Yes, that would be best,' Komet said again, restoring his cap to his head. 'I'm grateful for your help.' He hesitated. 'Younger sister, could I ask you not to mention this visit to Khun Simone? I wouldn't want to make her... nervous about seeing me.'

'*Mai pen rai,*' Ornsri nodded with a tight-lipped smile.

Komet breathed a sigh of relief as he got back on his motorbike. He wasn't used to divorcées—such women had a reputation for being forceful, even aggressive. Komet guessed they had to be tough to live with the knowledge they'd failed at a Thai woman's most important task: keeping a marriage together.

Things sounded promising but he still had ten places left to visit, and he needed to think up an excuse to explain how he'd spent the night searching for Bom and Deh, only to return to the office empty-handed.

Mark watched as Simone exhaled the smoke from her cigarette.

'One of my English students offered to pay me to check out this Australian guy who wanted to marry her,' she said, 'and I tailed the guy to a bar in Patpong and caught him on film fondling a topless waitress.' She raised her eyebrows. 'Word got around and more and more people came to me for help. The work paid better than teaching, but it was the thrill that got me hooked.' She smiled and stubbed out her cigarette. 'And that's how I ended up working as a private investigator.'

'Mild-mannered Melbourne school teacher hits Bangkok and turns into Australia's Mata Hari!' Mark said with a grin.

'Oh, hardly.' She pulled a face. 'The work's mostly research and surveillance, pretty mundane stuff. More Miss Marple than Mata Hari.'

'Who?'

'Miss Marple. You know, as in Agatha Christie novels?'

'Ah, I don't read much,' Mark said.

'Oh?' She seemed disappointed. 'Anyway, it's your

turn. How did you end up working in southeast Asia?'

'Where do you want me to start?' Mark held up their empty bottles and gestured for a waiter to bring another round.

She rested her chin on her hands and fixed her green eyes on him. 'Why did you become a cop?'

Mark shrugged. 'Like you, sometimes you fall into something and discover you're good at it.'

'When did you join up?' she asked.

'Ah…I was nineteen, so it was the end of 1985.'

'So you're thirty now?'

'Almost. My birthday's in November. Why? How old are you?'

'Same. Twenty-nine,' she said as the waiter set down the fresh drinks.

'Back in those days, you didn't get a lot of wogs on the force in Queensland,' Mark said. 'So I ended up doing a lot of "cross-cultural liaison". Some of the more…er…traditional men couldn't get their heads around the idea that beating your wife and kids was illegal in Australia.'

'Was that what your father was like?' she said gravely.

'God, no,' he laughed. 'My dad wouldn't hurt a fly! When I went to Italy, I couldn't believe his brothers. They're these wiry, tough bastards who live in the mountains, carry bloody great daggers in their belts and slaughter their own goats! It wouldn't surprise me if Dad came to Australia 'cause he wasn't tough enough for Calabria.'

'So your work was in domestic violence?' Simone said.

'For a while. Then I got transferred to a special squad set up to investigate child sex abuse. That's how I ended up in the Feds — my boss recommended me for a transfer to the paedophile unit at AFP.'

Simone looked poised to ask another question, but he held up his hand. 'Time out,' he said.

He left her lighting another cigarette and wandered from the terrace through to the men's room. Mark knew swapping life stories was part of the deal when getting to know a person. But his time with the special squad was best kept to himself.

Most sexual crimes against children were committed by extended family members or people known to them. But some victims — or 'survivors', as they preferred to be called — alleged they'd been lured by high-profile members of the community into private clubs for paedophiles. And while Mark made initial headway in pursuing these cases, witnesses would suddenly decide not to press charges, key documents would go missing, and obscure legal obstacles would emerge. Mark began to suspect an unholy alliance of church, state, big business and the law to protect wealthy perpetrators from prosecution. But he knew better than to share these thoughts and jumped when the opportunity to join the Feds came up.

But he didn't want to go over all that with Simone. He zipped up his fly and flushed the urinal. It only made him feel anxious about his current case to mull over unfinished business.

Jayne watched Mark walk away, unsure of what to think. Were they beginning a relationship, or just keeping each other on side for the sake of their respective investigations?

Mark's mention of Calabria made her think of the Mafia saying, *Keep your friends close and your enemies closer*. She didn't want to let him out of her sight.

Two young Ahka girls approached her table, their beanie-like hats covered in silver coins. The taller girl, about seven, carried cheap souvenirs on a tray suspended from a sash around her neck. The other held a bronze-coloured insect in her hand, fastened by one leg to her ring finger with a piece of red cotton, a tiny leash.

When Jayne spoke Thai, they became excited, asking her to teach them English words and giggling at the strange sounds coming from their own mouths. She was still chatting with them when Mark reappeared.

'Hey,' she said, 'I don't suppose you know the English word for this, do you?'

He looked into the girl's outstretched palm and shrugged. 'Nah, sorry.' He resumed his seat.

'Neither do I,' she laughed.

When she told the girls this, they grinned, the younger one cupping her hand over her mouth to hide her smile. Then they scampered off, leaving Jayne to stare after them.

'Do you want to move on?' Mark said, bringing her thoughts back to him.

She glanced at her watch. 'It's nearly midnight. You don't think we should be watching Kelly's place?'

'Nah. Since you saved me the effort of getting an ID on those cops, I can take a night off.'

She thought for a moment. 'How about we go to a show?'

'What kind of show?'

'It's a surprise.' She signalled for the bill.

Officer Tanin blinked, bug-eyes widening. There was no mistaking it. Officer Komet was sitting in the garden of the Mountain View Lodge with a farang woman.

Tanin ducked behind the trunk of a coconut palm. Although he was too far away to hear what the two were saying, he figured they must be speaking Thai as, to his knowledge, Komet didn't know any other languages.

The woman had fair hair and pale skin, and there was a lot of skin showing. Her dress had little strings over her shoulders, and when she leaned forward, Tanin could almost see her breasts. She shook her head a lot and waved her hands in the air when she talked.

The Mountain View was on Tanin's regular beat. The garden restaurant had a winding path across the lawn that led to the tables, each lit with candles inside domes of coloured glass. The path itself was lined with flowers, neatly trimmed to waist-height; and there was a pond in the middle, covered in pink lotus blossoms. It was quiet and romantic, a place where lovers met.

Tanin was confused. Was it possible Officer Komet had taken a mia noy? He knew Komet's wife was expecting a baby. But he didn't think farangs could be minor wives. It was very strange.

He wondered what Sergeant Pornsak would make of it. Word around the office was that he'd fallen out with Ratratarn, forced to do guard duty at the dead farang's house. Tanin hoped it wasn't serious: Pornsak had promised to look after him, and Tanin needed his help if he was to advance his career. He was trying to save enough money to get married.

Although Tanin looked up to Pornsak, the sergeant was always making scornful remarks about ban nok people and, like Komet, Tanin had grown up in a rural area. He tried to imagine the look on Pornsak's face if he knew that Komet—whom he dismissed as a hick—had a farang girl-friend. Pornsak was bound to be jealous.

Smiling at the thought, Tanin withdrew from behind the tree and backed away to his motorbike. He was tempted to drop in on Pornsak there and then, but it would keep until the end of their respective shifts. It gave him something to look forward to.

Mark cast a sideways glance at Simone who laughed as a drag queen dressed as Grace Jones took centre stage to sing 'I Need a Man'. A waiter wearing silver micro-shorts and the number 21 around his neck approached their table and, careful not to take his eyes off the guy's face, Mark ordered himself another scotch.

When the tuk-tuk had pulled up outside an ornate wooden house called the Lotus Inn, Mark assumed Simone was taking him to see some traditional Thai dancing. By the time he realised it was a gay bar, it was too late to suggest they go elsewhere without causing a scene. It wasn't that he had a problem with gays. But he didn't like having it shoved in his face.

The drag queen strutted around the stage, gyrating his pelvis and making lewd gestures with his tongue on the microphone. Half the time, Mark couldn't tell if these trannies were men or women. Some of their tits looked real, and one or two wore dresses so tight he could see every curve—and there were no bulges where their dicks should have been. Did they strap them up into the cracks of their arses? Or worse?

Mark downed his second scotch in one gulp and ordered another. The drag queen stepped down from the stage and started making his way through the audience. Still lip-synching, he stopped next to one guy, stroked the stubble on his shaved head and perched on his lap, his free hand working its way down towards the man's groin. The punter looked as if he was enjoying himself, but Mark didn't want to risk being the next victim. Mumbling an excuse to Simone, he made his way to the bathroom.

It was a bad idea. Stumbling through the washroom into the toilet area, Mark came upon two men in a corner by the urinal, shirts unbuttoned and hands down each other's pants. The men—one a westerner, the other a local—didn't even pause to look up as he brushed past them and locked himself in a cubicle.

Even with the music booming in the bar, he could still hear the two guys going at it through the door. Mark put the toilet seat down and sat back with his head against the wall, waiting for them to finish so he could return to Simone and suggest they get the hell out of there.

The two guys' groans grew deeper, louder, more intense. Mark sighed, wondering just how long it could take for a couple of poofs to jerk each other off, when he looked down and realised he had a hard-on.

He stared at his distended groin in shock and his head started to spin. He tried to will his cock to go down, to block out the sounds of the two men gasping towards climax. But his erection only grew harder, straining against the fly of his jeans, as the voices outside rose to a howl of satisfaction.

Mark slumped forward, listening to the men kiss loudly and laugh. He heard footsteps, the sound of running water, paper towels being pulled from the dispenser and muffled voices. Finally, he heard the bathroom door being opened. The music grew louder for a moment. Then he was alone.

He eased himself up and adjusted his jeans. Since his obstinate cock remained hard, he untucked his shirt and let it hang out over his belt. Unlocking the door, he walked to the wash basin and splashed cold water on his face. His reflection in the mirror stared back at him: shock, guilt, anger and lust.

He hesitated before helping himself to a paper towel, rubbing his face slowly at first, then harder and faster until the towel disintegrated in his hands. Scrunching the scraps into a ball, he flung it against the wall and shoved the door open, almost knocking out two men on the verge of entering. Another foreign poofter with his Thai fuck, Mark thought, angrily pushing past them. These guys had no fuckin' shame!

He paused at the exit and looked across the room to where Simone was sitting, hoping to catch her eye and signal for them to go.

'Fuck!' he said aloud.

She wasn't alone.

Jayne glanced at the glass of whisky in front of Mark's empty place at the table. He was missing the big finale when Whitney Houston, Tina Turner, Marilyn Monroe and Chiang Mai's petite Grace Jones joined together in a heartfelt rendition of 'When Will I See You Again?', a favourite in Thailand's gay bars. Then again, Mark didn't seem that comfortable with her choice of venue.

The Lotus Inn was one of the few places Didier would go to for fun. The clientele were well-heeled westerners and wealthy Asians, and the place got rave reviews in the *Spartacus* guide. The boys who worked as waiters and dancers could be bought for the night, of course, but the general ambience was more playful than sleazy.

The quality of the show was what had appealed to Didier. The sound, light and sets were dazzling; and the performers put enormous effort into their costumes and lip-synched so convincingly, you could almost believe they were really singing.

Jayne joined the applause as the performers took a bow then stepped down from the stage to mingle with the audience. With no sign of Mark, she helped herself to his scotch and searched for a cigarette.

'You want a boyfriend, Ma'am?'

She looked up at a short, muscular young man with the number 5 around his neck, his eyebrows raised in anticipation.

'It's OK,' she said. 'I'm here with my—' she hesitated. What was Mark to her? She decided to keep it simple. 'I'm here with my friend,' she said.

'*Pai len duay kan sarm kon dai,*' he said without missing a beat.

Jayne smiled, suspecting Federal Agent Mark d'Angelo wouldn't enjoy the threesome the boy had on offer.

'Thank you,' she said politely to save face, 'but we're very tired.'

As the young man departed with a wai, his place was taken by the Lotus's Marilyn Monroe.

'*Sawadee ka*,' she said. 'May I sit down for a moment?'

An approach by the boys was one thing, but in Jayne's experience the kratoeys weren't into women. Curious, she nodded for her to take a seat.

'I've seen you before,' Marilyn said in her falsetto voice. 'You're a friend of Khun Di, aren't you?'

Jayne glanced around the room, suddenly nervous.

'Y-yes,' she said, leaning close enough to smell Marilyn's floral perfume. 'Why do you ask?'

Marilyn picked up the drinks menu from the table and used it to fan her face. 'You see,' she said, 'I was at the bar when they found Khun Sanga's body.'

'Really?' Jayne whispered.

'Yes, it was just terrible!' She fanned faster. 'Oh, what they'd done to that beautiful boy! And the policeman, he made me...oh!' She raised the back of her hand to her forehead in a gesture worthy of her famous namesake.

'What policeman?' Jayne said, trying to remain calm. 'What did he make you do?'

'He made me look at the body!'

Tears sprung to Marilyn's eyes as the menu dropped to the table.

'That must have been awful,' Jayne said, rummaging through her purse for a clean tissue and handing it to Marilyn.

'What's worse,' she sniffed, 'the policemen, they made me sign a piece of paper saying I knew about Khun Sanga and Khun Di.'

'Knew what about Sanga and Didier?'

'That they were *faen kan*,' she said, the pitch of her voice rising. 'And now Khun Di is dead. And it's all my fault!' She hid her face in her hands and sobbed.

'Khun…Marilyn,' Jayne said, 'I'm sorry but I don't understand. You told the police that they were lovers. But you didn't tell them that Khun Di killed Khun Sanga, did you?'

'Oh, no!' She raised her head. 'But I didn't tell them they were lovers, either. The police already knew about Khun Di, but they wanted me to sign the paper, as if it was me who told them. And not only me. Other people, too. I wanted you to know that Khun Di was a good man and none of us would ever do anything to…to…' Her voice trailed off again.

'It's OK,' Jayne said, patting her arm.

Marilyn dabbed her eyes with the tissue. 'Since you were his friend, you should know the truth.'

Jayne cast her mind back over what she'd read in the police report. 'If you don't mind, Khun Marilyn, can I ask about your…ah…the name that appeared on your police statement?'

'Pairoj,' she sniffed. 'Pairoj Nilmongkol.'

Jayne took a pen from her purse and scribbled the name on the back of a coaster. 'And the man who forced you to sign it?'

'Police Lieutenant Colonel Ratratarn.'

Jayne put the coaster in her purse and slipped some money for the drinks under the table marker, standing up as Mark reappeared.

'Where have you been?' she asked. 'You missed the best part of the show and—'

He smothered the rest of her words in a kiss so hard it almost bruised her lips. Thrown off-balance, she leaned into his body to steady herself and felt his erection beneath his jeans.

'I want to fuck you so badly,' he whispered.

For Jayne, such an overt display of heterosexual lust in a gay bar was almost indecent.

'OK,' she said. 'Let's go to my place.'

Jayne grabbed the phone before it could ring a second time. Ornsri at reception said a Thai man wanted to meet her. She peered at the clock. Half past seven. Mark was snoring lightly beside her. She asked the man's name. There was the sound of muffled voices, before Ornsri whispered back.

'He says he's a friend of Khun Bom and Khun Deh.'

'Just a minute.' Jayne gently replaced the receiver and eased herself out of bed. She gathered her clothes from the floor and crept into the bathroom to get dressed.

Fighting the desire for a hot shower, she splashed her face, ran damp fingers through her hair, and put up the collar of her blouse to hide a bite mark on the side of her neck. She tiptoed back past the bed and picked up her day-pack and sandals. Mark stirred as she turned the door handle and she froze until she was sure he was still sleeping.

The man in the reception area looked familiar. His large eyes turned down slightly at the corners, giving him a sad expression despite the smile on his face. Ornsri nodded as Jayne entered and he leapt up to greet her with a wai. His clothes, though neat, were old, his grey slacks faded at the knees.

'*Kor thort krup*, Khun Simone,' he said, speaking Thai with a northeastern accent. 'My name is Komet. Sorry to disturb you, but I wonder if we might talk together in private for a moment.'

She returned his wai. '*Sawadee ka*, Khun…Komet, was it?'

He nodded.

'Have we met before?'

'Ah…' He smiled and gestured outside. A few guests were eating breakfast—a sleepy-looking woman picking at the remains of a banana pancake, a man studying the Lonely Planet guide in German—and Jayne followed Komet to a table in a quiet corner.

'Would you like something to drink?' she asked as they sat down, conscious of her own need for coffee.

'Just water, thank you.'

She summoned the waitress—one of Ornsri's daughters—who shuffled over at glacial pace to take the order.

'Khun Ornsri said you're a friend of Bom's,' Jayne said. 'And I think I recognise you…But I don't remember where we met.'

Komet coloured slightly and shift in his seat. 'Ah, Khun Simone, we haven't exactly met before. But I have some information for someone, and I think maybe you can pass it on.'

'What kind of information? To pass on to who?'

'To Khun Jen Kee Ni.'

There was no mistaking the transliteration of her name. In that moment she realised neither Bom nor Deh knew she'd changed hotels. Jayne felt her stomach sink. 'What makes you think I know this person?'

'Ah, maybe you don't know her,' Komet said nervously. 'Maybe I made a mistake. But it would be a pity because I have some important information about her friend

205

Khun Di who was killed last weekend.'

'What do you know about his death?'

She regretted the words as soon as she'd said them. Before Komet could answer, Ornsri's daughter reappeared, spilling coffee into the saucer as she set it down on the table.

'I read about the farang's death in the papers,' Jayne said when the waitress was out of earshot. 'What more does anyone need to know, Khun Komet?'

'They need to know that Khun Di wasn't killed because he was trying to resist arrest,' he said in a low voice. 'And they need to know he didn't kill Khun Sanga like the papers said.'

The sinking feeling in Jayne's stomach turned to butterflies. She wanted to drink her coffee, but didn't trust her hands to remain steady enough to pick up the cup. 'And how do you know all this?' she said.

'Because I work for the Chiang Mai police.'

Jayne remembered where she'd seen him before: he was the third man at the Kitten Club with Ratratarn and Pornsak, and before that, the guard at Didier's place the night she broke in. How could she have been so blind? She had a photo of the man in her backpack! It was the uniform—she hadn't recognised him without it.

She forced a smile. 'I'm sorry Officer Komet, but you must be mistaken. I'm afraid I don't know what you're talking about.'

She picked up her coffee. Over the rim of the cup, she saw him throw her a wounded look.

'Oh, th-that's a shame,' he stammered. 'I thought, that

is, I was hoping to find Jayne Keeney to tell her what I know. You see, my superior, Lieutenant Colonel Ratratarn, he's trying to find her, too. He's worried she knows about how he and the farang, Khun Kelly, worked together to kill her friend and Khun Sanga. I wanted to find her first, to warn her and, and to tell her the truth.'

He was good, Jayne thought. He was very good.

'And why would you want to do that? Didn't you say you're a police officer yourself?'

'Yes, b-but…but what they did is wrong!'

Was this a trap set by Kelly and the cops? Jayne didn't underestimate their intelligence, and for them to send a sweet-faced young rookie from Isaan to plead their case was a masterstroke. Yet something in Komet's demeanour made her think again. Neither spoke for a moment, the passion in his outburst lingering in the air between them.

'They're selling children,' he whispered, staring at the ground as he spoke. 'Not girls, children. Children who could have come from my own village…' He shook his head. 'Khun Di knew about it, so they killed him. That is, Lieutenant Colonel Ratratarn killed him. It says in the official report there were two bullets fired on the night, the first as a warning shot. But that's not true. There were two bullet casings at the scene, but only one shot. I know.' He looked up, imploring her with his eyes. 'I was there.'

Jayne averted her gaze, swallowing hard to fight back tears.

'And the so-called murder weapon,' Komet said, 'it wasn't behind the water trough. I searched there before the forensic team arrived. The lieutenant colonel planted it when I wasn't looking. He must've picked it up from Kelly, or the man Kelly hired to kill Khun Sanga.'

Jayne said nothing.

'Oh, yes, Kelly killed Khun Sanga,' Komet said. 'Not directly, but he was responsible. Sergeant Pornsak said Kelly drugged Khun Sanga before handing him over to be killed. Pornsak said the assassin came from Mae Sai. He called the man a *kha*, a barbarian. That's what they think, Pornsak and the lieutenant colonel. They think people from the hill tribes are savages. As for people from rural areas like me, we're all as stupid as cows.'

'Why are you telling me this?' she said.

'Because someone has to stop it. And I thought…I thought Jayne Keeney would help me. They say she was a close friend of Khun Di. And I thought even if no one else believed me, she would.'

'Don't you think she might worry that this is a plan to trap her? I mean, you say the police are looking for her. Why should she trust you?'

Komet shrugged his shoulders. 'Maybe she thinks Thai police are the same. Bad men. Corrupt. Hungry for money. Maybe many Thai people feel the same way…' His voice trailed off for a moment. 'But Thai police are not all the same. Some of us just want a job in the city, not to be a farmer any more. Farmers are poor, always struggling. We are young and headstrong when we turn our backs on our families. We look at our fathers' dark skin and dirty hands and say, "No! I don't want this! I want a job with a nice uniform and a regular paycheque!"'

He smiled his sad smile. 'We never dream the day will

come when what we wish more than anything is that we never left the farm.'

He reached into his pocket and took out a piece of paper. 'If you see Jayne Keeney, please give this to her. It's the same story I told you, only I wrote it down and signed my name.'

Jayne inhaled sharply and scanned the document, picking up enough of the Thai to see it checked out. She let out her breath in a sigh, no longer frightened.

'What about you, Khun Komet?' she said. 'What would happen if your superiors knew what you were doing?'

'No need to worry for me,' he said. '*Kam sanong kam.*'

'You're a very brave man,' she said.

'I'm a simple man, but it's not difficult to tell the difference between right and wrong, Khun Simone.'

'It's Jayne,' she said softly. 'My name's Jayne Keeney.'

Sergeant Pornsak dismounted from his motorbike, straightened his cap and marched inside to sign off from his shift. He assumed the air of a man charged with a secret mission. With the exception of Ratratarn from whom he received his orders, none of his colleagues could tell he'd spent the night counting fireflies in a dead farang's garden.

He made a show of checking his mobile phone for messages; there were none, but the digital chimes and bright flashing lights were guaranteed to attract a few envious looks. Officer Tanin who was standing by the noticeboard turned to see where the noise was coming from.

'Sergeant Pornsak,' Tanin said, 'I was hoping to see you. I—'

Pornsak cut him off by raising a hand, the other still pressing the buttons on his meu teu. He frowned as if some vital message appeared on the screen and nodded, before switching off the phone and restoring it to his belt.

'What is it, Tanin?' he said gruffly. 'I don't have much time.'

'It's Officer Komet, Sir,' Tanin said. 'I think he's got a farang girlfriend.'

Pornsak started. 'What?'

'I-I saw them, Sir, Officer Komet talking with a farang woman, at the Mountain View Lodge. In the garden. Around midnight.'

'Dog fucker!' If Komet had found the woman before him, that blew his best chance of getting back into Ratratarn's good books.

'She was very nice,' Tanin said, tracing the outline of a woman's body in the air. 'I saw them on my rounds and—'

With a glance at the roster, Pornsak left Tanin mid-sentence and rushed to the lieutenant colonel's office door.

'Sir!' He came to an abrupt halt and saluted.

'What do you want, Pornsak?' The lieutenant colonel sat behind his desk, a crease in his brow.

'Sir,' he said, panting slightly, 'Officer Tanin reports seeing Officer Komet conferring with a farang woman last night. I wondered if this meant we'd had a breakthrough in the case and—'

And I could be excused from sentry duty, he'd wanted to add, but the lieutenant colonel cut him off.

'What?' Ratratarn rose to his feet, fingertips splayed on the desk. 'Sergeant, what the hell are you talking about?'

'Komet, Sir. I had reason to believe he'd located the farang woman we've been looking for. Didn't he say any—?'

'Where's Komet now?' Ratratarn said.

'I checked on my way, Sir. He signed off an hour ago.'

'Find him. No, wait! Is Tanin still here?'

Pornsak dashed back to the front desk where Tanin was signing off and dragged the younger man back to Ratratarn's office.

'Sergeant Pornsak tells me you saw Officer Komet meeting with a farang woman last night,' Ratratarn said.

'Y-yes, Sir,' Tanin stammered. 'At the M-Mountain View Lodge.'

'Who was she?'

'I-I don't know, Sir,' Tanin said. 'I just saw Officer Komet talking with her in the garden. I thought she might be his girlfriend.'

Ratratarn shook his head. 'Tell me, Officer Tanin,' he said with exaggerated courtesy. 'Do you think you could recognise this woman again?'

'Hmm, maybe,' Tanin said.

'Maybe isn't fucking good enough.' Ratratarn's hand shot out across the desk, grabbing Tanin by the collar. 'Could—you—recognise—the—farang—woman—again?'

'Y-y-yes, Sir!' he cried.

'Good!' Ratratarn released his grip and sent Tanin reeling to the floor. 'Let's go to the Mountain View together.

211

I want to have a little chat with this farang woman about the nature of her relationship with Officer Komet.' He picked up his cap. 'Sergeant?'

'Sir!' Pornsak stood to attention.

'Find Officer Komet and bring him here at once. I want to know what the hell he's playing at…And Pornsak,' he added, 'let's surprise Officer Komet, shall we?'

Pornsak saluted, turned on his heel and marched back down the corridor. He wasn't sure what was happening, but at least he seemed to be back in favour with the lieutenant colonel. Only minutes ago he'd actually been jealous of Komet. But right now, Officer Komet Plungkham was the last person whose shoes he wanted to be in.

Ratratarn couldn't tolerate the thought of being duped by a junior officer from the ban nok. At the Mountain View Lodge, he learned only one farang woman had checked in on Tuesday, a French Embassy employee named Marie with a diplomatic passport to prove it. Ratratarn flashed the ID photo at Tanin who confirmed it was the woman he'd seen with Komet. He instructed the receptionist to summon her, brushing aside protestations that the guest didn't take breakfast for another half-hour.

The receptionist placed the call, her cheeks reddening as she apologised to the person on the line. Ratratarn noted the farang spoke Thai and was wondering what that said about Komet's strategy, when his mobile phone rang. He checked the caller's number.

'*Krup*,' he grunted. 'What is it, Pornsak?'

'Officer Komet's house is empty, Sir. No wife, nobody.

Could be they left in a hurry, too. There's still food on the stove.'

'Where's Officer Komet from? What's his hometown?'

'Nakhon Phanom,' Tanin piped up.

'Tanin says Komet's from Nakhon Phanom,' Ratratarn said. 'Check the bus terminal. Talk with the neighbours, see if they know anything. Find out what the hell's going on.'

As he hung up, a blonde woman approached the desk. At the sight of the two policemen, her scowl deepened.

Ratratarn mustered all the charm he could manage. '*Kor thort krup*, Khun Marie,' he said, 'I wonder if I might have a word—'

'Look,' she interrupted him, 'I already told the other officer I don't know anything.'

'What's that?' Ratratarn feigned innocence. 'Have you already spoken with one of my officers?' He shot Tanin a look warning him to keep his mouth shut.

'Yes, last night,' Marie said. 'I was on my way to bed then and now you've woken me up this morning. What is it with you people?'

Ratratarn opened his notebook at a random page. 'Excuse me, Madam,' he said, 'but according to our records, three farang women are to be interviewed. One says she's a victim of gem fraud, one reports theft of her credit card whilst trekking, and a third is wanted for questioning in relation to the death of a Canadian last weekend.'

'That was me!' she said. 'That's what your officer was asking about. But I explained that I only know what I read in the papers. He was very persistent. Even insisted on seeing my passport. Said he was looking for someone who might be in disguise.'

'And you didn't call the police in relation to a gem scam or a stolen credit card?'

'No, I didn't call the police at all.'

Ratratarn closed his notebook. 'My apologies, Ma'am. There's obviously been a misunderstanding. Rest assured I will see to it personally that those responsible are disciplined, and steps taken to ensure such mistakes do not occur in the future.'

The woman nodded curtly.

'I trust the spirit of co-operation between our two countries will not be adversely affected,' he added.

He smiled at his paraphrasing the platitudes of that arse-licker from the Canadian Embassy. But the woman thought the smile was for her.

'*Mai pen rai*,' she said.

'S-Sir, do you want me to follow up on the stolen credit card?' Tanin said as they returned to the car.

'What?' Ratratarn said. 'What the hell are you talking about?'

'The stolen credit card you mentioned, S-Sir. I have experience in this area and—'

'Shut up, Tanin.'

Ratratarn wanted to believe Komet was working in their collective interests, but he could smell a rat. Although Komet maintained he hadn't come up with any leads on Jayne Keeney from his survey of the town's hotels and guesthouses, he was onto something if he was going around interviewing Thai-speaking farang women about the dead Canadian.

Ratratarn recalled Komet giving him a list of places where women in Jayne Keeney's age group had been registered. Back at the Bureau he shuffled through the papers on his desk until he found it, scanning the list to see where else Komet might have been.

'Son of a bitch!'

The Mountain View Lodge wasn't even on the list. The document was a hoax.

Ratratarn collapsed into a chair and rubbed his temples. When Pornsak rang to report that, according to the neighbours, Komet's expectant wife had gone home to have her baby, Ratratarn saw an opportunity.

'It seems we were mistaken about Officer Komet,' he said. 'I've just found a report he left me on his interviews with various farang women, including the one Tanin saw him with at the Mountain View Lodge. He was taking initiative, Sergeant, which is to be commended—though in future such initiatives must be authorised in advance through the correct channels.'

'Sir?' Pornsak sounded confused.

'Go home, Sergeant. Come back for your regular shift tonight.'

'For more surveillance duty?' he asked plaintively.

Ratratarn decided to let him sweat. 'We'll see about that when you come in.'

The lieutenant colonel smiled as he switched off the phone. That took care of any loss of face he might have had with Pornsak, and Tanin was too stupid to worry about. That only left Komet.

When Pornsak said Komet's wife had gone away for

her confinement, Ratratarn realised the food on the stove wasn't the sign of an abrupt departure; it was the dutiful wife's parting gesture. And as Komet didn't know Ratratarn was onto him, no doubt he'd turn up for work that night as usual. All Ratratarn had to do was wait.

As soon as Komet left, Jayne ordered another coffee, wiped down the table with a serviette, and took what she needed from her backpack: pen, gluestick, stapler, dictionary, surveillance photos, and the police report she'd swiped from David Freeman. The report had been printed single-sided, making it easy for Jayne to lay out the alternative scenario, drawing arrows from the printed text on the right to her notes and photos on the left.

She began with the interviews conducted by police where Nou's body was found and made a note of her personal communication with Pairoj Nilmongkol. She went through the official account of Didier's death and its aftermath, picking it apart using the information Komet had given her. Here, she knew her source would carry more weight and noted:

> *Personal communication as per signed confession (see attached), Police Officer Komet Plungkham, Thurs 9 May 1996.*

Next she wrote:

> *Max Parker (Second Secretary, Australian Embassy, Bangkok), a close friend of M. de Montpasse, can testify to his character in order to counter police*

claims that amphetamines were found on the
premises.

Thinking of Max made her feel guilty, and she made a mental note to contact him.

On a blank page, she translated Komet's statement into English, pasting in photos of Kelly, Ratratarn and Pornsak as illustrations. She also noted 'confirmation by an independent witness' that Sanga was with Kelly around 1am on the night of his death, not long before his body was found at Man Date.

Satisfied with her handiwork, Jayne stapled Komet's statement to the inside front cover, added his photograph, then sat back and lit a cigarette.

'What's that?' Mark gestured at the smoke and screwed up his nose. 'Breakfast of champions?'

She tilted her head to kiss him, simultaneously pulling the police report closer. 'Hardly breakfast!' She folded her arms on top of it. 'It's nearly midday.'

'That explains why I'm so hungry,' he said. 'Any chance of getting some food around here?'

'You'll have to ask her.'

At a nearby table, Ornsri's daughter was cutting square paper napkins into smaller squares and stuffing them into bamboo holders, a bored look on her face.

Mark went over to confer with her, while Jayne slipped the report into her backpack. On instinct, she felt compelled to keep her latest findings a secret.

'Nah, nothing doing here,' Mark said, sauntering back to her table. 'Want to go out for something?'

'Ah, I've got a few things to do. Why don't we meet up again for dinner tonight?'

He cocked his head. 'Anything wrong?'

'Nothing a hot shower and a decent sleep won't fix.'

Mark handed her the room key and kissed her. Jayne felt a twinge of guilt as he left but resisted the urge to run after him. She slipped 100 baht under the napkin holder and returned to her room.

She'd felt elated after her meeting with Komet; his confession confirmed her every instinct about Didier's death. And it had been enormously satisfying to pick the police report to pieces, substantiating her case with evidence even David Freeman would have to concede raised 'reasonable doubt' about the official account. But she didn't know how she could use that evidence without putting Komet in danger. The word-of-mouth statements from Pairoj and Nalissa amounted to little on their own. Komet's confession held it all together, not only because he was a material witness to the conspiracy, but because of who he was. A repentant rookie. A cop with a conscience.

When she asked what would happen if word got out about their meeting, Komet used the same phrase as Nalissa. *Kam sanong kam—What goes around, comes around*. Much as she admired his courage, Jayne did not share his faith in karmic retribution. If she went public, it would be her fault if anything happened to him.

She thought of talking it over with Mark, but she still wasn't sure how committed he was to the whole idea. He hadn't mentioned Didier since the night they met and seemed uneasy if Jayne brought up his name. It was almost as if he were jealous.

Then it occurred to her that since Mark had promised to release information on the murders to the media once he arrested Kelly, Jayne could draft a press release on his behalf. Something that drew on Komet's evidence and was substantial enough to provoke an inquiry, yet worded in such a way as to protect him. She'd give a copy to Mark at dinner and know from his reaction whether or not he was serious about keeping up his end of their deal.

She finished her cigarette, took out a pen and opened her notebook.

Mark proposed they meet at the Riverside. Simone looked tired when she arrived, though seemed in good spirits. As they drank cold beers at a table on the river's edge, she pointed out quirky translations on the menu.

'How about some "drunken nuts" for starters,' she grinned, 'or maybe "ripped mango with salted sauce"? Or "cold Chinese crystal slide pork roll"—what the hell is that? Oh, here's a good one under European food: "canelloni vegetariani".'

'Doesn't sound like anything my Nona used to make,' Mark grinned.

She placed their order in Thai and lit a cigarette. 'Tell me about Cambodia,' she said.

Mark raised his eyebrows. The question was out of the blue, but he knew it was bound to come up sooner or later. Simone wasn't to know that talking about Cambodia was picking at a wound that never healed. 'What about Cambodia?'

'All I know is you were there. Why did you go?'

'It's a long story.'

'We've got all night.' She smiled.

'OK then.' He took a deep breath. 'Cambodia was supposed to showcase the AFP's potential under the new legislation,' he said. 'With the UN peacekeepers gone, the country was becoming a new hub of paedophilia in the region, and I figure the Australian government felt guilty, since they'd backed the peace plan to begin with. I was sent to investigate some cases to do with street kids.

'See, Cambodia attracts a particular kind of paedophile. Not the situational offenders you see at the Kitten Club—the place's too dangerous for a cheap holiday destination. In Cambodia you get what we call preferential offenders. These guys are wealthy, well-connected and highly organised. And they're into boys rather than girls.'

She frowned. 'Go on.'

'Well, to keep it short, my work resulted in an extradition order for an Australian businessman on child sex charges. It should've been cut and dried, but the Cambodian authorities insisted on trying him under local law, even though they didn't have any bloody laws covering child sex offences. They had to charge him with rape of a minor. And they couldn't prove whether the victim was fifteen or sixteen at the time of the assault—half the Cambodian people can't tell how old they are. Sullivan said the kid told him he was sixteen—the age of consent—and they dropped the charges. It was a fuckin' farce.'

'Sullivan?' Simone said. 'You worked on the Sullivan case? That was huge! The Thai papers were full of the story.'

'Yeah?' He was pleased she'd heard of it. 'Shame about the outcome though.'

'Actually, I remember public opinion was pretty divided. A lot of people thought Sullivan was the victim of an anti-gay witch-hunt.'

'Oh, for fuck's sake, Simone!'

He didn't mean to shout, and seeing the look on her face, mumbled an apology.

'No, go on,' she said, 'I'm interested in your opinion.'

He took another breath. 'To be honest, that bleeding heart attitude pisses me off. The vast majority of cases we prosecute involve girls abused by family members. I mean, some of the shit I had to deal with in Brisbane...No one accuses us of being anti-family there. But as soon as the charges involve young boys, we're accused of being anti-gay.'

'Maybe it's the definition of "young" that creates problems,' Simone said. 'If the kid told Sullivan he was sixteen, then isn't he legally entitled to have sex? It seems to me that people feel differently about heterosexual and homosexual sex, even when it's consenting.'

'Look, I really don't want to argue with you about this,' Mark said, trying to control his temper. 'As far as the AFP's concerned, homosexuality's not the crime. We're out to get paedophiles, regardless of who they are.'

'But the media—'

'Stuff the media,' he said, struggling to keep his voice down. 'That's not what I'm talking about. I'm talking about cops—and what we do. We're not the ones with a double-standard.'

Simone stared at the table.

'Look,' he said more gently, 'maybe the media is anti-gay. Maybe it's easy to get the wrong impression from what makes it into the news. But Simone, that's not what motivates me to do my job. I don't give a shit whether an offender's straight, gay or whatever. If they're fucking children, it's a crime.'

Simone nodded, still staring at the table. 'You're right,' she said. 'Sorry. It's just that, you know, some of my closest friends are gay. My best friend...' Mark heard a tremor in her voice.

'It's OK,' he said. 'Besides, judging from what you've told me about your friend, I reckon he'd agree with me.'

'He might,' she said thoughtfully. 'Then again, Didier took a pretty sophisticated view...'

She stared out over the river as if she'd forgotten Mark was there, and he knew she was thinking about her Canadian mate. It pissed Mark off that the guy had such a hold over her. So Didier had a sophisticated viewpoint—and his own wasn't?

The tension was broken by the arrival of their meal. Mark had encouraged Simone to order so he could try her favourite Thai dishes, and the food enabled him to steer the conversation back onto safer ground.

'This is *yam pladook foo*—catfish salad,' she said, pointing to a plate on which Mark was hard pressed to detect any fish. 'The fish is mashed up and deep fried,' she added, as if reading his mind. 'It's fantastic with the green mango sauce. This one's called jungle curry—watch out for the whole spices as it packs a punch. And this—' she indicated another plate '—is cold Chinese crystal slide pork roll.'

'Spring rolls?'

'Looks like it.'

Mark laughed, relieved to lighten the mood.

Half an hour later, they pushed their empty plates aside. 'That was fantastic,' he said.

Simone murmured in agreement, rummaging through her bag. 'Before I forget, I've got something for you,' she said, handing him a piece of paper. 'I took the liberty of drafting a press release. It covers the stuff I told you—about Didier's death, I mean. I thought you might be able to use it—save you doing it yourself.'

Mark scanned it, unsure whether he was flattered by her active interest in his work, or pissed off by her presumption.

'Sure, whatever,' he said, putting it in his pocket. 'Thanks.'

'And I want to come with you tomorrow night. Not when you arrest Kelly, of course,' she added quickly, 'but for the pay-off. I've been thinking about it. I could be outside getting photos of the cops as they arrive, while you're inside, picking up from where I leave off. You've got a camera that records the date and time of the photo?'

He nodded.

'Well, think of how good it would look if we had a sequence showing their arrival *and* the pay-off.'

He shook his head. 'I don't think it's a good idea.'

'Please,' Simone said. 'It'd mean a lot to me.'

'I can't do it,' he said. 'It goes against procedure and I won't jeopardise the operation.'

'And why would my involvement jeopardise the operation?' She sounded more hurt than angry. 'I've done all the right things by you. I've given you names, my surveillance photos. I thought my skills were an asset to your operation.'

'Of course,' he said, shifting in his seat. 'But—'

'Surely the AFP enlists the services of freelance private investigators from time to time?' she continued. 'Can't you see it like that?'

'I don't know,' he said.

'I promise I'll be careful,' Simone said. 'Please, Mark. I want to work with you on this—to support you.'

Mark hesitated, knowing he should refuse. But this was precisely the personal engagement he'd wanted from her.

'You'll be in the same place as last time?' he said.

She nodded.

'And you'll leave as soon as the cops go inside?'

'Assuming it's safe,' she said.

'I mean it, Simone. You've gotta get out of there as soon as possible.'

She held up her hands. 'Whatever you say.'

'OK then,' Mark sighed.

Simone got up from her seat, put her arms around his neck, and kissed him on the cheek. 'Thank you,' she said.

'I thought kissing in public wasn't the done thing,' he said, squirming out of her hold.

Simone chuckled and walked off in the direction of the ladies' room.

Mark's gaze followed her. He wanted to win the case against Kelly and the cops, but he also wanted Simone. Was it too much to aim for both?

Not since he was a child had Komet slept so peacefully, lying like spoons with his brothers on a sleeping mat beneath the mosquito net. Maybe he'd dreamt of those times. On waking, he half expected to hear the roosters noisily ushering in the dawn and the chickens fussing, impatient to be released from the rattan basket where they were kept at night.

Instead he heard a radio, children's voices in neighbouring yards, the hum of traffic, the cries of food hawkers. He got out of bed not to a glowing dawn, but to the fading light of dusk.

Komet warmed and ate the whole pot of rice porridge Arunee had left for him, before getting ready for his shift. He took more care than usual with his uniform, polishing his belt buckle, smoothing down the epaulets on his shirt, and adjusting the red braid over his left shoulder so it was perfectly straight. He shined his shoes as a finishing touch, and oiled and combed his hair before placing his cap firmly on his head. As he told Jayne, he'd joined the Chiang Mai police force as a means of getting out of Nakhon Phanom. But that evening, for the first time, he wore his uniform with pride.

It didn't trouble him when, on arriving at the bureau, he bumped into Officer Tanin and found him even more skittish than usual. Tanin gave him a convoluted story about seeing him with a farang woman at a hotel the previous evening and the lieutenant colonel being angry about it. Pornsak was looking for him, too. Komet simply smiled in reply, leaving Tanin staring after him, open-mouthed, as he went to sign in for the evening.

Nor did it worry him when a grim-faced secretary at the front desk said he was to report to the lieutenant colonel. The woman looked nervous on his behalf but, again, Komet smiled and made his way to Ratratarn's office. He had a strange sense that everything was going according to plan. Not a plan of his own making, but a plan nonetheless.

Komet could tell from Ratratarn's face that the lieutenant colonel was onto him. He wasn't sure if Ratratarn knew about his meeting with Jayne Keeney, but he knew he'd been taken for a ride. His body was tense with fury, his upper lip in a half-formed sneer. And in his narrowed eyes, Komet could detect a trace of grudging respect.

'Good to see you again, Officer Komet,' Ratratarn said in response to his perfunctory salute.

Komet recognised the tone. The lieutenant colonel wielded courtesy and charm as weapons so that the blow, when it came, hit harder.

'No, don't close the door,' Ratratarn said. 'There's been a new development in our investigation into Khun Sanga's murder. A witness wants to meet by the Talat Tohn Payorm. I want you to come with me.' He took his cap from the desk and gestured for them to leave.

'Sir,' Komet hesitated, 'I understand from Officer Tanin that there may have been some confusion earlier as to my whereabouts. I was surprised to hear this, Sir, as I was at home, sleeping as usual, for the better part of the day.'

Ratratarn seemed taken aback, though whether it was because of what he'd said or the fact he'd volunteered any information at all, Komet couldn't tell. 'We'll discuss that later,' the lieutenant colonel said.

In the station carpark, Komet headed for the squad car.

But Ratratarn stopped him before he could open the passenger door.

'No, not that one,' he said. 'I don't want to spook the witness. We'll take the other.'

Komet nodded and walked to the unmarked vehicle reserved for surveillance work.

They drove in silence, west of the old citadel walls, past the Maharaj Hospital and Wat Suandok, before reaching the Ton Payorm Market. It was deserted at this time of night, save for the rats—Komet saw their eyes reflected in the headlights. North of the crossroad was Chiang Mai University, the campus also quiet as the students were out on their long holidays.

Komet slowed the car, but Ratratarn gestured for him to continue.

'We're meeting on the other side of the bridge,' he said. 'Turn left and find somewhere to park.'

Komet kept his face blank but his heart skipped a beat. South of the university, on the opposite side of the canal to the market, was an open zoo that students used as an observation centre. Surrounded by a high mesh fence, it was even darker than the campus. There was barely enough room to park between the boundary of the zoo and the retaining wall of the canal. Unable to open his own door, Komet slid across the passenger seat to get out after Ratratarn.

Komet paused, taking a deep breath to allow his sense of calm to return, before edging around to the front of the car. The flame of a match briefly illuminated Ratratarn's face. The man drew back on his cigarette. Komet's eyes slowly adjusted to the darkness.

'What else did Officer Tanin tell you?' Ratratarn said suddenly.

Komet had to think for a moment. 'Only that you've been appraised of my work, Sir, my interviews with the farang women.'

'Son of a—' Ratratarn tossed his glowing cigarette in the canal. 'Damn it, Komet! What the hell are you playing at?'

'Just doing my job, Sir. Trying to locate the farang woman, Jayne Keeney, as ordered. Sir.'

'Do I detect insolence in your tone of voice, Officer?' Ratratarn circled him like an animal stalking its prey.

'No, Sir,' Komet said. Insolence was too strong a word for it. What he felt towards the lieutenant colonel was indifference.

'I knew it!' Ratratarn slapped his thigh. 'You've been working in secret to try and impress me, haven't you Komet? Even left me with a list of dead-end leads so there was no chance anyone else might steal your thunder, right? Well, Officer, let me tell you...'

The lieutenant colonel continued to circle, prattling on about protocol and lines of authority. But Komet was only dimly aware of what he said.

The words of the Fourth Buddhist Precept came to him in his father's voice. *You shall not lie.*

But surely, Komet thought, by keeping silent, one can avoid lying altogether.

You must ask yourself what is the truth, my son, he heard his father say. *If you fail to correct false assumptions, then have you not lied without uttering a single word?*

Ratratarn stopped pacing, waiting for Komet to

respond to a question he hadn't heard.

'I'm sorry, Sir, you're mistaken,' he said. 'I wasn't looking for the farang woman to impress you. I was trying to find her to tell her the truth and—'

He should have anticipated the blow, but didn't. The next thing Komet knew, he was on the ground, tasting dirt and blood.

'You dog-fucking cocksucker!'

Ratratarn was on top of him. Komet could smell the smoke on his breath.

'You little shithead!' he spat. 'Do you really think you can fuck with me?'

The kick to his lower back was swift and accurate. Komet cried out as pain shot the length of his body, bile mixing with the blood in his mouth.

'You have no fucking idea.'

Another kick. This time to his stomach. Komet recoiled in agony, lying in the mud of his own vomit.

'You with your self-righteous little rebellion. Striking a blow for the rural underdog, are we?'

Ratratarn used his fist this time, delivering a punch to the side of Komet's head 'Don't you go cold on me,' he said. 'I haven't finished. Listen, you little fuck, you know first-hand what it's like to live in a lost country. Politicians talk of Thailand as a nation. But we know better, don't we?'

Komet felt a boot to his shin, a blow designed as much to rouse him as to cause more pain.

'We know there's Bangkok, and then there's everyone else. There's no nation. Just a parasite of a capital, sucking the blood of the rest of us for its own survival.'

Ratratarn grabbed Komet by the hair and twisted his battered head so they were eye to eye.

'They're killing us, Komet. Slowly, but surely. We're being sacrificed. A once glorious country for the sake of one shithole of a city. Does that seem fair to you?' He jerked Komet's head around further. 'Because it doesn't seem fair to me.'

He let go and Komet hit the dirt, gravel digging into his cheeks.

'I'm not prepared to sit back and take it.' The lieutenant colonel's voice now sounded calm, almost reasonable. 'It's no use playing by the rules. They make rules in Bangkok for their own sake, not ours. We need to make our own rules, Komet, our own order. Don't you see? We have to do it to survive.'

Komet spat the blood and bile from his mouth and, with enormous effort, raised his head from the ground.

'L-Lieutenant C-Colonel,' he whispered hoarsely.

'Yes, boy.' Ratratarn crouched down and tilted his head.

'Tell me,' Komet said.

His voice sounded far away, as if it were coming from the bottom of the canal.

'How…does it help us to survive, letting f-foreigners pay money to fuck our children?'

He closed his eyes, this time anticipating the blow. He thought of Arunee, of his unborn baby, of his father and, strangely, of Khun Di, the dead Canadian.

And then came the sweet relief of darkness.

Jayne strode to the Nawarat Bridge then down the steps to the promenade along the river. Though the path was lined with streetlamps, only a few worked, and she chose to sit in the shadows where she wouldn't be seen. Mark had wanted her to stay but, pleading exhaustion, she'd left him at his hotel. Still smarting from his outburst at dinner, she didn't feel like sleeping with him that night. She wasn't sure she wanted to sleep with him ever again.

She lit a cigarette. It was unlikely their relationship had a future, certainly not while Mark thought she was someone else. But coming clean at this point would be messy and required a level of risk she wasn't prepared to take. She had to keep him on side. Her desire to see Didier exonerated depended on it. But Mark was jealous of Didier—she could tell—and she also had to placate him. When he'd barely glanced at her press release, she'd resorted to flattery and emotional blackmail. Jayne needed to ensure that in the aftermath of his big-time operation, her case against Kelly and the cops wouldn't be forgotten.

And it wasn't only their relationship that made her uneasy. Jayne also had doubts about Mark's management of the case. He insisted there was a straight line between the problem and its solution. Paedophilia was a crime and those who perpetrated it were criminals. Solution: arrest those responsible and put them on trial. In this, he had both the letter of the law and common sense behind him. What made Jayne sceptical was that Mark clung to this belief despite his experience in Cambodia.

Didier would say such responses failed to take into account the complexity of the problem. 'They're missing the point,' he'd told her when they'd talked about the Sullivan case. 'For every paedophile put behind bars, there's at least one other to take his place. For every child rescued from a brothel, the ratio is much higher. In the poorer areas, there'll be five, maybe ten others. And those in power will keep turning a blind eye, because they benefit the most from maintaining the status quo. It's not about individuals. It's about the whole, rotten system.'

'So what's the solution?'

Didier shrugged. 'We must find a way to eradicate poverty.'

'Oh, great!' she had snorted. 'It's good to see you setting realistic goals.'

'But it's true, *mon amie*,' he said with a sad smile. 'The arrest of one Australian paedophile might keep people in your country happy, make them feel good because their government looks like it's doing something. But it won't change anything.'

'Surely it's better to do something rather than nothing?'

Didier looked so disappointed she regretted her words.

'Maybe you're right,' he said. 'Maybe I'm not realistic. But for me...well, it's like wearing glasses. I can take them off—' he removed his spectacles and waved them in the air

'—but I can never look at the world again without knowing what I see is out of focus.'

'Meaning what?'

'Meaning I cannot support doing something when I know it will not work.'

In that, along with everything else, Didier set his sights on the biggest possible picture. The path he plotted between the problem and its solution was as circuitous as Mark's was direct. Caught between the two, Jayne saw merit in both but was satisfied by neither.

This dissatisfaction was symptomatic of her life. She'd believed Didier would have been her ideal partner if only he was straight. Yet when he'd started making love to her—removing what she'd thought of as the only obstacle to her happiness—he called her bluff. What made a credible fantasy didn't work at all in reality. By contrast, Mark turned her on—her body couldn't get enough of him—but he failed to engage her in other ways. He didn't read, he baulked in the face of an argument and, although he'd deny it, he was homophobic.

Jayne stared at the neons of nearby buildings reflected in reverse on the water. She'd have to keep playing along, but her heart wasn't in it.

The sound of voices caused her to look back towards the bridge. A group of children clustered around a working streetlamp, using tiny lassoes on the end of bamboo poles to trap the insects that swarmed to the light. The same light illuminated an elderly woman, her silver headdress and indigo leggings identifying her as Akha. She paused, mid-shuffle, to spit a scarlet jet of betel nut juice into the brown river. It was a difference so subtle you could miss it: in Australia, you didn't see the very young and very old on the streets this late at night.

In search of other subtleties she might have overlooked, Jayne went back over events from last Friday. One thing for certain was that Didier had identified Kelly. Did this mean he'd had a change of heart—decided there was value to pursuing individual offenders after all? Or did it mean something else entirely?

She checked the time. It occurred to her to pass by the Kitten Club—on her way home, more or less—to reassure herself that it was business as usual. She stood up, brushing the grass from her jeans as she walked back to the road. Checking on the club gave her something to do. And anything was better than sitting around, mulling over questions that had no answers.

Among the strip of bars behind the Royal Princess Hotel, she guessed she'd find a tuk-tuk driver willing to take her to Loh Kroh. Within fifteen minutes she was back at her surveillance post in the abandoned police box. She set up her camera out of habit and, checking her watch, decided to give herself an hour—until midnight—to scope out the place.

She could hear music playing inside the club whenever the door opened, but there was none of the rowdiness of earlier in the week, nothing that might bring Kelly to the door.

After almost three-quarters of an hour, feeling tired, Jayne was about to pack it in when a motorbike pulled up, driven by a uniformed police officer. For a moment she thought it was Komet. But as the man dismounted, facing her as he adjusted his belt, she saw with alarm that it was Sergeant Pornsak.

Finger hovering over the camera, she released the shutter. In the stillness, the click was unusually loud. Pornsak looked up and, frowning, began walking across the road in her direction.

Jayne froze, aware that she was totally defenceless. She didn't even have the protection of her Christian charity worker disguise. She pressed herself into the darkest corner of the booth, kicking instinctively as something brushed her foot. When she saw what it was, she had to bite her hand to stop herself from crying out. Landing with a thud near the entrance to the sentry box was a large, ginger-coloured rat.

It quickly recovered from the fall and paused to sniff the air. Jayne broke into a cold sweat, aware from the sound of footsteps that Pornsak was getting closer. Both cop and rat seemed poised to pounce and she couldn't decide which would be worse. But then the creature pivoted in a half-circle and scuttled out into the street.

The footsteps came to a halt. Slowly turning her head so she could see through the slats, Jayne's gaze fell on Pornsak's gunbelt. He was so close that he'd see her if he peered over the edge of the police booth. Holding her breath, she heard him snigger and watched him turn and retrace his steps.

She exhaled and reached for her camera, trembling so much she released the shutter again. But Pornsak had already made it to the Kitten Club, and the noise was drowned out by music as he opened the door and disappeared inside.

Almost dizzy with relief, Jayne shoved the camera in her backpack. With only a cursory glance to make sure the coast was clear, she leapt out of her hiding place and sprinted several blocks before stopping to catch her breath. Waving down a passing tuk-tuk with a 100 baht note, she mumbled directions to her hotel, still shaking as the driver took off.

Police officer killed, body dumped

CHIANG MAI—The body of police officer Komet Plung-kham was found in a rubbish skip at the Ton Payorm Market in the early hours of this morning.

The body was discovered by Officer Komet's colleague at the City Police Bureau, Sergeant Pornsak Boonyavivat, during a routine inspection of the area.

Officer Komet's body show-ed signs of having been badly beaten. A preliminary report from the Scientific Crime Detection Division suggests the 25-year-old policeman died from a fractured skull.

Police sources say the Tohn Payorm Market has been under surveillance for some time as a meeting place for those involved in the illegal production and sale of amphetamines to students at nearby Chiang Mai University. While Officer Komet's role in the police operation is unclear, early reports suggest his death may have been drug-related.

Jayne might have missed the story altogether, had she not checked the forecast to see when the storm might break. The report was tucked away on page 14 of the midday edition of the *Chiang Mai Daily*. Both the placement and brevity of the article spoke volumes where its content did not: Ratratarn had found out Komet was working to under-mine him and, with Pornsak's help, got him out of the way.

Jayne had been right to worry about the young man's safety. But that was no consolation. Perhaps if she'd told

Mark, he might have been able to offer Komet some form of protection. But it was immaterial. Komet was dead. Ratratarn had sent a message, loud and clear. If you fuck with the Chiang Mai police, you die.

Jayne stared out from the cafe across the garden to the sky. The clouds hung low as if threatening to smother the city. She was seized by an urge to jump on the first available flight out of Chiang Mai, to get away from all that had happened in the past week. She rubbed the scar on her arm and remembered the blood and the pain, fearful that something like that could happen again. Or worse.

The thought gnawed at her that if Didier had let her in on his investigation into Doug Kelly, she might have been able to save him, shown him how to cover his tracks. Or would she have tried to talk him out of it, told him to walk away as she was now poised to do?

Jayne couldn't let him down. The sky above remained the same, grey and menacing. But it was as if a cloud had lifted in her mind. She saw with perfect clarity what she had to do and, despite the implications, she felt calm at the prospect.

She returned to her room and clipped the column on Komet's death from the paper. She then glued the article inside the back cover of her report and added her own note on the event. Satisfied all was in order, she wound off the film in her camera and slipped the canister into her purse.

On her way out, she left a message at Mark's hotel to say she'd call him later. After dropping off the film for processing, she made her way to the post office to make a long overdue call to Max in Bangkok.

'Jayne?' he gasped. 'Oh, thank God. Where are you? No, don't tell me—you're still in Chiang Mai.'

'Don't be cross with me, Max.' He sounded far away beneath the static. 'I'm OK. Really. I've teamed up with a cop from the AFP, teamed up in more ways than one, and—'

As soon as she spoke, she regretted it. She should have left her relationship with Mark out of it. Max, though, seemed to have missed the innuendo.

'What are you talking about? David had some crazy story about you taking a document of his by mistake and both of us tried to track you down at the Silver Star.'

'Oh, yeah,' she said lightly. 'I'd better go back and settle my account.'

'It's taken care of,' Max said impatiently. 'Why didn't you leave me a forwarding address?'

'Look, I haven't got much time,' she said. 'I'll explain it all later, I promise. What you need to know is that I've solved the case.'

'What?'

'Nou's murder, and Didier's,' she said. 'I've got proof, Max. A whole wad of evidence to show how the Chiang Mai cops conspired with an Australian, Doug Kelly, to kill Nou and frame Didier. They were trying to discredit him because he was going to expose a child sex racket that Kelly operates with police protection.'

There was a moment of what Jayne took to be stunned silence on the end of the line.

'God, I don't know whether to laugh or cry,' Max said finally. 'I mean, it sounds absurd, but that's precisely the sort of thing Didier would stumble into. So he's innocent!'

'I'm glad we see eye to eye on that at last.' She sensed him squirm.

'Of course I'm relieved,' he said quickly, 'but it's almost too much to take in. I mean, where does this leave you?'

'I'm going to send you a parcel with all the details,' she said. 'Mark—that's the AFP officer—is poised to arrest Kelly tomorrow morning. He wants to bring the cops down, too, by leaking the story to the press, including the stuff about Didier.'

'Going after the Thai police doesn't sound like the sort of thing the AFP would condone.'

Max's comment confirmed her suspicions.

'I don't know much about the official side of things,' she said. 'Let's just say I have my doubts. That's why I want to send you this parcel, Max. You're the only person I can trust.'

'You might think flattery will get you everywhere, my dear,' he said tersely, 'but I don't like the sound of this one bit. You promised to come back once you'd spoken with David.'

She muttered a profanity about his Canadian counter-part that made Max laugh in spite of himself.

'Look, I'm sending this parcel to you as one friend to another, but if anything should happen to me, I need you to promise you'll pass it on to Gavan at the *Bangkok Post*. Will you do that?'

Max made no effort to conceal his alarm. 'What do you mean, if anything should happen to you?' he cried. 'For heaven's sake, Jayne! You broke your promise to return to Bangkok and now you expect me to—'

'I'm sure there's nothing to worry about.' She kept her tone calm. 'But I need you to promise. Do it for Didier.'

Her words had the desired effect.

'Is there nothing I can say to dissuade you from doing whatever it is you're planning to do?' he said feebly.

'Frankly, no.'

'Jayne, I couldn't bear it if anything happened to you.'

'I'll be fine. Look, I'm running out of coins. I'm at the post office now and I'll send this parcel express. You should get it tomorrow morning. Please don't reveal the contents to anyone unless…I'll call again tomorrow at midday, OK?'

'Good luck, my dear,' he cried as the warning beeps sounded.

'Thanks—'

The line went dead.

Ratratarn frowned into the receiver and asked the secretary to repeat what she'd just said. He'd heard correctly. A farang woman by the name of Jayne Keeney was waiting to see him. Hanging up the phone, Ratratarn reached for his pistol and placed it on the desk behind a pile of papers. Then he sat back and waited for her to enter.

Her hair colour no longer matched their official description. She wasn't tall for a farang and apart from her green eyes, there was nothing striking in her appearance. She looked ordinary, able to pass for a tourist in the street. Ratratarn supposed that was how she'd succeeded in evading them.

She paused inside the doorway. Folding his arms, he waited for her to speak. After a lengthy silence, he cleared his throat.

'Please, Khun—Jayne, wasn't it?'

She bowed her head.

'Please close the door behind you and take a seat.' He gestured to a chair in front of his desk and forced a smile as she took her place. 'You wanted to see me?'

'*Kor thort ka,* Sir,' she said, 'I thought *you* wanted to see *me.*'

Ratratarn eyed her sharply. Her Thai was near perfect. She used the courteous form of address, referring to herself as 'little sister', and kept her eyes downcast as she spoke. He couldn't tell whether she was nervous or impertinent.

'It's true we wanted to interview you,' he said, 'a routine matter. We were gathering background information on the Canadian who murdered Khun Sanga Siamprakorn last weekend. But the investigation is now closed. I'm afraid your visit was unnecessary. I apologise for any inconvenience.'

'It's no inconvenience, Sir,' she said.

'Well, then…' Ratratarn waved his hand, giving her an excuse to leave. She remained in her seat.

'Is there something you wanted to tell me?' he said.

'Well, yes, Sir,' she said. 'I wanted to tell you a story.'

Ratratarn snorted, sat back and lit a Krung Thep.

'May I join you?' The woman held up a packet of her own.

He pushed his ashtray, half-filled with butts, across the table. Jayne lit a cigarette and, still averting her gaze, began to speak.

'It's a very strange story, Sir. It's about a man who had a dark secret. He entrusted only one friend with this secret, but then another person guessed it. The man was desperate to guard his secret, but didn't think he could do it alone. So he asked his friend to help him and together they had the person killed. The man thought all his problems would be over. But instead of giving him peace of mind, it only made things worse as now he had both a secret and a murder to hide.'

She paused to exhale smoke.

'Then the man had an idea. He could cover up the murder by having someone else killed and making it look as if they were responsible. He did this, again with the help of his friend, all the while thinking it would protect his secret. But, of course, it only made matters even worse as now he had a secret and two murders to hide.'

Ratratarn wondered where she was taking this.

'With each of these incidents,' she said, 'the man attracted more and more attention to himself, to the point where a young police officer got wise. You may not believe what happened next, Sir, but—crazy as it sounds—the man and his friend decided to kill the police officer to protect the original secret. Needless to say, he was worse off than ever, as now he had a secret and three murders to hide. A case of *chang tai thang tua bai bua put mai mit*, wouldn't you say?'

Ratratarn frowned. 'A case of covering a dead elephant with a lotus leaf?'

'Well, of course,' Jayne said, 'humans are a lot easier to hide than elephants—at least, until the bodies start piling up.'

She sat back in her chair and, for the first time since she'd entered the office, her gaze met Ratratarn's own through their cigarette smoke.

'So, how does your little story end?' he said.

'That depends, Sir. There are a number of possible endings. See if you like this one. After the death of the policeman, the man's friend decides he can't stomach any more killings. Realising the man's secret was never worthy of his protection in the first place, the friend turns on the man, exposes his crimes and is hailed as a hero throughout the land.' She extinguished her cigarette. 'What do you think of that ending, Sir?'

'Hmm,' he said, deciding to humour her. 'I don't think that's a very realistic ending, do you? I mean, wouldn't it be in the friend's interests to continue protecting the man by eradicating all who threatened him?'

'I guess that depends on who's serving whom,' she said thoughtfully. 'If the man with the secret is the one calling the shots, then the friend will continue to protect him. But what if the friend's in charge?'

Ratratarn raised an eyebrow. 'Then it would be up to the friend to take control of the situation,' he said.

'One might question why he hasn't done so already,' she said.

Ratratarn spoke as if thinking aloud. 'Business relationships are complex,' he said. 'Money made by unsavoury means can be purified when put to the right uses. The reverse is also true: money provided for good purposes can do terrible harm. It's all a question of order and distribution.'

'That's a very interesting theory, Lieutenant Colonel.' She sounded genuine. 'Tell me, what can you do with blood money to make it clean?'

'There are village investment schemes—' He stopped, aware of her eyes on him again. Though there was no insolence in her voice, it was clear in the look on her face.

'Enough!' he said, angrily butting out his cigarette. He moved the papers on his desk aside so the pistol was in view, the barrel pointing at her. 'No more stories, Khun Jayne, no more theories. Just tell me everything you know.'

The gun terrified her. The blood seemed to drain from her face and for a moment, she looked as if she might cry. Then the ghost of a smile played across her lips.

'Exactly what do you have in mind, Lieutenant Colonel?' she said. 'Another farang suspect accidentally shot dead while to trying to avoid arrest?' Her voice trembled, but she was no longer looking at the gun. She was looking at him.

'You'd better make sure you have a second empty bullet casing to leave at the scene,' she added, 'just like you did for Didier.'

Ratratarn narrowed his eyes and looked from Jayne Keeney to the pistol and back again. 'Actually, I have plenty of options,' he said. 'You know, it's not uncommon for an ignorant farang to wander into the wrong part of town and end up with a bullet in the head.'

He clucked his teeth. 'Sad as I am to admit it, there are some bad elements in this place and attacks on foreigners can be horrific. Face blown away, all personal effects stolen. Makes it difficult, if not impossible, to make a positive ID on the victim. Terrible tragedy that. Family back home might never know.'

She swallowed hard, her face paler than ever. 'Be a shame to mess up your office,' she said, gesturing towards the gun.

Ratratarn admired her attempt at bravado, but the tremor in her voice gave her away.

'Oh, this!' he said, picking up the pistol and waving it from side to side. 'This has multiple uses, you know. Quick blow to the back of the head and—oh dear!—looks like my visitor has passed out. Better hand her over to Sergeant Pornsak to drive her home. Should the corpse of a farang woman turn up the following day, Sergeant Pornsak will be adamant it couldn't be the same woman, since he saw to it personally that she got to her hotel safely.'

'Ah, y-yes, Lieutenant Colonel,' she said quickly, her voice shaking. 'I meant to talk with you about Sergeant Pornsak. I presume he was acting on your orders when he went to the Kitten Club on his own last night.'

Ratratarn did a double take. The last time he'd seen Pornsak was at the canal when he'd left him to get rid of Komet's body. Pornsak knew better than to meet with Kelly alone. She had to be bluffing.

'Look, I'm getting tired of all these…these allegations,' he said. 'Tell me what you know.'

She took a deep breath. 'Think of everything you hope I don't know,' she said, 'and believe me, I know it.'

'No fucking way—'

'Kelly's role in Sanga's death, your role in Didier's, every piece of manufactured evidence. I know it all—apart from the details of Officer Komet's death,' she corrected herself. 'But I assume you got Pornsak to take care of that. He had a certain expression on his face when I saw him last night—like a hunter fresh from a kill. Look, I'll show you.'

She held her hands palms outward and gestured towards her bag. Ratratarn tightened his grip on the gun, but nodded for her to continue.

'You see what I mean?' she said, holding out the photograph.

Ratratarn stared at a picture of Pornsak poised to enter the Kitten Club, date and time recorded in one corner. The sergeant did have a look on his face that seemed more smug than usual.

'I must admit,' she said, placing the photograph on the desk to face him, 'I thought it was odd. I mean, the pay-off with Kelly isn't due till tonight, right?'

'Damn that motherfucker Komet!'

'Sir, if I might make a suggestion,' she said, the polite tone returning to her voice. 'There's a way of solving all our problems—a solution that's in our mutual interests and doesn't require...ah, violence.'

'I'm listening.'

'Do you need that,' she gestured at the weapon, 'to improve your hearing?'

'No,' Ratratarn replied with a sneer, 'but it often improves the ability of the person I'm interviewing to articulate themselves.'

He sat back in his chair, the gun still pointed at Jayne.

'Here's the idea,' she said. 'You hold a press conference to announce new findings into last weekend's deaths: namely, that it was Doug Kelly and not Didier de Montpasse who was responsible for the murder of Sanga Siamprakorn. You'll need to issue a statement fully exonerating Didier and expressing the heartfelt regrets of the Chiang Mai police over his death, etcetera, etcetera.'

'This is a joke, right!' Ratratarn said.

'On the contrary, Sir. I'm making a significant concession in not demanding you retract the charge that Didier was resisting arrest when he was shot, since we know that wasn't the case.'

Ratratarn said nothing. In a strange way, he found the farang woman's attempt to cut a deal with him amusing.

'Secondly,' she continued, 'regarding Officer Komet, you say something to the effect that he was tragically killed in the line of duty, and his expectant widow will be fully provided for by the police pension fund.'

The woman wasn't just naive, Ratratarn thought, she was delusional.

'And tell me, Khun Jayne,' he said with exaggerated interest, 'what compelling grounds do the Chiang Mai police have for complying with these demands of yours? What could you possibly offer in exchange for such...such extraordinary requests?'

'The guarantee of my silence.'

'What?' he snorted. 'That's it?'

She shrugged.

'I'm afraid you overestimate your importance.' The game was no longer amusing him. He stood up and moved beside her, allowing the gun barrel to rest against her temple. 'I have myriad ways to guarantee your silence.'

He saw her swallow hard, sweat breaking out on her forehead.

'Ah, I-I have no doubt about that, Sir,' she said, the fear returning to her voice. 'I underestimate neither your resourcefulness n-nor your intelligence, which is why I've sent all the information I have to a friend in Bangkok. He's been instructed to release the information to the press if something happens to me.'

'You're bluffing,' he growled.

'I don't want to be a hero,' she cried. 'Not like Didier and Komet. I'm not that courageous. So I created my own life insurance policy.'

Ratratarn knew she was telling the truth, but still wasn't willing to believe she posed any real threat.

'Let's say something does happen to you,' he said, 'and the story goes to press. What makes you think the Chiang Mai police can't handle it with an official denial?'

'I've got witnesses admitting they were forced into signing statements.'

'Their word against ours.'

'I can place Khun Sanga with Kelly around the time he was killed.'

'Circumstantial,' Ratratarn said.

'And, of course, I have Officer Komet's sworn statement disclosing all the facts of the case as fraudulent.'

Ratratarn hesitated, but only for a moment. 'Komet was corrupt. His statement is a fabrication.'

Jayne bit her lip. 'Well, I'd hazard a guess my report would at least prompt the Canadian Embassy to re-open its investigation into the death of Khun Didier.'

'I can take care of those cocksuckers!'

Ratratarn saw her swallow again and compose herself.

'Then it would seem I was mistaken,' she said with a forced nonchalance. 'I-I thought I had sufficient grounds to make a deal. But I can see now, Sir, I'm no threat to you whatsoever.'

He snorted.

'In which case,' she said, 'I assume that makes me free to go.'

Ratratarn frowned. By that logic, she had him cornered. But perhaps that was the solution: to appear so indifferent—so completely unthreatened by her—that he let her go. He restored his pistol to its holster.

'It seems you've wasted your time, Jayne Keeney,' he said, resuming his seat.

'Yes.' The colour slowly returned to her cheeks. She picked up her bag but stayed seated, bag perched on her lap.

'There's one other thing, Sir. You'd know yourself the Thai government recently introduced new anti-prostitution laws with harsh penalties for those dealing in children. I'm curious why you don't move in and arrest Kelly. I mean, a high-profile raid at a time like this—it would do wonders for the image of the Chiang Mai police.'

'Why should I give a shit about those sons of bitches in Bangkok?' he snorted.

'No reason, Sir,' she shrugged. 'It's just, well, I've been trying to figure out why a sovereign government would allow foreign law enforcement agents to conduct an operation within its territory at the expense of its own police force.'

Ratratarn narrowed his eyes. 'What the hell are you talking about?'

'I've been trying to imagine the reverse-case scenario,' she continued as if he hadn't spoken. 'To imagine the

Australian government allowing Thai agents to override the jurisdiction of local police in a rural area of my own country. But I can't see it happening. The local police wouldn't stand for it. They'd argue—quite rightly—that they were perfectly capable of managing matters. I also suspect they'd go out of their way to expose such arrogance for what it is by mounting their own, far superior operation.'

Ratratarn stared at her, his mind ticking over with the implications of what she was saying. If the Australians had plans to move against Kelly without involving the Chiang Mai police—he and his men would look like idiots. The press would have a field day, and the powers that be in Bangkok would use it as yet another excuse to undermine the local authorities.

'I can tell you everything you need to know,' she added quietly.

'And why would you do that?'

She met his gaze squarely, all pretence of politeness gone. 'Let's talk again about that deal, shall we?'

Mark readjusted the pens in his pocket until he was confident the hidden camera would stay in place, checking the effect in the mirror. It was amazing, the technology these days. The camera was the size of a cigarette packet, the lens designed to look like an ordinary shirt button. He could operate it by remote control without taking his hand out of his trouser pocket.

'The name's Bond,' he said to his reflection. 'James Bond.'

He smoothed down his hair and straightened his shoulders. Then he laughed, mussed up his hair, extinguished the light and returned to the main room. He unlocked his guncase, ready to clean and load his weapon, when the phone rang.

'Did you get my message this morning?' Simone said, her voice shaky.

'Yeah. Are you OK?'

'Ah, yeah, I felt a bit sick earlier…must have been something I ate. But I'm fine now.'

'Are you sure? I mean, maybe you shouldn't come tonight—'

Mark hesitated, conscious of sounding too eager. He felt more uneasy than ever about letting Simone be part of this.

'I'll be there,' she said firmly.

'I could lose my job over this.'

There was a moment's silence.

'I'd never let that happen, my love.'

In spite of his misgivings, Mark flushed with pleasure. It was the first time she'd spoken to him with such tenderness.

'OK, OK,' he sighed. 'We'll stick with Plan A.'

She seemed satisfied, though something in her voice still didn't sound right. 'Are you sure you're OK?' he said.

'Absolutely!' she said with sudden vehemence. 'We'll make our way there separately. What time are you planning to go inside the club?'

'I need to get there before the cops. That means going in around eleven forty-five.'

'So, will you meet me in the surveillance booth just before eleven-thirty?'

'I wasn't planning to—'

'Please, Mark. You've made it clear that I have to get

out of there as soon as the cops are in the club. But I'd really like to see you before…before it all happens.'

He thought about it for a moment. 'Look, I'll do my best to drop by the booth at half past eleven. Otherwise I'll call you from Bangkok. The embassy's organised a six o'clock charter flight for me to bring Kelly in. After that, we could…that is, I was hoping we could meet up again in Bangkok.'

'Of course,' she said softly. 'I'll just cross my fingers that I'll be seeing you sooner rather than later.'

Despite the affection in her voice, Mark frowned as he hung up the phone. Simone sounded anxious, almost frightened. Even the first time they'd met, when he'd sprung her on surveillance, she hadn't been afraid. Startled perhaps, but not frightened.

Mark resumed cleaning his gun, and prayed he wasn't making the biggest mistake of his career. He resolved to meet her in the booth before he went inside the club—to reassure himself as much as her that everything was going to be all right.

Jayne placed her camera on the shelf in the abandoned police booth, checked the view and adjusted the focus. She had to stay busy, keep her emotions at bay. She reached for her bottle and drank a mouthful of water. She'd come this far—she wasn't going to panic now.

She poured some of the bottled water into her hand and doused her face. She recalled her meeting with Ratratarn and imagined she could still feel the spot where he'd pressed his gun. She splashed more water on her face and before she could stop, the bottle was empty and the front of her blouse soaked through. She stared at the empty plastic container in her hand, before flinging it into a corner of the booth.

'Get a grip, Keeney!' she said aloud.

She pulled at the front of her blouse. The dampness could probably pass as sweat. Then again, it was only just after eleven. With any luck her shirt would be dry by the time Mark arrived.

At the thought of Mark, Jayne groaned. She was used to being on the other side of the equation, the wronged party, not the one that did wrong. While she'd only exposed his operation as a last resort to bring Ratratarn around, she had betrayed Mark's trust. And he'd never forgive her if he found out.

Jayne told herself that cutting a deal with Ratratarn was the only way any justice would be done. And if that meant sacrificing their relationship, then it was a small price to pay. But she knew she was kidding herself. She'd never even trusted Mark enough to tell him her real name.

She wiped her face with her damp blouse and checked her watch again. The following half-hour was critical. She had to get Mark into the booth and keep him there until Ratratarn and his men made their move—a margin of fifteen minutes at most. In her negotiations with Ratratarn, it was the least controversial point.

'*Nae jai*, Khun Jayne,' the lieutenant colonel had said with his reptilian smile. 'I agree. It would be best if the Australian police agent wasn't inside the premises when it is raided. It might cause a conflict—' he paused for effect '—a conflict of interests, I mean. And no one wants any added complications.'

Mark glanced at the deserted street, before ducking into the booth where Simone was waiting, crouched by her camera.

'Hey!' he said in a low voice. 'How are you—?'

Before he knew what was happening, she grabbed him by the shoulders and pulled him down towards her. Caught off-balance, he fell onto his knees, his mouth colliding with hers as she tried to kiss him.

'Jesus, Simone!' he hissed, pulling back and squatting on his haunches. 'You've got a bloody lousy sense of timing.'

'Sorry, Officer,' she said with a grin.

She reached out a hand but Mark ignored it, swivelling out of reach to brush the dirt from his pants. 'Honestly,' he muttered, 'what the hell were you thinking?'

'I'm sorry,' she said again. 'I'm nervous. It feels as if... as if there's something strange going on tonight.'

'What?' He raised his head sharply. 'What do you mean? Have you seen anything?'

'Not exactly.' She looked through the lens of her camera. 'It's more of a gut feeling...' She turned back to him. 'I don't know, maybe it's this weather. If the storm doesn't break soon, I'm going to suffocate in this humidity.'

'Yeah, well, we could sit and chat for hours about the weather,' he said impatiently, 'but we've got work to do.'

He started to rise to his feet, but Simone held up her hand.

'What is it?' he whispered.

'Hang on...' She looked through the camera again.

'I can't see anything,' he said, peering through a gap in the slats.

'I thought I heard something, but...no, it's OK. What were you saying?'

Mark shook his head. 'I don't remember. Look, I have to get going. Are you all set?'

'Yeah.' She placed her hand over the camera. 'Where's your equipment?'

He patted his shirt pocket. 'The lens is in the button.'

'You're kidding?' she grinned. 'That's amazing, you must feel like James Bond.'

Mark managed a smile.

'It didn't get dislodged, did it?' she added. 'I mean, when I knocked you...'

She waved vaguely and Mark found himself growing

impatient again. Frowning, he squatted with his back to the wall to check the camera was still in place, becoming aware of the sound of vehicles in the street.

'What time is it?'

He looked up. Though she directed the question at him, Simone's attention was fixed on her camera.

'Eleven-forty,' he said, glancing at his watch again. 'Why?'

He saw her swallow, her face pale. 'I think they're early,' she whispered.

'Son of a bitch!'

Mark pivoted, peering through a gap in the woodwork to see two police cars pull up outside the Kitten Club.

'Shit!' He leapt up. 'I've gotta get in there before they—'

With a strength that took him by surprise, Simone grabbed him by the wrist and jerked him back down again.

'I don't think they're here for the pay-off,' she hissed.

'What are you talking about?'

'Look at them, Mark. There's a whole squadron arriving!'

Police vehicles were flooding into the street in force, motorcycles and several vans in addition to the two squad cars, blocking off either side of the Kitten Club. There must have been around forty uniformed cops. Mark watched as they took up positions, some around the back of the building, others forming a barricade between the entrance and the street.

'I don't believe it!' he groaned. 'They're going to raid the place.'

As he spoke, a man he recognised as the ringleader of the protection racket, Lieutenant Colonel Ratratarn, got out of one of the squad cars. Beside him was one of the other guys Simone had identified—the sergeant, Pornsak—his gun already drawn. Under Ratratarn's orders, a group of about ten officers armed with rifles fell into line behind them.

Still crouched on the ground, Mark slowly drew his own weapon from the holster above his ankle.

'Put that thing away!'

The fury in Simone's voice stopped him in his tracks.

'But,' he said, 'I've gotta go and—'

'And do what?' she hissed. 'Look at the firepower out there. You go out waving a pistol in the air and—'

She stopped abruptly as two police officers scuttled across the road and crouched down within metres of where they were hiding, their rifles pointed at the club's entrance. Another two flanked the front door. Simone was right: the situation was potentially explosive.

'But I've gotta do something,' Mark whispered.

His voice was drowned out by a cracking sound as Pornsak kicked in the door of the club. With Ratratarn at the helm, the troops surged forward and entered the place. A burst of music came from inside the club, before screaming and shattering glass drowned it out.

Seconds later, a panic-stricken group of patrons poured outside, only to be pounced on by the cops waiting for them. Most customers were middle-aged farangs— Australians, Germans, Dutch, Americans judging from their accents—though there was also a clutch of embarrassed-looking Japanese, one of whom dropped to his knees and had to be lifted into a waiting van by two police officers. A fit-looking man with white-blond hair made the mistake of resisting the officer who approached him, before the thrust of a rifle butt in the stomach brought him to heel. A punter who tried to escape by tumbling headfirst out of a side window found a gun barrel in his face.

As the men were seized, they were steered over to the police vans and bundled inside. Several were crying. Others frantically pulled their shirts over their heads to hide their faces. One American loudly protested his innocence and demanded to speak to his lawyer.

Some of the cops who'd entered the club with Ratratarn re-emerged with more patrons in tow—those too far from the door or too drunk to flee when they'd burst in. One was bleeding from a cut above the eye, another clutched at his bloodied nose, while a third had to be dragged to the van between two officers. The Thai man who'd been the auctioneer four nights earlier was among those arrested, as was Kelly's bouncer, who allowed himself to be led away by a skinny officer whose neck he could have crushed with one hand.

Mark couldn't bear to watch any longer. Returning his gun to its holster, he slumped against the wall of the booth with his head in his hands. After several minutes, he heard the vehicles moving and the sound of a siren. He looked up to see Simone still staring at the spectacle through her camera lens.

'What's happening now?' he said dully.

'One of the vans is full. It's pulling out. Looks as if

they're arresting everyone in the place, though I haven't seen Kelly yet.' She paused. 'God, I can't believe how quickly these guys get around.'

'What's that?'

'The media. They're arriving in droves. There's a Channel 4 van pulling up and a couple of others—'

A volley of gunshots rang out from inside the club.

Mark sprang up, instinctively placing an arm around Simone's shoulders. Trembling beneath his touch, she kept her gaze through the camera. He looked again through a crack in the wall. Everyone in the street—the cops, their captives, the press—seemed to hold a collective breath. Mark felt for his gun with his free hand as Ratratarn marched out of the club.

The lieutenant colonel made a beeline for one of the squad cars, reached through the window and grabbed the radio handset. In the eerie silence that descended on the scene, Mark could hear him barking orders.

'Can you understand what he's saying?' he whispered.

'He's calling for an ambulance,' Simone said.

Nervous chatter started up in the crowd and the journalists took it as their cue to get to work. A small clique surrounded Ratratarn and began firing questions at him, while the cameramen and photographers set about getting visuals. At first Ratratarn seemed to be fending off the journalists' inquiries. But when the ambulance arrived, he signalled for them to wait by the entrance while he accompanied two paramedics inside the club.

After a minute or so, Ratratarn reappeared in the doorway, ushering out a police officer who was carrying a young girl. Mark recognised her as the one whose virginity had been auctioned off. The officer cradled the girl in his arms like a baby, and Mark suspected this whole episode was staged for the press. Indeed, no sooner was the first officer's photo taken in a barrage of flashing cameras than the second appeared, his arms around the shoulders of another child. Then six other young girls were herded out, one dressed as a baby bride. Pale and frightened, they shuffled through the crowd, clutching at each other and shielding their eyes from the glare of the cameras. The two police officers—both handsome men, no doubt hand-picked by Ratratarn for the occasion—slowed and smiled benevolently for the photographers before steering their pathetic little wards into the waiting squad cars.

A second procession followed, led by Ratratarn. A combination of police and ambulance officers carried two stretchers between them, a couple more cops bringing up the rear. The photographers switched their attention to the bodies on the stretchers, covered from head to toe in blankets. In what seemed to Mark like another orchestrated detail, the left arm of one corpse had been allowed to slip from under the covers, revealing the chocolate-brown shirt of a police uniform.

Standing between the two stretchers, illuminated by the glare of television lights and camera flashes, Ratratarn gave a brief statement in Thai, before a wave of his hand sent the press scampering back to their vehicles.

As the bodies were loaded into the ambulance, the remaining police van drove away with its siren on, escorted by a cavalcade of motorcycle cops. Ratratarn's squad car pulled out in the wake of the ambulance; the clamour of sirens resonated through the streets.

Two police officers posted as sentries set about cordoning off the entrance to the club with orange plastic tape, watched by a small crowd of onlookers, mostly Kitten Club staff who hadn't been arrested. A jacket lay in a heap in the middle of the street, dropped by one of the punters, and the air was hazy with churned-up dust.

Mark was still staring at the scene when he felt Simone standing beside him.

'Kelly's dead,' she said flatly.

'The second body on the stretcher?'

She nodded. 'I heard Ratratarn tell journalists that Kelly pulled out a gun and shot one of their officers. They returned fire and he was killed.'

'Oh, shit!' Mark said. 'Do you know—?'

But Simone rushed out of the booth into the street. He jammed his pistol back into its holster and followed to find her retching into the gutter.

Kelly's death was a slap in the face so violent, it made Jayne throw up. While Mark went off to find a tuk-tuk, she forced herself to go back over the details of her conversation with Ratratarn.

'All your conditions will be met,' the lieutenant colonel had said. 'I give you my word. Take it or leave it.'

She'd taken it, and now another two men were dead. One corpse was Kelly and she suspected the other was Sergeant Pornsak. She'd seen Pornsak kick in the door and enter the Kitten Club when the raid began, but she hadn't seen him come out.

Ratratarn told journalists at the scene that Kelly's death was accidental. It was clear to Jayne, though, that he'd never intended to arrest Kelly at all. Kelly had too much dirt on him and Ratratarn would never have risked putting him on trial. The raid on the club had been little more than a pretext for getting Kelly out of the way. That it meant having to account for the deaths of two foreigners—Didier and Doug Kelly—at police hands in the space of a week was a measure of Ratratarn's confidence.

As for Sergeant Pornsak, something told Jayne that his death, too, was part of Ratratarn's plan. The lieutenant colonel didn't flinch at sacrificing his own sidekick. It was the thought of how narrowly she'd escaped the same fate that overwhelmed her.

By the time she cleaned herself up, Mark had returned with a tuk-tuk. He directed the driver to take them to the Riverside, squeezing her hand reassuringly as they drove through the streets. The first few fat drops of rain began to fall as they pulled up. A brilliant flash of lightning illuminated the sky and within seconds, the trickle turned into a downpour. It was only a short dash across the road to the shelter of the bar, but they were soaked by the time they reached it.

Mark found them a table by the edge of the balcony, which was under cover but only just; the rain bounced off the railings onto their feet. The house band, cranking up the volume to compete with the storm, was performing 'We Are the Champions'. Over Mark's shoulder, Jayne could see the lead singer—a bare-chested Thai man with a shaved head and handlebar moustache—belting his heart out in homage to the late Freddie Mercury. Jayne liked the band, but the song was so much at odds with how she knew Mark must be feeling, she silently begged them to stop.

'We are the dickheads, more likely,' Mark said, tilting his head towards the band. 'Are you up for a drink?'

'God, yes! Whisky.'

'Make mine a double.'

When their order arrived, Mark raised his glass. 'Here's to yet another resounding victory for the forces of good over the forces of evil,' he said. 'Not.'

He gulped the contents and signalled the waiter to bring another. 'I'm warning you, Simone,' he said, 'I intend to get plastered tonight. Can you handle that?'

In lieu of a reply, Jayne drained her own glass. The

whisky felt like fire in her empty stomach and she held her breath until the blaze subsided.

'Will you be OK for a minute?' Mark took a mobile phone from his pocket. 'I have to make a call.'

Jayne nodded and watched as he headed for the relative quiet of the bar's main entrance. The Thai Freddie Mercury was singing 'Can anybody find me somebody to love?' The lyrics made Jayne maudlin. She lit a cigarette.

Lightning flashed like a strobe, followed by thunder-claps that reminded Jayne of the shots fired at the Kitten Club. Suddenly feeling cold, she shook the droplets from her hair and rummaged through her backpack for a jacket.

Condensation on the whisky refills had formed pud-dles on the table by the time Mark reappeared.

'You know you smoke too much,' he said, nodding at her cigarette as he sat down. He took his glass in hand. 'Another toast,' he said. 'This one's to the Chiang Mai police.' He drank half the contents in one gulp. 'I've gotta hand it to those bastards. They knew just when to strike. Totally fucked up my plans.'

'So what will you do now?' Jayne said, moving the ash-tray to the corner of the table furthest from Mark.

'Oh, I'll be flying out tomorrow morning a little later than planned, and I'll be travelling solo since Kelly can't make it.' He laughed cynically and finished his drink. 'I still can't believe it,' he said, shaking his head. 'I mean, the timing was un-fucking-believable. You'd think they knew exactly what I was planning down to the last minute.'

Jayne stared into her glass.

'And now Kelly's dead,' Mark said, 'leaving no one to

testify to the cops' role in all of this. Without the photo of the pay-off, we don't have a leg to stand on. Everything we've got is circumstantial. Or else it comes down to our word against theirs. And after tonight's performance, I'd have to say the smart money'd be on the cops, wouldn't you?' He waved at a waiter and held up his glass, then leaned across the table and took Jayne's free hand. 'I'm really sorry, Simone,' he said softly. 'About your friend, I mean.'

'I'm sorry, too,' she said, 'for both our sakes. I know how hard you worked on this, Mark.' She squeezed his hand. 'But maybe it's better this way.'

She felt his muscles tense beneath her touch.

'What do you mean?'

'Well, you said yourself the Thai government's getting tougher on child prostitution. And this raid proves they're serious about it.'

Mark snatched his hands away. 'What? We both know Ratratarn doesn't give a shit about child prostitution. He's corrupt!'

Jayne glanced around the room. 'Even so,' she said in a low voice, 'it's ultimately up to the Thais to deal with that. I mean, it *is* their country.'

'What are you saying? That we should all go home and let them sort it out for themselves? Jesus, Simone! That flies in the face of everything I've worked for—not to mention the whole philosophy underlying the Australian laws.'

The arrival of the waiter with another round of drinks gave Jayne a moment to choose her words.

'Of course there's value in your work,' she said carefully. 'The problem is, you can launch a police operation in this part of the world on perfectly reasonable grounds, only to find that things are far more complicated than they seem—'

'I can't see what's so fucking complicated!' Mark interrupted her. 'Corrupt cops shouldn't be allowed to get away with murder.'

'Oh, what?' she said, losing her patience. 'And that doesn't happen in Australia? For Chrissake, Mark, you worked in Brisbane! What about all the scandals under the Bjelke-Petersen government?'

'It's not the same thing!' he said.

'On the contrary, there's a lot in common between what happened in Brisbane in the eighties and what's happening in Chiang Mai today. If I remember rightly, the Queensland police were found to be instrumental in running illegal prostitution rackets there, too.'

Mark took a swig from his third whisky. 'So there's police corruption in Australia as well as Thailand. So what? That doesn't make any of it right.'

'No,' Jayne said, 'it doesn't. The point is, you shouldn't beat yourself up over what happened here.'

He scoffed.

'No, really,' she said. 'Truth is, you probably had about as much chance of bringing down Ratratarn as a Thai cop would've had going up against...oh, what was the Queensland police commissioner's name?'

'Terry Lewis?'

'Yeah, Terry Lewis.'

Mark narrowed his eyes. 'You didn't seem to feel that way before.'

'What do you mean?'

'I mean that a few nights ago, you were all for trying to bring down Ratratarn and the other cops. Why the sudden change of heart?'

'I guess I didn't realise what we were up against. Or maybe I just didn't want to admit it.' She forced a smile. 'I mean, who'd have predicted Ratratarn would bite off the hand that feeds him?'

She realised, too late, that it was a mistake to try to make light of it.

'Jesus, Simone! We're talking about the arsehole who killed your friend. Don't you care about that any more?'

'Of course I care!' She felt her face redden.

'Then how the fuck can you joke about it?' Mark banged his empty glass on the table. 'In fact, how come you're so bloody calm about the whole thing? It's as if what happened tonight didn't really come as a surprise to you at all.'

It took all the nerve Jayne had to look him in the eye. 'What are you implying?'

Mark held her gaze and Jayne was sure he could see right through her. The whisky in her stomach turned to acid and she felt a trickle of sweat run down her back. She couldn't even trust herself to butt out her cigarette, sure her trembling hands would give her away.

But in the next moment, Mark appeared to deflate. 'I'm sorry,' he said, slumping back into his chair. 'I didn't mean anything by it. It's just that I'm…I'm so pissed off…and tired. I'm so tired…'

'It's OK,' she said, stubbing out her cigarette and reaching for his hands.

He looked up with such a sad smile that Jayne could have kicked herself. Mark didn't need her to rationalise why the operation didn't work. He only wanted her reassurance that everything was going to be all right—even if they both knew it wasn't.

'Why don't you finish this,' she said gently, pushing her third, untouched whisky towards him, 'and we'll get out of here.'

'Thanks,' he said. 'Look, I really am sorry—'

'Shh,' she stopped him. 'Don't worry about it.'

'I just wish…' His voice trailed off as he brushed away a tear of frustration with the back of his hand. 'I just wanna go home.'

Mark knew he'd be sent back to Canberra. He'd probably be given a desk job and forced to suffer the indignity of debriefing with a counsellor. While he might have fallen just short of career suicide, he was assured of social death. It was a measure of how strongly he felt about Simone that he could face the prospect at all. If nothing else came of his disastrous time in Chiang Mai, at least he had her.

Mark slowly woke and winced at the memory of the night before. Not because he regretted the sex—far from it. But he regretted not having made more of an effort to disguise how much he'd needed it, how much he needed her. Despite her apparent calm, Mark knew Simone had ghosts she needed to lay to rest. She didn't need the added burden of nursing his as well.

He opened his eyes and became aware of two things in the same moment: his head hurt and Simone wasn't in the bed beside him. He rubbed his forehead and glanced towards the bathroom. The door was open, but the light was off and there was no noise coming from inside. With a frown, he pulled back the sheet and staggered to use the toilet.

He then pulled on a pair of boxer shorts, phoned reception and asked if there were any messages. Drawing a blank, he called the hotel restaurant, waiting five minutes before being told Simone Whitfield was not having breakfast.

His scowl deepening, Mark returned to the bathroom in search of something for his headache. It was only then he saw the envelope propped up against his shaving kit. He picked it up and tore it open. The note inside was written on a single page of hotel stationery.

> *Dear Mark,*
> *There is no easy way of saying this, so I'll get to the point.*
>
> *Your instincts were correct: the Chiang Mai police knew about your move against Kelly, which is why the Kitten Club was raided when it was. They knew because I told them.*
>
> *I did it as a last resort, believing it was the only way that any sort of justice would be done. You have to believe me when I say it was business, not personal.*
>
> *I know you won't be able to forgive me. But I'm telling you this because what happened here in Chiang Mai was not your fault.*
>
> *I wish that things could have worked out differently for us.*

The note slipped from his grasp as Mark leaned on the bathroom cabinet, his head spinning.

Fuck finding it unforgivable! What Simone had done was criminal. No matter how much she tried to dress it up, she hadn't just betrayed him, she'd undermined an Australian Federal Police operation. If she wanted it to be 'business, not personal', then he'd give it to her from both barrels. At the very least, he'd have to bring her in for obstruction of justice, if not goddamn treason.

With a roar of indignation, Mark yanked at the drawer of the bathroom cabinet and sent it crashing to the floor, its contents spilling onto the tiles. He angrily sifted through them, more in need of painkillers than ever, when he caught sight of the note again. It had fallen face down, revealing a postscript on the reverse side.

P.S. Simone Whitfield was an alias. I'm sorry, Mark.

'Oh, the fucking cunt!'

He screwed the piece of paper into a ball, threw it on the floor. There was no way he could go after her now—not without being made to look like a complete arsehole. He kicked the drawer into pieces.

'Shit!' He said at last and slumped down on the floor. His right hand landed on a strip of sought-after painkillers. He swallowed two of them dry and sat with his head in his hands, waiting for them to kick in.

Through the cracks in his fingers, he saw her note at his feet and wondered why she'd bothered to leave it at all. She could have just slipped away. It would have been cowardly, but that stuff happened all the time. If he'd woken up and found her gone without an explanation, he would have blamed himself for being too full-on and scaring her off.

He picked up the piece of paper and smoothed it out on the tiles.

> *…what happened here in Chiang Mai was not your fault.*

She'd saved him on that score, too.

> *I wish that things could have worked out differently for us.*

And he never even knew her name.

Ratratarn stood to one side of the lectern and scanned the conference room, estimating the crowd at around forty. Local and national television and print media were well represented and, to his satisfaction, there were also a few foreign correspondents. His gaze wandered over the faces until he saw Jayne Keeney standing towards the back of the room. She'd dressed for the occasion—camera around her neck and notepad in hand—but they both knew her presence had nothing to do with any journalistic aspirations. He nodded to her in such a way the press liaison officer could easily mistake it for his cue.

'Ladies and gentlemen,' Officer Chonsawat began, 'may I have your attention, please. Police Lieutenant Colonel Ratratarn Rattakul, commanding officer in charge of last night's operation, will now read a statement. He will then take questions, but please keep them brief as we have limited time.'

He bowed and stepped aside. Ratratarn placed his notes on the stand and cleared his throat.

'As you are aware, the Chiang Mai Police City Bureau raided an establishment in Loh Kroh late last night, known as the Kitten Club, managed by an Australian, Douglas Kelly.'

He paused to allow Chonsawat to read the same statement in English.

'The raid was a turning point in an operation carefully planned by Chiang Mai police over several months, which included intensive surveillance and undercover activities. We believed Khun Doug Kelly organised and profited from the sale of children for sexual purposes, and the raid was timed to coincide with the introduction of strict new anti-prostitution laws.'

Ratratarn paused again, savouring the moment.

'Code-named Operation Jasmine, the raid sends out the strongest message to those who seek to engage in and profit from the heinous crime of child sexual exploitation. Such crimes will not be tolerated!'

He pounded his fist on the lectern.

'Neither the police nor the citizenry of Chiang Mai will rest until those who exploit young children are made to pay for their crimes—until the world understands such criminal elements are not welcome in Chiang Mai.'

A murmur of what he took to be admiration went through the crowd.

'The raid was highly successful,' he continued. 'Eight children were rescued and thirty-six farang offenders were arrested and charged under the new laws. Trial dates are set for later this month.'

While he paused for the translation, he adopted a grave expression.

'Shortly after police entered the Kitten Club, Khun Doug—the primary target of the operation—produced a weapon and began firing, killing one officer. When police returned fire, Khun Doug was himself killed. The Chiang Mai police deeply regret his death. Nevertheless, this misfortune will not stand in the way of ongoing police efforts to stamp out child prostitution in Chiang Mai and to bring those responsible—farang or Thai—to justice.'

He indicated to Chonsawat that he was ready to take questions. First to jockey into position was a young reporter from Channel 4.

'Sir,' she said, wielding her microphone like a dagger, 'Can you comment on rumours that the farang brothel owner killed in the raid was also going to be charged for the murder of Khun Sanga Siamprakorn?'

Ratratarn inclined his head as if to check his notes, hiding a smile. It was all going to plan, the 'rumours' having been leaked by his own office earlier that morning.

'I can confirm,' he said, 'that our findings into last weekend's murder have been revised on the basis of new evidence, which suggests the late Khun Doug organised the assassination of Khun Sanga to protect his child sex racket.'

To Ratratarn's gratification, the disclosure sent the journalists into a near-frenzy. The foreigners strained to hear the English translation as the Thais surged forward, clamouring for attention. Several punched frantically at mobile phones, others scribbled hasty notes, while two men from rival newspapers engaged in a heated argument.

Holding up his hand in a call for order, Ratratarn gestured for another question from the floor, this time from a farang.

'Frank Reeves,' the man said, 'Reuters. Sir, what does this development mean for the Canadian, Didier de Montpasse, previously held responsible for the crime?'

Ratratarn indicated to the interpreter that he would answer the question himself.

'All of you present today will receive a copy of a statement exonerating Khun Didier of any involvement in Khun Sanga's death,' he said. 'The police will also be issuing a formal apology through the Canadian Embassy for the unfortunate incident leading to Khun Didier's accidental demise.' Sensing farang journalists were poised to pursue the matter, he added, 'For the record, Khun Didier's body will be released later this afternoon. Any further inquiries on this should be taken up with the press liaison officer or the Canadian mission in Bangkok. Next!'

'Sir, can you tell us about the young girls rescued in last night's raid?'

This question from Khun Nalinee, Chiang Mai correspondent for the *Nation*.

'The eight girls, aged between nine and sixteen years, have been placed in the care of a local welfare organisation,' he said, 'with a view to returning them as soon as possible to their families.'

'Are they local girls?' she said.

'To my knowledge, one or two are Burmese, the others are from the northeast.'

'Isn't it likely the girls were sold by their families into prostitution and therefore risk ending up in the same situation again?'

'As we have limited time, Khun Nalinee,' Ratratarn said, 'it's only fair to allow an opportunity for others to ask questions, don't you think?'

He ignored her withering look and turned to a reporter

from the local television station. 'Yes, Khun Wipawee.'

'Do any of the rescued children have AIDS?' she said breathlessly.

Ratratarn smiled indulgently, as if moved by her concern for the girls' welfare. 'One can only hope not, but rest assured, the girls will be individually assessed and their needs met by the appropriate agencies on a case by case basis.'

He gestured at a journalist from the *Chiang Mai Daily*.

'Sir,' the man said, 'have police released the name of the officer killed in last night's raid?'

Ratratarn nodded solemnly. 'He was Police Sergeant Pornsak Boonyavivat.'

The hush that followed his reply was broken by a voice at the back of the room.

'Françoise de Calan,' the woman said in a European accent, 'Agence France Presse. Sir, can you comment on whether there is any relationship between Operation Jasmine and the death of another one of your officers, Komet Plungkham, two nights ago?'

A ripple of interest went through the crowd, heads turning to see who had asked such an odd question.

Ratratarn acknowledged Jayne Keeney with a nod. 'Yes, Khun…Françoise, was it?' He made no effort to hide the sarcasm, and cleared his throat again. 'The body of Officer Komet Plungkham was found in a rubbish skip at the Ton Payorm Market two days ago—allegedly discovered by the late Sergeant Pornsak. I say allegedly,' he said, 'because recent evidence suggests Officer Komet was the victim of foul play.'

There was more commotion as a new round of mobile phone calls were made.

'It would appear Sergeant Pornsak was extorting protection money from Khun Doug,' Ratratarn said. 'Our surveillance team has photographic evidence of him entering Kelly's club as recently as Thursday night. On the basis of this and other findings, we believe that Officer Komet was on the verge of exposing Pornsak's nefarious activities when he was killed.'

Ever the zealot, Khun Nalinee's voice rang out in the crowd.

'What's to say other officers weren't involved in the protection racket as well as Sergeant Pornsak?'

It was a question Ratratarn had anticipated. 'In the wake of last night's victory against the forces of corruption—which, I reiterate, saw thirty-six foreigners arrested and eight children rescued from sexual slavery—it is my sincere hope that the Chiang Mai police will finally receive due recognition, both in Thailand and abroad, for their efforts to eradicate child prostitution in this country.

'Furthermore, to let the reputation of the entire constabulary be tarnished by the actions of one bad apple is an insult to the memory of brave men such as Officer Komet.'

That ought to shut her up, he thought.

'On that basis then, Sir, may we take it the Chiang Mai police will provide for Officer Komet's widow and their unborn child?'

Ratratarn scowled as Jayne Keeney once again pushed him to make a public declaration on a point in their agreement.

'Of course!' he snapped. 'That goes without saying. I have time for one more question.'

He nominated a benign-looking woman before him.

'Poona Sivaraksa,' she said, '*Thai Rath*. Sir, you said earlier that Khun Doug ordered the assassination of Khun Sanga. Can you explain, then, the reason for the mutilation of Khun Sanga's body?'

'It would appear Khun Doug, through his hired thug, wanted to make the death look like a crime of passion, hence, the castration and the triangular shapes carved into the face. We believe the latter feature was designed to draw attention to Khun Didier, a known farang homosexual.'

He gathered his notes together. 'Thank you. That is all.'

Ratratarn signalled for Chonsawat to take his place. As he left the dais, he knew the trial of the farangs would prolong interest in the case for a while, but that it would soon die down and he could go back to business as usual.

At the end of the day that was all Ratratarn wanted.

Jayne watched the lieutenant colonel work the crowd like an evangelical preacher soliciting donations. She noted how he modulated his voice, speaking with calm detachment at first, building to righteous indignation, then sober as he spoke of the deaths of Kelly and Pornsak. His timing was perfect. He had the audience in the palm of his hand and there was no mistaking the pleasure he derived from it.

She had to press him to go public about Komet. But once that was done, she saw no reason to stay. Ratratarn had turned every detail to his advantage, even citing *her* photo of Pornsak as evidence of the sergeant's nefarious activities. He'd probably already labelled it as a police exhibit and filed it under 'Operation Jasmine' in his office.

She made her way outside in search of a taxi to meet Max's flight from Bangkok. The mid-morning light was clear and bright. With the exception of a few puddles in the deeper potholes, there was little evidence of the deluge of the night before. The streets that had been hastily deserted now thronged with people going about their normal business.

Jayne thought of Didier and Nou, of Komet and Mark, of all that had happened in the past week. And she wondered if she might do the same as Ratratarn and get on with her life.

Max and Jayne had arrived at the morgue on the Saturday afternoon at the same time as Nou's family. Though described in the press as a local boy, Nou was from Ayuthaya and his father, brother and a female relative had come to Chiang Mai to claim his remains. While they waited for the paperwork to be completed, Jayne chatted with the woman. Max shifted his weight from one foot to the other until a pause in their conversation gave him the opportunity to take Jayne aside.

'Do you think we should ask about holding joint funeral rites for Didier and Sanga here in Chiang Mai?' he said.

'I don't think it's a good idea,' Jayne whispered back.

'You don't think Didier would've wanted it that way?'

'Maybe, but I'm pretty sure Sanga's family would feel differently,' Jayne said. 'The young woman—Veera, the one I've been talking to—says she's Nou's fiancée.'

Max didn't press for details, but later Jayne filled him in over drinks in the bar of their hotel. According to Veera, the betrothal had taken place seven years ago, and they were only waiting for Nou to earn enough money before they married and started a family.

Jayne reckoned Nou probably agreed to the engagement to keep his parents happy, but Max was troubled. Had Didier known about this? And could this have been behind his own desire to have children? Max still felt guilty about having interfered in Didier's plans.

'You know Didier wanted to have children with you,' he said.

Jayne held onto a lungful of smoke longer than usual. 'Really?' she said, breathing out. 'How do you know?'

'He told me,' Max said, 'but I…I warned him off telling you. I told him it wouldn't be fair on you, but I was jealous and…' Without intending to, he started to cry. 'I'm sorry, Jayne.'

She rested her cigarette in the ashtray, patted his arm and passed him a paper serviette. 'It's OK, Max. I'm flattered Didier felt that way. Really. Thanks for telling me. But you're right—it wouldn't be fair on me. It wouldn't be fair to ask me to be a parent when what I really want to be is a partner, a lover.'

'Oh?' he sniffed. This veiled criticism was at odds with Jayne's fierce loyalty towards Didier and Max felt he was missing something.

'Does this change of heart have anything to do with your friend the Federal Police agent?'

'No,' Jayne blushed and looked away. 'That didn't work out.' She was about to take another drag of her cigarette, when a look of panic flashed across her face. 'Listen, Max, promise me you won't mention that AFP guy to anyone.'

'Why?'

'Please. I'll tell you the whole story once I'm sure he's left the country. But in the meantime, promise not to tell anyone, OK?'

Max wouldn't normally have let her get away with it. But after all she'd been through, the least he could do was respect her privacy.

He hadn't known what to expect when he flew up from Bangkok to meet her. She looked terrible, although that was partly because she'd dyed her hair and it didn't suit her at all. She hugged him tightly, admitted she was tired, but brushed off his concerns.

She remained dry-eyed at the morgue and applied herself with businesslike efficiency to organising the funeral—though he took it as a good sign when she dyed her hair back to its normal colour.

At the funeral, it struck Max that anyone who didn't know better would assume Jayne was Didier's widow. She greeted most of the mourners by name and introduced Max as the ceremony's benefactor. He recognised some of the guests from Jayne's report: Deng, who ran the bar behind the Night Bazaar; Mana, whom police cited as a witness in their report; and Pairoj, aka Marilyn. Jayne also introduced Bom and Deh, and the two boys blushed with pride as she explained their role in Didier's acquittal.

It was an extraordinary story—a real coup on Jayne's part to have put it all together—and Max still hoped to use the information in some way. Jayne was adamant about not releasing it to the press—there was a young policeman's widow to protect—though there were other avenues available to him. Diplomatic channels. Opportunities for an informal dinner with Thai government officials. Max felt he owed it to Jayne and to Didier to give it a try.

The funeral attracted a large crowd and Jayne was heartened by the turnout: if the Thais believed Didier had killed Nou, they wouldn't have come to farewell his spirit. Max had contacted Didier's university colleagues, while Jayne sent word out among his friends. The local grapevine accounted for the rest.

Jayne wore a crimson *pah biang* sash over her white blouse and black skirt out of respect for Didier's love of Thai culture. Marilyn turned up in an ankle-length black dress and patent leather stilettos, complemented by a beaded handbag and matching pillbox hat with tulle veil. As all the other mourners had opted for the traditional white, Marilyn stood out like a bee on a jasmine vine, providing Jayne with a rare moment of levity for the day.

They'd chosen to give Didier a Buddhist funeral. Didier was brought up Roman Catholic, but they felt their friend would have wanted a Thai ceremony. Max made a generous donation to Wat Phrapaeng to secure the services of its monks, and Jayne chose the casket, a red and white box she ordered from a specialist stall.

She also had a photograph of Didier enlarged and framed in black, to be displayed throughout the service. It was from a picture he'd kept by his bedside table, him and Nou on holiday on Koh Samui. A week in the sun had turned Didier's skin to burnished gold and he was looking at the camera, eyes smiling, easily mistaken for someone without a care in the world.

The monks, swathed in saffron-coloured robes, their shaved heads smooth as doorhandles, began the rites by gathering in a circle and chanting over Didier's body. The abbot dipped what looked like a large paintbrush into a silver bowl of scented water and blessed the dead and everyone present by flicking the water over their heads. At this point, the white-robed Buddhist nuns checked the body in the casket. The monks kept up the chanting as the coffin was carried to the temple courtyard and placed under a shelter made of palm branches. Hours later, they were sitting on the lawn, still chanting, as people fell into line to pay their respects to Didier.

The casket was designed for the body to sit in upright, like an enclosed throne, with Didier's photo propped on one side and a pyre below. Before the cremation took place, mourners were invited to leave offerings, gifts to accompany Didier into the afterlife.

In deference to his friend's Catholic past, Max had transcribed the words of Psalm 23, adding it to the pile as the procession circled around the casket. Among the flowers, incense, candles and sweets, Jayne placed her gift, a copy of the Chandler novel, *Farewell, My Lovely*.

She choked back tears as the procession finished—her grief would keep until she was out of the public eye—and the time came to light the fire. Jayne walked over to Max, the photograph of Didier under one arm. She placed her free hand on his shoulder.

'They want you to do it,' she said, gesturing towards the coffin.

Max stared at her in alarm. Her eyes were clear and her voice was steady.

'Everyone knows you paid for the funeral, Max, and they're very grateful. I know it's difficult, but it's a real honour to be asked. Can you manage it?'

He straightened his shoulders beneath her touch. 'Will you come with me?'

She nodded and took his hand. They walked slowly towards the funeral pyre. A monk stepped forward and offered a flaming torch to Max.

'Rest in peace, my friend,' Max whispered as he held the torch against the kindling.

Before the flames reached the casket, he let go of Jayne's hand, turned and walked out of the temple grounds.

She was alone by the time the fire died down. Most guests had left for Man Date where Deng had arranged for the monks to perform another ceremony to prevent Nou's ghost from haunting him. Nalissa had gone to work, but told Jayne she would join the wake at the Lotus Inn, an idea of Marilyn's which promised to be as spectacular a tribute to Didier as the funeral had been a solemn one.

Within a few days, the monks would put Didier's ashes in an urn and inter it in a small concrete stupa in the temple compound, after which she and Max would return to Bangkok. Before she returned to the hotel to check on him, she had one thing left to do.

Jayne stooped to scrape a handful of warm ashes into an envelope. She attracted curious looks from the wat's young novices, but no one tried to stop her. She placed the envelope carefully in her backpack and walked to the street to hail a tuk-tuk.

'The Lamphun Road,' she said to the driver.

'You want to go all the way to Lamphun?'

'*Mai chai*,' she shook her head. 'Just drive along the

'll tell you when to stop.'

The Chiang Mai-Lamphun Road ran along the east bank of the Mae Ping, affording Jayne a view of the town at its finest. The spires of its numerous wats sparkled gold in the late-afternoon sun, the river was liquid copper and the distant mountains lavender.

People sauntered along the riverbank: school children in uniform; young men wearing baseball caps; mothers with toddlers learning to walk. Among them was a Yao woman in an indigo turban and tunic with ruffles of red wool. As the tuk-tuk passed, Jayne saw the red pom-poms of a baby's cap peeking out from a sling on the woman's back. It struck her that while Chiang Mai might have an ugly side, the light that afternoon was at its most flattering.

'*Pai loei mai?*' The driver's voice cut into her thoughts.

'Yes, keep going,' she said.

He veered left where the road turned away from the river and within minutes reached the place Jayne was looking for: a stretch lined with yang trees, transformed into Buddhist shrines to prevent them from being cut down. On their last night together she'd seen Didier gazing at a picture, his face lighting up at the sight of those trees.

She asked the tuk-tuk driver to pull over and wait. She crossed the road and deliberated for a moment before choosing a tree with generous shade and an orange sash of modest size around its trunk. She wedged incense sticks and a single candle into the dirt and lit them with her cigarette lighter. Next she emptied the packet of Didier's ashes into the palm of her right hand and carefully poured a circle around the base of the tree. Then she squatted in front of the smoking incense and candle.

'Look, Didier, I know I'm supposed to pray or chant or something,' she said, 'but you know I don't go in for that stuff. I'm only doing this because—'

She hesitated, cleared her throat.

'I'm doing this because we never had a chance to say goodbye.'

Her voice cracked and the tears she'd held back all day streamed down her cheeks. She let them fall.

A pool of wax formed at the base of the candle.

'I'll always miss you,' she whispered. 'But I have to let you go.'

She looked up at the stretch of trees.

'And I thought this was the best place to leave you.'

Jayne gathered her things and stood up. She straightened her shoulders, turned, and walked away without looking back.

ACKNOWLEDGMENTS

Thanks first and foremost to Andrew Nette, my lover, friend and travelling companion, greatest champion and toughest critic, who read more versions of this book than anyone else and provided loving and practical support every step of the way.

Thanks also to my friend, mentor and partner in crime Christos Tsiolkas, for passionate encouragement and helpful feedback.

While I accept responsibility for all faults and flaws, this is a much better book for the expert advice and support of Melanie Ostell at Text Publishing. I'd thank her *profoundly* except that she's eradicated adverbs from my writing.

I appreciate the help of all those involved in the Victorian Premier's Literary Awards for encouraging this book with the award for unpublished manuscript in 2004.

A number of friends and peers were roped in as readers at various stages in the writing process and include Diana Baker, Susan Fry, Dimity Hawkins, Cath Keaney (who provided an adulterated version of her surname to the main character), Dr Jane Maree Maher (ditto for the character's first name), Helen Morgan and Julian Savage.

I'm grateful to my other brother Luke, whose vast general knowledge was an invaluable resource; and to my parents Olgamary and Haydn for giving me the confidence to think I could write books in the first place.

Thanks also to: Greg Carl for taking me to the bars

behind the Night Bazaar; Kathryn Sweet for checking Thai transliterations; Randall Arnst for translations of the health warnings on Thai cigarette packets; the late Jen Lipman for information on the structure of the Thai police; Sisters in Crime Inc. for giving the thumbs-up to the first Jayne Keeney story; Susan Hampton, my first editor; Haydn Savage and Susan Fry for last-minute research in Chiang Mai (*much* appreciated); and Richard Fleming for legal advice.